PRAISE FOR

Hope Ignites

"A heartfelt romance that readers will adore! . . . *Hope Ignites* possesses everything a reader wanting an escape will ever need."
　　　　　　　　　　　　　　　　　　　　—*Fresh Fiction*

"Delivered on everything I was hoping for and more . . . I can't wait to see where this series will go next."
　　　　　　　　　　　　　　—*Under the Covers Book Blog*

"A fast-paced romance that is full of passion, excitement, and a beautiful love that is worth fighting for."
　　　　　　　　　　　　　　—*Guilty Pleasures Book Reviews*

PRAISE FOR

Hope Flames

"Jaci Burton's books are always sexy, romantic, and charming! A hot hero, a lovable heroine, and an adorable dog—prepare to fall in love with Jaci Burton's amazing new small-town romance series."
　　　　　　—Jill Shalvis, *New York Times* bestselling author

"A heartwarming second-chance-at-love contemporary romance enhanced by engaging characters and Jaci Burton's signature dry wit."
　　　　　　　　　　　　　　　　　　　　—*USA Today*

"If you're looking for a sweet, hot, small-town romance, *Hope Flames* fits the bill perfectly."
　　　　　　　　　　　　　　　　　　　　—*Dear Author*

continued . . .

Changing the Game

"An extraordinary novel—a definite home run!"
—*Joyfully Reviewed*

"A must-read."
—*Fresh Fiction*

The Perfect Play

"Holy smokes! I am pretty sure I saw steam rising from every page."
—*Fresh Fiction*

"This book delivers."
—*Dear Author*

"A beautiful romance that . . . leaves us begging for more."
—*Joyfully Reviewed*

"Hot, hot, hot! Romance at its best! Highly recommended! Very steamy."
—*Coffee Table Reviews*

"The romance sparkles as the sex sizzles."
—*RT Book Reviews*

FURTHER PRAISE FOR THE WORK OF JACI BURTON

"Passionate, inventive . . . Burton offers plenty of emotion and conflict."
—*USA Today*

"A wild ride."
—#1 *New York Times* bestselling author Lora Leigh

"Jaci Burton delivers."
—Cherry Adair, *New York Times* bestselling author

"One to pick up and savor."
—*Publishers Weekly*

continued . . .

Hope
Burns

JACI BURTON

JOVE BOOKS, NEW YORK

THE BERKLEY PUBLISHING GROUP
Published by the Penguin Group
Penguin Group (USA) LLC
375 Hudson Street, New York, New York 10014

USA • Canada • UK • Ireland • Australia • New Zealand • India • South Africa • China

penguin.com

A Penguin Random House Company

HOPE BURNS

A Jove Book / published by arrangement with the author

Jove Books are published by The Berkley Publishing Group.
JOVE® is a registered trademark of Penguin Group (USA) LLC.
The "J" design is a trademark of Penguin Group (USA) LLC.

For information, address: The Berkley Publishing Group,
a division of Penguin Group (USA) LLC,
375 Hudson Street, New York, New York 10014.

ISBN: 978-0-425-25978-8

PUBLISHING HISTORY
Jove mass-market edition / October 2014

PRINTED IN THE UNITED STATES OF AMERICA

10 9 8 7 6 5 4 3 2 1

Cover photography by Claudio Marinesco.
Cover design by Rita Frangie.
Text design by Kelly Lipovich.

Because family is everything, and mine is most important to me, these are the ones I love the most:

To Kevin, Michelle, Kaylynn, Matt, Julie, Alex, Ashley, Ashley, and Brant.

And as always, the man who makes home and love the most special words of all, my husband, Charlie.

Chapter 1

THIS WEDDING WAS going to be a disaster.

Molly Burnett didn't know what had possessed her to agree to come back to Hope for her sister Emma's wedding. Love for her sister, of course. But she knew what was at stake. She never came home, hadn't been home since she'd left when she was eighteen.

That had been twelve years ago. She'd moved around from town to town, state to state, never setting down roots. Permanence just wasn't Molly's thing. And she sure as hell had never once come back to her hometown.

Until now. Even as she drove past the city limits sign her throat had started to close up, her breathing becoming labored. If she hyperventilated, crashed the car, and died a week before Emma's wedding, her sister would never forgive her.

Then again, with all the sputtering and coughing her ancient Ford Taurus was doing, it might just do itself in before she had a chance to crash it into anything.

"Come on, George," she said, smooth-talking the car. "Hang in there." She didn't have a new—or a newer used—car in her budget. Old George, currently fifteen and she hoped heading toward sixteen, was just going to have to suck it up and keep working.

At the next stoplight, George shuddered and belched rather loudly, making the two little kids sitting in the backseat of the car next to her point and laugh. She gave them a smile, then gently pressed the gas. Obviously having cleared his throat, George lumbered on and Molly sighed in grateful relief. Gripping the steering wheel and forcing deep, calming breaths, Molly drove past the First Baptist Church, her favorite donut shop, the florist, and Edith's Hair Salon. So many places still stood, all of them so familiar.

And yet a lot had changed in twelve years. So much progress, so many new businesses had cropped up. New restaurants, the hospital was bigger than she remembered, and they'd widened the highway. When she'd lived here, there'd been only one shop to stop at for gas and sodas along the main road. Now there was one at every corner.

She purposely turned off the main road, determined to avoid the high school. Too many memories she wasn't ready to face yet. She headed toward the main strip of town. There was a new bakery, and on impulse, Molly decided to stop and buy some goodies for the family.

She headed inside, the smell of sugar and baked goods making her smile. This place definitely reminded her of home, though it hadn't been Cups and Cakes last time she was home. Red and Helen Osajeck had owned the Hope Bakery for as long as she could remember. Her mom had told her they'd retired several years ago and sold the bakery.

She wondered who owned this place?

She browsed the display case, her stomach rumbling.

"Can I help you?"

She stood, and smiled at the familiar face from back in high school. With light brown hair and brown eyes, she was still as pretty now as she had been in school.

"Megan? Megan Lee?"

Megan frowned as if trying to place Molly's face, then grinned. "Molly Burnett? I can't believe it's you. Are you back in town for Emma's wedding?"

"I am."

"Then welcome home. I'm so glad to see you after all these years."

"Thanks." She looked around. "And you work here?"

"Actually, I own the shop. I bought it two years ago after the Osajecks' retired. I worked for them all through high school, and during breaks from college. I wanted to own my own bakery, and the opportunity fell into my lap when they decided to sell. And of course, you don't want to hear all those details."

Molly grinned. "No, really, that's fantastic. Congratulations. Also, it smells wonderful in here. I'm going to have a hard time figuring out what to buy."

"Thank you. Have you gotten settled in yet?"

"No. I'm just driving into town, and thought I'd stop and buy some goodies on my way."

"You've come to the right place, then. May I make some suggestions?"

"Definitely."

Megan took out a box, and between the two of them, they filled it with éclairs and cream puffs.

She left the store, having survived her first reunion with an old friend from Hope. She made her way outside, stopping short as she spotted a very fine male ass bent over, inspecting her car.

"Can I help you?"

He straightened, and Molly almost dropped the box of baked goods.

The last person in Hope she wanted to see today—or ever—stared back at her.

Carter Richards, her first and only love, and the main reason she'd left Hope all those years ago.

"Hey, Molly."

"What are you doing here, Carter?"

"My auto shop is just a few doors down. I was outside and I saw you get out of the car."

Recovering, she walked over to the driver's side, placed the box on the hood, then opened the door. "And you thought this would be a good place for a reunion? Really, Carter?"

She hoped he wouldn't notice her hands shaking as she slid the box onto the passenger seat and climbed in, shutting the door.

He leaned his forearms inside the car. "That's all you have to say?"

"I think we said all we needed to say to each other twelve years ago."

She turned the key and winced at George's attempts to fire on all cylinders. She tried again, and this time, the car fired up. Sort of. It mostly wheezed.

Dammit. Come on, George. I just need you to start this one time.

"Let me help you with that."

She shot him a look. "I don't need help. I can do this."

She tried again. No go.

"Molly."

Carter's voice was soft, laced with tenderness and concern. She wanted him to disappear. She wanted to pretend he didn't exist, just like she'd tried to erase him from her memories. She wanted to be anywhere but here right now.

"Slide out and let me give it a try."

With a resigned sigh, she opened the door and got out. Carter slid in and fiddled with the ignition.

"George is a little touchy."

He turned to face her. "George?"

Crossing her arms, she nodded. "Yes. George."

His lips curved, and her stomach tumbled. God, he was even more good-looking now than he'd been in high school. He had dark hair, and those mesmerizing green eyes. He wore a polo shirt that stretched tight over his well-muscled biceps. Why couldn't he have turned out bald and fat and hideously ugly? Not that it would have made a difference anyway, because he still would have been Carter.

When George's engine finally turned over, tears pricked Molly's eyes.

Carter got out and held the door for her. "There you go."

"Thanks."

He shut the door, then leaned in again. "Molly . . ."

She looked up at him. "Please don't."

He nodded and backed up a step so she could pull out of the parking spot, which she did with a little too much fervor. As she drove away, she stared at him way too long in her rearview mirror.

Forcing her attention on the road ahead, she gripped the steering wheel and willed the pain in her heart to go away.

It was in the past. Carter was in the past, and that's where he was going to stay.

CARTER WATCHED MOLLY drive away, that old junker she drove belching out smoke and exhaust like it was on its last legs.

He shook his head and leaned against the wall of the bake shop, needing a minute to clear his head before he went back to work.

He'd been thinking about Molly for a while now, knowing she was coming back to Hope. She had to, because she was in Luke and Emma's wedding. He hadn't expected to see her today, though, when he'd stepped outside to take a break from all the damn paperwork that was his least favorite part of being owner of several body repair shops.

He'd always liked watching the cars go by on his breaks.

When he'd seen an unfamiliar one—an old beat-up Taurus choking out a black trail of exhaust, then wheezing as it came to a stop in front of the bakery—he couldn't help but wonder who'd drive a piece of shit like that. Surely the owner had to realize the poor junker should be shot and put out of its misery.

His heart slammed against his ribs as a gorgeous brunette stepped out of the car. She had on jeans, a white T-shirt, and sandals as she hurried into the bakery as if she didn't want to be recognized. She even kept her sunglasses on, but there was no mistaking who it was. Not to him, anyway.

He could never forget the curve of her face, the fullness of her lips, or her long legs. It might have been twelve years, and she might have changed from girl to woman, but Molly Burnett was someone Carter would never forget. His pulse had been racing, and he knew damn well he should turn around and go back to his office. But for some reason his body hadn't been paying the slightest attention to what his mind told it, and he pushed off the wall and started down the street toward the bakery.

He debated going inside, then thought better of it and decided to figure out what the hell it was she was driving. So he'd walked over and studied the car.

A '99 Taurus. Christ. He wondered where Molly was living, and how the hell that car had made the trip. It had dents all over, patchy rust spots, the muffler was nearly shot, and the tires badly needed replacement—like a year ago.

In retrospect, he should have let Molly be, should have kept his distance from her. But when he'd seen her, he'd closed his eyes for a fraction of a second, transported back to the last time he'd heard her voice. It had been in hurt and anger. The last words they'd said to each other hadn't been kind ones.

And maybe he wanted to change all that.

But it hadn't gone at all like he'd expected. She was still hurt, still angry with him, even after all these years.

Carter dragged his fingers through his hair and made his way down the street toward the garage, then back to his office. He shut the door and stared at his laptop, but all he could see was Molly's long dark hair pulled up in a high ponytail, and her full lips painted some shimmering pink color. She was tan, and her body had changed over the years. She was curvier now, had more of a woman's figure.

But she was still the drop-dead gorgeous woman he'd fallen in love with all those years ago.

He'd thought he was over her, that what he'd once felt for her in high school was long gone. But they'd had a deeper connection than just being first loves.

And seeing her again had hurt a lot more than he'd thought it would.

Chapter 2

IT HAD TAKEN several miles to stop shaking and get her nerves under control again, but Molly was fine now.

Just. Fine.

Carter wasn't even in her thoughts anymore.

Much.

She finally came to a stop at her grandmother's old house, the house Emma now owned and shared with her fiancé, Luke McCormack.

She pulled into the driveway and turned off the engine, staring at the one-story brick and frame house.

A lot of sweet memories were built into this home. She and Emma playing in the front yard while Grandpa mowed the grass. Her grandmother letting her help bake a pie. Molly had learned some of her not awesome but adequate baking skills from her. No one was as good a cook as her grandmother.

She missed her grandparents, but was glad Emma had decided to live here, instead of letting the house go to strangers.

At least one of the Burnett sisters was comfortable calling

Hope home. Molly would never feel at home in Hope again. Too many bad memories.

She got out of the car and headed to the door, smiling at the sound of the old familiar doorbell.

She heard barking, and Emma's voice.

The front door opened and two rather large dogs came running out, one an exuberant pit bull. She knew Annie was still young, but she was huge and nearly knocked her over. Daisy, the lab, was just as excited to see her, though she was a little more reserved.

"Hi, kids." Molly bent down and was rewarded with wagging tails and licks to her face.

"Oh, you're here." Emma came out, looking gorgeous as always, her brown hair in a ponytail. She still wore her scrubs from work as owner of the veterinary clinic in town.

Molly stood as Emma pulled her into a tight hug. "It's been too long, Molls."

Molly closed her eyes, loving the feel of her big sister's strong arms holding her. "It has. I've really missed you."

Emma pulled back, the dogs winding around both their legs. "Come on, girls, give us some space."

Molly laughed. "They're both so adorable."

"Aren't they?" Emma picked at the top of her scrubs. "And I'm so sorry. I probably smell like medicine and animals. I had a late emergency at the clinic, so I just got home about ten minutes ago. I was afraid you were going to get here before me. Oh, and Luke's at Taco Bueno, your favorite, picking up dinner."

Molly grinned, her stomach rumbling at the thought. "You remembered."

"Of course." Emma slung an arm around Molly's shoulders. "Let's go inside."

The dogs followed. Emma shut the door. "I'm going to dash and take a quick shower. Why don't you bring your bags inside?"

"I can stay at Mom and Dad's, you know. I'm sure you and Luke want to be alone."

Emma was headed toward the hall. "Luke and I have a lifetime of being alone. You'll only be here a short while, so

I want to see you as much as I can. Besides, you're my maid of honor, and we have so much to catch up on with the wedding plans."

"This is true."

"Plus, Luke and I have a long vacation in Hawaii coming up after the wedding. So we'll have blissful alone time."

"Yeah, how did you manage to swing that, being the sole owner of the vet clinic?"

"One of the docs I know who works at a clinic in Tulsa is going to cover for me. He's a great guy who's been out of school two years and works with a large group. He's looking to buy his own practice, so he wants the solo experience."

"That'll work out well for both of you."

"I know, right? I'll be back in no time. Make yourself at home. There's iced tea in the fridge."

Emma disappeared, and Molly exhaled. She loved her sister, loved seeing her. Usually it was Emma who came to visit her, at least once a year, and they talked on the phone quite a bit, although definitely a lot more recently as they planned the wedding together. Molly felt like a horrible sister for not coming home sooner to help with the ceremony and the other celebrations surrounding it, especially being the maid of honor. She'd told Emma she wouldn't mind if she wanted one of her friends to handle that responsibility, but Emma had insisted, and fortunately Molly was good at organizing, even long-distance.

But she did have to come home for the wedding. That part she couldn't handle from afar.

So now here she was—back in Hope, after all these years. Despite her best efforts to stay away forever, she knew someday she'd have to return, so she'd just have to suck it up and deal with it.

Deal with *him*. And all the bitter, painful memories.

Shoving unwanted thoughts of the past aside, she grabbed her bags—plus the box of baked goods—and brought them inside. She put the box on the counter and laid the bags near the door to the hall, then went into the kitchen, found the cupboard where the glasses were located, and pulled the iced tea from the fridge, pouring herself a glass to drink while she waited for Emma. In the meantime, she wandered and took a look around the house.

It had been a long time since she'd been here, but all the details of the place were etched into her memories. The yellow wallpaper in the kitchen had been replaced by bright new paint, and the old linoleum with new tile. The countertop was new as well, as were the cabinets. But the wood floors in the living room were the same. They'd been refinished and restained, and they looked good. The dark wood pillars holding up the archway leading into the hall were still standing as well.

Emma had brightened and renewed their grandparents' home, but still managed to retain the old charm. Leave it to her sister to manage to retain the memories while bringing the home into the twenty-first century.

The front door opened, and Emma's fiancé, Luke, stepped in. He gave her a wide smile. "Molls. You made it."

"I did." She'd met Luke last year when Emma brought him to Little Rock. Molly had instantly fallen in love with his quiet strength and infinite charm. Emma and Luke were perfectly suited to each other, and it was clear how much he loved her sister. "I hear you were sent on a taco mission."

Luke passed her, giving her a peck on the cheek as he made his way into the kitchen. "I was. Taco Bueno has become one of our favorite places to eat, especially on nights when we both have to work late."

Molly inhaled the scent of flavored meat and beans. "I can't tell you how many of those tacos and bean burritos I ate when I was in high school."

That, at least, was one memory that wasn't painful.

"Not as many as I did," Emma said, coming out to greet Luke with a swift kiss. Her hair was still wet and she'd changed into yoga pants and a tank top.

"Did you go to a tanning salon?" Molly asked.

Emma wrinkled her nose. "No. But I'm trying out a spray tan. What do you think? Too orange?"

"No. Actually, it looks really good on you. I hate you for that."

Emma grabbed plates and Luke poured tea for both of them, then they pulled up seats at the kitchen table. "I don't know why. You're tan. Have you been swimming or something?"

"There's a pool at my condo. It's my leftover-from-summer tan."

"Oh. Perfect. You have that sun-kissed look. Not surprising since you live down south now. The weather must be great in Austin."

"It's good there. I like it."

Emma grabbed a taco. "For now, right?"

Molly shot her an enigmatic smile. "For now. I have a great job doing accounting and marketing for a music company. You should visit. It's an amazing city."

"We should. When the dust settles post–wedding and honeymoon, we'll take a road trip. If you're still there." Emma winked

"Great." It was a known fact that Molly never spent more than six months to a year in one spot. Then, wanderlust or an uncomfortable itch to move on set in—she tried to never put a label on it—and she'd find yet another job in another city.

It made her parents crazy, and it worried Emma. But for Molly, it had become the norm. She liked moving around. It gave her a chance to see different parts of the country. What was so wrong about that?

She bit into the burrito and rolled her eyes heavenward. After she swallowed, she looked at Emma and Luke. "I missed these—so much."

"I imagine you get some great burritos in Austin," Emma said.

"Oh, definitely. And I know these are from a fast-food chain and all, but Taco Bueno has memories associated with it."

Emma grinned. "Stopping for a taco after school."

"And on Friday nights," Molly said with a grin. "It just reminds me of home."

"You wouldn't miss them if you'd come home once in a while."

She answered with a shrug. "I'm here now. And they were worth the wait."

They ate and she listened to Emma and Luke discuss their days. She and Emma talked at least once a week, so she was familiar with their jobs. Luke was busy as a local cop in Hope, and Emma had her hands full running the vet clinic. They were both successful, and ridiculously in love with each other. Luke scraped taco sauce off the corner of Emma's mouth, and Emma listened intently to Luke's story about a rear-end collision he'd worked today, offering sympathy as he told them about one of the occupants' injuries.

The way Emma looked at Luke was the same way Molly used to look at—

No point in going there. That had been a long time ago. She never even thought about him anymore.

"So tell me what's on the agenda for this wedding shindig," Molly said after they cleaned up the remnants of their fast-food fest. Luke had taken the dogs outside, leaving Emma and Molly to catch up in the living room.

"You and I are going to head to the bridal salon for a final fitting tomorrow. We should be fine, and we'll bring the dresses home. Ours will go to Mom's, of course, because we'll be getting ready there the day of the wedding. Oh, and we're meeting Jane and Chelsea at the bridal shop."

"Okay."

"Luke's brother Reid flies in from Boston tomorrow as well, but Luke's taking care of picking him up. The rehearsal dinner is Friday, then the wedding at the country club on Saturday. We're going to do a brunch Sunday with the families, then Luke and I head out on Monday for Hawaii."

Molly grinned. "My guess is that you and Luke are way more excited about Hawaii than anything else."

Emma laughed. "You would guess right. Though I am looking forward to being married. Finally. It's taken a lot of planning, but it's going to happen."

Molly grasped her hand. "I'm so happy for the two of you, Em. Luke's a great guy."

"He is. And thanks. I want the same thing for you, Moll."

"Oh, well. You know, I'm not even close to being ready to settle down."

"And why is that? With all the traveling you've done, haven't you found one place that suits you yet? Or a guy who makes you want to put down roots?"

"Uh, no." There'd never be a guy who'd make her want to stay in one place. Never. She'd planted her flag in a guy's heart once, and love had devastated her. She never wanted to go there again. "I like my freedom too much."

"And speaking of guys . . . you are aware Carter is in the wedding, right?"

Just the mention of his name made her pulse kick up several beats. "Of course. You told me."

"I know you two broke up in high school, but you've never talked about it."

Molly shrugged. "Nothing to talk about, really."

Other than the utter destruction of her heart.

"He is Luke's best friend. Are you sure you're okay with this?"

No, she wasn't okay with it. She was hoping he'd be out of town and unable to make the wedding. Too much to hope for, of course. And running into him at the bakery had been an awful start to her trip. One she wasn't going to mention to her sister. "Of course, Em. I'm fine with it. High school was a long time ago, you know. I'm so over Carter."

She'd never be over Carter, or what had happened between them. But this was Emma and Luke's wedding, and she was going to be an adult about it. Nothing was going to spoil Emma and Luke's big day.

Her heart was just going to have to suck it up and take it. Then, after the wedding, she'd hightail it out of Hope and never look back.

Just like she'd done twelve years ago, when she'd left town to escape the heartbreak.

Only this time, she wouldn't be heartbroken, because she'd never allow that to happen again.

Chapter 3

AFTER RUNNING INTO Molly yesterday, Carter had buried himself in the dreaded paperwork. It was only because he'd interviewed a guy for the vacant body repair position that he'd happened to be in Hope during the day and then decided to just spend the rest of the workweek here because of the wedding stuff going on. And because he'd happened to be here, he'd also happened to see Molly, something he'd hoped to avoid until the wedding.

Of course if he'd just stayed at the shop, he could have prevented her unhappiness, and his damn bad mood. So he had no one to blame but himself.

And the interviewing wasn't going well, either. He was beginning to think he was never going to find a decent body guy. Good thing he had some of the other guys to fill in, and if worse came to worst, he could do some of the bodywork himself, though that wasn't his preference. Every now and then he enjoyed getting his hands dirty, but overseeing the shops was enough of a full-time job these days.

When he'd first started out, he'd worked for Mo Bennett, who owned the shop he was at today. Carter always had a feel for cars, had started learning about them with his dad when he was a kid. His dad had worked for Mo, and Carter had come in with him on weekends, sitting by and watching until he was old enough to get under the hood and tinker on them himself. Mo had hired him at sixteen, and by the time he turned twenty-two and Mo was ready to retire, Carter had gotten a loan and bought the place. Over the years Carter expanded the garage and brought in auto body guys, then branched out and bought another shop several years later.

Now there were four Richards Auto Service garages, one in Hope and three more in surrounding areas, including nearby in Tulsa. He'd worked his ass off to become a success, put himself in debt up to his eyeballs, but he was in the black finally. He might not get to work on the cars, which he loved, as much as he used to, but he'd made enough to buy a house and he lived comfortably enough that he could sleep at night without worrying about money.

These days if anything kept him up at night it was his personal life—or lack of personal life. The absence of a special woman. Not that finding the right woman had ever been front burner for him before. He'd dated plenty, and women had come into and gone out of his life without a lot of fuss.

Maybe it was seeing Molly again that reminded him of the plans they'd made twelve years ago. Plans that had never come to be. Plans he'd put on hold while he concentrated on work, on building his business.

He shoved aside the paperwork and stood, stretched his back, and decided to go take a look out in the shop. Sitting at his desk gave him too much time to think, mainly about things he shouldn't be thinking about.

Diving headfirst into an engine or body repair would clear his head, and that's just what he needed on a day like today.

MOLLY PARKED GEORGE in the driveway of her parents' house, needing a few minutes to catch her breath before she went inside to face the hordes.

Catching up with Emma had been fun, but she had to admit

she'd been distracted, her thoughts straying to her meeting with Carter yesterday.

Of all the people she hadn't wanted to run into, she'd walked outside the bakery to find him leaning over her car.

He'd looked good. No, he'd looked hot, with jeans that fit his oh-so-fine ass perfectly, a polo shirt that defined his muscled biceps. He was lean and fit, and he wore his dark hair shorter than he had in high school, but those green eyes of his still mesmerized her.

And he'd been . . . nice. How dare he be nice to her, after what he'd done?

It felt like all the air had been sucked out of her lungs, and even now—a day later—she still found it hard to breathe when she thought about him. As she'd driven over here, she was afraid she was going to run into him, which was ridiculous. Hope was a small town, but it wasn't that small.

She needed to get a grip or her mother, who was observant of all things, was going to notice. Then she'd get questioned incessantly, and she wouldn't be able to deal with it.

She took several deep breaths, relying on her yoga training to calm herself inwardly and block out the negative.

It wasn't really working, because every time she closed her eyes, Carter's face swam before her.

She was just going to have to fake it as best she could and hope the impending wedding extravaganza stuff would take precedence over any of her peculiar behavior. Besides, it wasn't like anyone was used to her being around anyway. How would they know what was normal for her these days?

She opened the front door into a house filled with people. Aunts and uncles had arrived, as well as Emma's friends, Chelsea and Jane.

Home. She had grown up here, yet it didn't feel like her home anymore. Too much time had passed, and even though so many things looked familiar to her, like the fireplace where she and Emma used to sit and sing together, and the kitchen table where they'd eat breakfast before school, a lot had changed. There was new carpet and new living room furniture, and Mom had changed the paint scheme on some of the walls.

Life goes on without you, Molly. Deal with it.

"Molly, you're here!"

Her mother hurried over, a bright smile on her face.

Her mother's love and smiles, however, would never change, and she was so grateful for that.

Molly dropped several boxes of donuts on the kitchen counter along with the foam cup filled with coffee she'd picked up at Megan's shop this morning.

Her mother grasped her hands. "Let me look at you."

"You just saw me a month ago when you came to visit."

"Shh. I know that. But I still miss you every day." Her mom gave her the once-over. "You look beautiful, as always."

Molly laughed. "Thanks, Mom. You're good for my ego."

Her parents' dog, Pokey, a miniature dachshund, came over to sniff her.

"Hey, Pokey, how's it going?" She bent down to love on the dog, picking him up to hold him. Her parents brought Pokey along whenever they came to visit, so she had a little taste of having a pet whenever she saw them, since most of the apartments where she lived didn't allow animals.

"He's happy to see you."

She ran her fingers over Pokey's back. "I'm happy to see him, too. And everyone else. The house is full of people."

"Come on, put the dog down and say hello to everyone."

Not that she'd have a choice, since her mother firmly held her hand and dragged her around like she was eight years old. She listened to the admonishments of her aunts about how it had been way too long since she'd been back in Hope, and was firmly hugged by her uncles.

When she had endured enough, she kissed her mom on the cheek, then headed out back where Emma, Jane, and Chelsea were enjoying coffee.

"Hi, everyone."

"Molly. It's so great to see you. It's been too long." Chelsea got up to give her a hug, and Jane, did, too.

"It's great to see you both," Molly said. This part, at least, was easy. She might not have seen Chelsea and Jane for a long time, but they'd talked a lot on the phone and Skyped over wedding details the past several months, so it was nice to be able to sit down with them in person.

"I see you already got yours," Emma said as they all took seats.

Molly lifted her cup. "I couldn't wait, since I was on donut-fetching duty this morning."

"Lucky you," Chelsea said. "Emma's mom called me at seven this morning and gave me a grocery list."

Emma's eyes widened. "She did not."

"She did. Juice and milk and oh, she needed two loaves of bread. She was going to go herself, but there were people at the house and she didn't want to be rude."

Emma snorted. "I'm surprised I didn't get that list. And I'm really sorry she just assumed you'd run errands for her. I'll talk to her."

"You'll do no such thing. You're the bride, honey," Chelsea said. "We're the minions. It was no problem, and the store's on my way over here."

Emma blew out a breath. "Thank you. This will all be over soon. I promise."

"Is the stress getting to you?" Molly asked.

"Just the past week or so. It had been fairly calm and organized before that, but now it seems as if there's some crisis, or some detail that needs attending to every day."

"It has been intense, Emma, but you have to trust us all," Jane said. "We'll take care of it. We have taken care of everything so far, haven't we?"

Now Molly felt even guiltier that she hadn't been here for all those details. She should have never agreed to be the maid of honor. She sucked at this. She hadn't even come to the wedding shower. Chelsea and Jane had been lifesavers, handling everything in Molly's absence and telling her not to worry that she couldn't make it.

"Yes, you have taken care of everything."

"And now Molly's here, which is what you were worried about the most," Jane said, offering Molly a genuine smile.

Which made Molly feel even worse, because Jane and Chelsea didn't pass judgment on her stupid idiosyncrasies. Like her abject fear about returning home.

"Emma, can you come here for a minute? Aunt Louise wants to take a picture of you with all of us."

Emma shot a panicked look at all of them before smiling and standing. "Sure, Mom."

After Emma went inside, Jane turned to them. "I'm glad Will and I did the small wedding. Between his job and mine, and both the kids, we had enough to deal with."

"Hey, you had a party at the house, at least," Chelsea said. "It was a great one, too."

"Yes. With catered barbecue." Jane looked to Molly. "I got barbecue sauce on my dress. There are lovely photos of a very inappropriately placed stain."

Molly laughed. "But did you have fun?"

"We did. Our friends were there, our families were there, we love each other, and it's done. Now we're one family—me, him, and my kids. Correction—our kids."

"How's the adoption process going?" Chelsea asked.

"Good. Faster than I thought it would."

"You're adopting?" Molly asked.

Jane shook her head. "Will's adopting my kids from my first marriage. Long story short, my ex abandoned us, he lost his parental rights. Will loves those kids like they're his, and they love him as well. He wants them to be his."

Molly sat back. "How do the kids feel about him adopting them?"

"We had a lot of heart-to-hearts. They're sad about their father, but they understand now that he's not coming back into their lives. And they love Will. He's their father now. They want him and they want his name. It's what I want as well, but ultimately, the kids had to be on board with it. Even though they're young, they had to believe in Will and love him like a father, which they do."

"Sounds like you have a perfect family."

Jane smiled. "Oh, far from it. We're a work in progress, but it's right for us. There's a lot of love, and that'll get us through anything."

Molly once thought love was enough as well, but it hadn't been. It hadn't even been close. Then again, she'd mistaken something else for what she thought was love. Passion and the stupidity of youth.

She wasn't a teenager anymore but she wasn't stupid, either. She'd grown up a lot over the years and she'd learned to be more cautious. She'd never confuse passion with love again. Too many mistakes could be made.

"So, how are you liking Austin?" Chelsea asked.

"I love the pace there. It's very hip and music oriented. I think I might stay there awhile."

"That would be a first for you, wouldn't it?"

Taken aback, Molly could only stare at Chelsea.

"Sorry, I tell it like it is. I don't mean any offense. But you move around a lot, don't you?"

"That's true. I've got a case of wanderlust, I guess. I always think a place is the perfect fit—until something better comes along."

"Kind of like Chelsea and men," Jane said with a smirk.

Chelsea shot Jane a look. "Hey. I am not at all like that. Besides, it's been three months since I've been out on a decent date."

"Uh-huh," Jane said. "Define *decent date*."

"Dinner and a good movie. Followed up by drinks at his place or mine, and a hot kiss to end the evening."

"Or hot breakfast the next morning?" Jane waggled her brows.

"No, that would be a *perfect* date. I'd be satisfied with decent at this point."

Molly laughed. "A bit of a dry spell?"

"Honey, you don't know the half of it. It's like every available man in this town has pulled up stakes and moved to Alaska."

"I find that hard to believe," Jane said. "I've fixed you up with several eligible men. You're just too picky."

Chelsea studied her nails. "I am picky. And I have high expectations." She fluffed her gorgeous red hair. "But I'm worth it."

"There you go," Molly said, taking another sip of her coffee. "Never settle for less than the best."

"Is that what you're looking for, Molly?" Jane asked. "The best?"

"Me?" She laughed. "I'm not looking at all."

Chapter 4

HANGING OUT WITH the guys was so much more fun than dealing with women and all the baggage they brought to the table. Carter knew he'd be hung from the nearest tree if his mom ever heard him say that—or any of his ex-girlfriends. But none of them were here right now. Just his best friend Luke, Luke's brothers, Reid and Logan, and Will Griffin, all of them groomsmen in the wedding.

They were currently sitting in the No Hope At All bar, run by Sebastian Palmer, or "Bash," as everyone called him.

"This round of tequila shots is on me," Will said, ponying up the money.

Bash lined up the shots, including one for himself. He'd closed down the bar for the day, since he was in the wedding, too.

"I'm monitoring all your drinking. If you show up drunk for the rehearsal dinner, it's my ass on the line," Bash said.

"To Bash," Will said.

They all downed their drinks. "No, wait," Will said. "That wasn't my toast. Another round."

"You all suck," Reid said, shaking his head. "You can't even get drunk right."

"Oh, and you can?" Luke crossed his arms. "Wait. Tell me. They drink better in Boston, too."

"Hell yeah."

"You wanna take him out back and beat the shit out of him?" Logan asked.

Luke laughed. "That might be fun."

"You two don't scare me anymore like you did when we were kids. Besides, I can drink you both under the table and then kick both your asses."

Logan snorted. "I'd like to see you try."

"I'll lay money on Reid," Carter said, giving Reid a critical once-over. "He looks like he's been doing Krav Maga. His arms are beefier than the last time he was here."

Luke frowned. "You'd take my little brother over me?"

"Somebody has to."

Reid slapped him on the back. "Thanks, Carter."

Bash rolled his eyes, but poured the drinks. "Last one. I'm locking up the tequila."

"Does that mean you're pulling out the whiskey next?" Carter asked with a grin.

"You wish, Richards. No, this is the last round. Then I'm making coffee, so none of our law enforcement officials sitting here—or their friends—arrests us.

"I could get us a highway patrol escort," Will said. "Then none of us have to drive."

"Yeah, but we'd still be drunk," Logan said, taking the glass Bash had poured. "So do your toast, Will, and we'll be good boys. Because nothing's worse than a pissed-off woman."

"True that," Will said, then turned to Luke. "To your last day as a single man."

Luke groaned. "Again."

"Try and do it better the second time than you did the first," Logan said.

"It'll help that the second wife is a much better choice than your first one," Carter said.

"A-fucking-men to that," Luke said. "Let's drink."

They took their shots, then Bash cleared the bar and poured them all sodas and coffee.

Carter grimaced as he took a sip of the coffee Bash had poured for him. "The tequila was better."

"You say that now," Logan said. "Until Emma's mom knocks your drunken ass down over dinner."

"Good point." He drank two cups of coffee, had a soda, and by the time they left, felt clearheaded. He was glad he hadn't driven Rhonda today, though. He'd bring her to the restaurant tonight. Not that he wanted to show off for anyone in particular.

Okay, maybe he did.

After they left the bar, he went home, showered, changed into his navy blue suit that he didn't much want to wear, but when Georgia Burnett told you to wear a suit, you wore a suit. She said they were going to church tonight, and even though it was just for rehearsal, they were still going to be in God's house and you had to dress up.

You didn't get on Georgia's bad side. After picking out a tie, he climbed into Rhonda and headed over to the church. He pulled into the lot and parked, then got out, straightened his tie, and walked through the front doors.

It was quiet except for the sounds of voices coming from the front of the church. Emma and Luke were already there, along with Reid and Logan. Logan's girlfriend, Desiree, was there as well. And there was no mistaking Chelsea's fiery red hair as she sat in the front pew next to Jane.

And over where Emma's parents were talking to the minister stood Molly, wearing a dress that hugged her body all the way to her waist, then flowed out from her hips. The dress had bright flowers on it, but honestly, all he noticed were her bare shoulders and her tan skin. Her hair was loose, waves cascading halfway down her back. She sported high heels that had no business being worn in a church, showcasing legs he had no business thinking about in a church, either.

"Got some sins to confess, buddy?" Bash slapped him on the back and gave him a smirk.

"Probably."

"Why don't you save it for another day? Let's get this shindig going. I'm starving."

"So what you're saying is, you're just in it for the food."

"Oh, no. I'm totally here for Luke and Emma's happily-ever-after. I'm all about the love, man."

They walked down the aisle. "It's not good to lie in church, Bash."

Bash gave him a lopsided grin as they made it to the front of the church.

"Is everyone here?" the minister asked.

Emma's mother looked around. "Yes, I believe so."

"Then we'll get started. For those who don't know me, I'm Reverend Barry Greenwood, and I'll be performing the service tomorrow. I like things informal, so please call me Barry."

Barry got things in order in a hurry. He sent the bride, her parents, and the bridesmaids down to the back of the church, and Luke and the guys set up at the front. Luke stood first in line, followed by Logan, his best man, then Reid, Carter, and Will.

"I'll be first in line to grab him if he makes a run for it," Will said with a grin.

"I don't think he has any intention of running. Look at his face."

Will looked around the guys, then shook his head. "You're right. He's like a lovesick puppy."

"Kind of disgusting, isn't it?" Logan asked.

Carter rolled his eyes. "You're even worse the way you're looking at Des."

Logan grinned. "She's been on a movie shoot for six weeks and just got back three days ago. How am I supposed to look at her?"

"I'm surprised you're even here," Reid said, glancing down the aisle at Desiree. "She looks hot."

"I could kick your . . . You're lucky we're in church, kid."

Carter laughed, but then Bash started up the aisle with Emma's mom, so they all had to straighten up. He delivered her to the front row, then Evan, Luke's friend on the police force, escorted Martha down the aisle. Though Martha wasn't technically family, she was the McCormacks' housekeeper and the closest thing Luke, Logan, and Reid had to a mother since their own had abandoned them. And she had a grin a mile wide at being considered the mother figure at Luke's wedding.

The bridesmaids started down, with Barry informing them about how to walk.

"Not too fast, ladies. This isn't a race. But don't take all day, either."

Carter was fascinated with Molly's walk, especially since she did everything in her power to avoid making eye contact with him as she made her way down the aisle and over to where the rest of the bridesmaids were standing.

Jane's six-year-old daughter Tabitha was going to be the flower girl. She had such a serious face as she practiced walking down the aisle with a plastic basket. Tomorrow, it would be filled with flowers.

Cute.

Then Emma's dad walked her down the aisle. Luke cleared his throat.

"It's just the rehearsal, Luke. You don't get to choke up until tomorrow," Logan said.

"Yeah, yeah."

They went through the motions, with Barry explaining what would happen at every step. It went pretty fast, which was good, because, like Bash, Carter was hungry. So when Barry told them they were good to go, everyone headed out to the restaurant.

Bash rode with him.

"Taking Rhonda tonight, huh?" he asked on the way.

"Yeah. She's my date." Nothing like taking your '67 Mustang Shelby as your date for the night. She was also going to be his date tomorrow. Less complicated that way. He typically didn't bring a date to a wedding, and he especially didn't need or want one at this event. He had enough issues to deal with.

They were going to have dinner in Tulsa at the Polo Grill on Utica Square. Emma's parents had provided the rehearsal dinner, and Georgia Burnett had fine dining down to an art form. She'd booked a private room, so they all gathered in there, where cocktails were provided.

Carter headed for the bar to order a whiskey, straight up, determined to ignore Molly the rest of the night.

Except she was dragged to the bar by Jane and Chelsea and Emma before he had a chance to get out of the way and go hide among his friends.

"Carter. You brought Rhonda with you tonight," Chelsea said.

"Yup."

Molly cocked a brow, then looked around. "Who's Rhonda?"

"His car."

She smirked. "You named your car?"

He shot her a look. "*You* named *your* car."

"That's different," she said with a shrug.

"In what way?"

"Never mind."

He took another drink, figuring the less said, the better, since their first meeting didn't go all that well.

"Oh, you have to see Rhonda," Jane said to Molly. "You'll understand then. Let's go outside and you can show her, Carter."

Such a bad idea. But Emma already had Molly by the hand, pulling her toward the door, so he downed the contents of his whiskey in one swallow, then followed the women outside.

There was no doubt about it, Rhonda was impressive. He always kept her gleaming, and her navy body paint with white stripes stood out in the crowded parking lot. She got a lot of looks from passersby as well.

"Oh. So that's Rhonda," Molly said.

"Yup."

"I can see why you'd name her. She's a beauty." Molly turned to face him. "It was always your dream to own a '67 Shelby."

He was surprised she remembered. "Yeah, it was."

"You must be doing very well."

"I'm doing okay."

"He's doing better than okay. He owns four auto repair shops now," Emma said with a wide smile. "Worked his butt off over the years. At least that's what Luke tells me."

"Worth the hard work for something like Rhonda. She'd go very well with my hair," Chelsea said with a wink.

"I'll take you for a ride in her sometime."

"It'd be more fun if I got to drive her."

Carter shook his head. "No one drives Rhonda but me."

Chelsea sighed. "You're no fun, Carter."

He slanted his gaze toward Molly, who looked as miserable as he felt.

"We'd better go back inside before people start missing us," Emma said.

Carter held open the door as the women walked inside. He caught a whiff of Molly's scent—something vanilla—as she walked by. He got in line behind her as they made their way back to the private dining room, trying not to notice the tension in her shoulders, the stiffness in her back, or the sultry sway of her hips that was more natural than affected, because she was definitely tense walking in front of him.

When they got back to the room, she went one way, and he went the other.

Wasn't this going to be fun?

He did a lot more drinking than eating during dinner, and it was a good thing he didn't have to give any toasts because he was starting to feel the effects of the whiskey. Emma's parents toasted, wishing the couple well, and Martha and her husband, Ben, did as well. He barely tasted the food, which was a shame, because the steak looked really good.

All he could think about was Molly, who kept her focus on her sister. She smiled at the appropriate times, and laughed when someone told a joke. But her laugh didn't meet her eyes, and she no doubt wanted this to be over as much as he did.

He was just going to sit here and wait for everyone to leave and have another drink.

"You okay?" Luke asked as the party broke up and everyone started to leave.

Carter looked up, smiled, and nodded. "I'm fine. I'll see you tomorrow."

"Okay."

After everyone left, he headed to the bar and asked for another whiskey. Then another. He was going to have one hell of a headache tomorrow, but he'd deal with it.

Tonight, he just wanted to forget.

MOLLY CLIMBED INTO her car and turned the starter, listening to George cough as he struggled to come to life.

She also noticed Carter's Mustang still sitting in the parking lot. Everyone else had left.

She shouldn't care, but she'd noticed—out of the corner of her eye when she shouldn't have been looking, but couldn't seem to help herself—that he'd been downing a lot of whiskeys tonight. She also noticed—even though she shouldn't— the look on his face.

Misery. Unhappiness.

Not her problem. She was miserable and unhappy being here, too.

George sputtered and conked out on her.

Dammit. She'd just wait five minutes, like usual, and start him up again.

She should have just ridden with her parents as they'd suggested. But her independent streak refused to allow her to sit in the back like she had when she'd been a kid. She wanted the option to flee if necessary.

Currently, there'd be no fleeing.

As she counted down the minutes, she stared at Carter's car—or, Rhonda, as she was called. She sure was pretty. She hoped Carter wouldn't stumble out of the bar drunk as hell and bash Rhonda into some tree.

Not that it would be her problem if he did.

She tapped her fingers on the steering wheel.

Well, hell. Taking her keys out of George's ignition, she slid them into her purse and went back inside, figuring it wouldn't hurt to just check.

Maybe he was meeting someone here, like a date, and she could just duck out, satisfied that some woman would be driving him home.

She spotted him sitting at the end of the bar—alone—nursing a drink. He did not look sober at all.

Indecision made her chew on her lower lip. She could call Luke and have him come pick Carter up, but the guy was getting married tomorrow. The last thing he needed was to come fetch his drunk friend.

Damn Carter for putting her in this position. She wanted minimal contact with him until she left town, which was only a couple of days away. And now . . .

She walked with purpose down the bar and stopped in front of him.

He lifted his gaze toward her and frowned. "Molly?"

"Are you drunk?"

"Yes. I don't know. No. Yeah, probably."

She rolled her eyes and held out her hand. "Give me your keys."

He gave her a drunken half smile. "Are you going home with me?"

"Not on your life. Give me your keys, Carter."

He dug into his pocket and put the keys in her hand, then closed her fingers over them. "Your hands are still soft." He turned her hand over. "And you still bite your fingernails, Moll."

She jerked her hand away from his grasp. "Come on. Let's go."

He slid off the barstool. "Okay."

Grateful that at least he was cooperative and not belligerent, she walked out to the parking lot and opened the passenger door of the Mustang. The delicious smell of leather greeted her. "Get in."

He got in, then frowned up at her. "You're driving?"

"Yes. You've been drinking a little too much tonight, Carter."

"Right. Shouldn't drive Rhonda."

She slammed the door a little forcefully, then went around

to the driver's side, experiencing a slight thrill as she slid into the seat and adjusted it.

When she started it up and felt the rumble, she couldn't resist a smile. Oh, yeah. The Mustang was a beauty, all right.

She shifted Rhonda into first and pulled to the end of the driveway, carefully looking both ways before pulling out into traffic and heading for the highway.

"I assume you still live in Hope."

"Yup." He gave her his address and was at least coherent enough to provide directions to his house. "Thanks for driving me home."

"Not a problem." The problem was going to be coming back to get George tomorrow amidst all the wedding stuff going on. But she'd deal with that tomorrow.

She took the exit leading to Hope, then followed Carter's directions to his house.

Carter was quiet on the ride back to town. Thankfully, because she had absolutely nothing to say to him.

Surprisingly, he had a nice house with a sizeable yard and a big driveway. She pulled in and put on the emergency brake, then shut off the engine. Then she got out and came around to the passenger side and opened up the door.

"Come on. Let's go inside."

Carter got out of the car, then laid his hands on her shoulders. "I'm sorry, Molly."

Not the first time she'd heard that, and she wondered exactly what he was apologizing for. Tonight, or for twelve years ago. She decided to ignore the warmth of his hands on her. He was drunk, and at least he was nice about it, so tonight he got a pass.

"It's okay. Let's go inside."

She fumbled around on the key chain and found what looked like the front door key, so she opened the door, then flipped on the light. From what she could see, it was a nice, spacious house.

But that was as far as she was going. "Are you okay?"

He turned to her and gave her a nod. "Yeah. I'm fine. Thanks."

"I need to take your car with me so I can get home. You think you'll remember that in the morning?"

He gave her a goofy smile. "Of course. I'm drunk, not shitfaced."

She shook her head. "Good night, Carter."

"'Night, Molly."

She pivoted and walked away, then got in his car and drove off.

Their interaction had been so civil.

And so much had been left unsaid.

She felt worse now than ever.

Chapter 5

MOLLY'S BREATH CAUGHT as she stood in the back of the church with her sister

Emma had always been beautiful, but today she was the most gorgeous woman Molly had ever seen. In a cream-colored off-the-shoulder gown with a slight train and tons of intricate lace, Emma was a vision.

Luke was going to go crazy when he saw her.

Their mom had already shed copious tears, and they'd had to fix her makeup twice, until Emma told her if she cried one more time and made Emma tear up one more time, she was going to make her go sit in the car until after the wedding. Mom had straightened up after that and promised no more tears, at least until during the wedding. Emma had cast a pleading look at Molly, who held up her hands in surrender.

"I can't make her not cry."

Emma sighed. "It's a good thing I'm wearing waterproof mascara. I don't want to look like a raccoon in the photos."

"You're going to look breathtakingly beautiful in every picture," their mother had said, which had made Emma tear up again. And then Mom had started blinking back tears.

"Mom," Emma said. "You're supposed to be the rock here."

"I know. But one of my babies is getting married today. I don't know where all this emotion is coming from."

Fortunately, Reverend Barry had showed up and told them it was time to start. They all lined up and Molly smoothed down any imaginary wrinkles in her deep purple dress, then picked up her flowers and stood in front of Emma. She turned and blew her sister a kiss, so very glad she was here.

At least for today, she was happy to be home.

It was time to walk down the aisle.

As the music started up, she was suddenly transported back twelve years, when she and Carter had made plans for their own wedding. Of course, it had been kind of a rush. They hadn't anticipated getting married that quickly. But things had happened, and when it had, they both decided they wanted to get married right away.

They were in love, after all, so why wait? They knew they wanted an eternity together.

Until disaster happened. And then her world had been crushed, and everything had fallen apart after that.

That's when she realized that someone saying they loved you meant nothing, and she'd gone dead inside.

She shook it off. Now wasn't the time to think of the past, but the future. Namely, her sister's future. She followed Des down the aisle, trying to remember Reverend Barry's instructions about keeping the appropriate pace.

The church was filled with people, but she kept her focus on the altar, making sure to not look in the direction where all the guys were lined up in their tuxes. There was no way she was going to make eye contact with Carter.

Instead, she looked straight ahead and made sure to smile, because pictures were being taken, and she wouldn't ruin Emma's day by scowling.

She made it to the altar and turned, watching cute little Tabitha all dressed up, smiling broadly and sprinkling flowers across the carpeted aisle. Then everyone stood as Emma and their dad started down the aisle. Everything else was forgotten as her beautiful sister and Luke stood together and made their vows to love and honor each other forever. And after Reverend Barry pronounced them husband and wife and they kissed, Molly's heart squeezed.

Despite her views on love and marriage, she felt right about this ceremony. It was so obvious Luke and Emma belonged together, and watching them seal the deal with a passionate kiss only confirmed that. Molly sighed in contentment.

They exited the church, but stayed behind for photos. Fortunately, she was paired up with Logan, though she was conscious of Carter nearby, who looked utterly, devastatingly handsome in his black tux with white shirt and purple flower tucked in his lapel.

She tried her best not to notice him, but it was difficult as they all shuffled for photos, and then she had to sit in the pew while Logan, Luke, and Reid took a photo together and they all sat and watched as the bride and groom took one spectacular picture.

"They look perfect, don't they?" Carter asked.

He was sitting behind her. She nodded, not looking at him.

"You look beautiful today, Molly."

"Thanks." She got up and made her way over to her parents, then stood for the family picture with them and with Emma, then with Emma and Luke. It seemed to take an eternity at the church, and it felt like Carter's gaze stayed on her the entire time, but when she happened to glance his way again, he was huddled up with Bash and Will and not even looking at her.

Likely it was all in her head, tension and nervousness at his proximity getting the best of her today. She'd known she'd have to spend the entire day with him, and she'd built it up that she'd be shoulder to shoulder to him for the duration, when it was anything but.

She could survive today. She could put up with anything, because after tomorrow, she'd be on her way back to Austin, and she'd never have to come back to Hope again.

After they finished up the photos, they climbed into the limos. This time, the bridesmaids and groomsmen rode together, and the bride and groom rode alone. Which meant more time in a confined space with Carter. Des and Logan

snuggled up together, as did Will and Jane, which made sense
since they were couples. She chose a seat over in a corner of
the limo, and didn't it just figure that Carter ended up sitting
next to her. Bash and Chelsea were preoccupied arguing about
something, leaving her and Carter alone.

It was a good-sized limo, but there were quite a few of
them in there, so it wasn't like they could all spread out.
Which meant Carter's thigh was pressed alongside hers.

It had been twelve years since he'd touched her. Since she'd
touched him. In those last moments before she'd walked away
from him forever, they'd shared tears and words neither of
them could take back. Now, silence stood like an impenetrable
steel wall between them.

"The wedding was good, huh?" he asked, obviously reaching for something, anything to say.

"You don't have to talk to me."

"We have to talk, Molly."

She lifted her gaze to his. "No, we don't."

"There's a lot that needs to be said."

"No, there isn't." She purposely kept her voice low so the
others wouldn't hear their conversation. But damn if she'd
smile at him.

Instead, she looked straight ahead, wishing she were seated
near the window so she could focus on the scenery, and not
the partition separating them from the driver. She couldn't
eavesdrop on everyone else's conversations, because that
would be rude, which meant her only recourse was to either
talk to Carter, or stare ahead like a zombie.

And it was a twenty-five-minute drive to the reception
venue.

Great. Maybe she should close her eyes and take a nap. Or
maybe Carter would, since he'd had so much to drink the
night before.

"Shouldn't you be tired or something?" she finally
asked him.

He frowned. "No. Why should I be tired?"

"You drank a lot last night."

"Oh, that." His lips curved, drawing her attention to the

fullness of the bottom one, something she definitely did not want to look at, or remember. "Nah, I'm fine. Had a whopper of a headache this morning, a minute of panic when I couldn't find Rhonda."

"Rhonda is just fine, and parked in Luke's garage."

"Thanks for the rescue and the ride home, by the way."

"You're welcome." She looked away again, but then shot her attention back on him. "You wouldn't have really driven home in your condition, would you?"

"No. I'd have either called a taxi or one of the guys to give me a ride. I am a responsible adult now, Molly."

She snorted in disbelief, louder than she'd intended to, which caused nearly everyone in the limo to look her way.

Great.

"What's so amusing over there?" Chelsea asked.

Searching for something . . . anything . . . she finally blurted out, "Oh, nothing. Carter told a joke."

"Well, now you have to share," Logan said.

"Was it a dirty joke?" Will asked, causing Jane to poke him in the ribs.

"Thanks a lot," Carter whispered to her.

She clasped her hands together in her lap. "You're so welcome."

Now that everyone's attention was focused on Carter, she could relax. And she could tell he was squirming, which made her even happier.

"Let's see," Carter said. "What was that joke again? Oh, right. I remember now. A husband and wife came back from their honeymoon, and they weren't speaking to each other. The best man asked what was wrong.

" 'Well,' the groom said. 'When we made love the first night, I forgot what I was doing and left fifty bucks on the pillow.' "

" 'Ouch,' said the best man. 'I'm sure she'll forgive you, though. Surely she couldn't expect you to save yourself for marriage.' "

" 'It's not that,' said the groom. 'The problem was, she gave me twenty bucks in change.' "

Despite herself, Molly snorted again, and everyone else

laughed as well. She lifted her gaze to Carter, who winked at her.

Damn him. She wasn't going to like him ever again. She was a lot more comfortable hating him. He'd been in that dark place in her heart for twelve years, and that's where he was going to stay.

They arrived at the reception hall and there was a decided chill in the air. She was glad Emma had thought to have the matching long-sleeved shrugs added to their gowns, because she might need hers before the end of the night. October could be so unpredictable in Hope, and while the day had dawned warm and sunny, it was growing cooler in the evenings and these skimpy dresses weren't going to provide much in the way of warmth.

They made their way into the reception area, and Molly took in all the beautiful decorations. Emma and their mom had seen to all the planning, with a lot of help from Martha and the bridesmaids as well. It was gorgeous, with abundant fall colors, including eggplant and burnt orange as well as deep yellows and browns. Champagne was flowing and the bar was open. People were filing in and the deejay was already playing music.

Molly made her way to the bar to get a glass of wine. She met her dad there.

"How's it going, sweetheart?"

"Fine, Dad. How about you?"

"Happy to have one of my baby girls married. And how about you?"

"Happy to not be one of your baby girls who got married today."

He laughed, then put an arm around her and tugged her close. "Plenty of time for that. You just haven't found your knight in shining armor yet."

She didn't want to tell her father she didn't believe that knight existed, so she just nodded. "Right."

"I'm glad you're here."

At this moment, with her dad kissing the top of her head, so was she. "Me, too."

She didn't miss a lot about Hope, but she did miss her parents and her sister. If she could have packed them up and had them travel the country with her, life would have been perfect. But she couldn't, so she made do without them. At least her mom and dad visited her a couple of times a year, as did Emma when she could. She was grateful for that.

She rounded up the wedding party and got them to stand at the entrance to the ballroom so they could flank Emma and Luke when the deejay announced their arrival.

The doors opened, and the deejay called for everyone's attention.

"Ladies and gentlemen, put your hands together and direct your eyes to the open ballroom doors while I introduce Luke and Emma McCormack!"

Luke and Emma entered, their smiles wide, clasping their hands together as everyone cheered.

Her sister was married. Wow. That was kind of surreal.

She grinned.

They made their way to the head table and sat. Champagne was poured, and Logan got up to make his toast.

"I know my brother well, and if anyone was ever against marrying—again," he said, to much laughter, "it was Luke. Until he met Emma, the one woman he couldn't live without. When you find that right person, that one person who you're meant to be with no matter what happens, then you know. And with Luke, he's always known it was Emma. So raise your glasses and toast to Luke and Emma."

Everyone toasted and drank.

Molly had been preparing a speech, but it was going to be hard. Still, she knew as the maid of honor it was her duty, so she took the mic next.

"I haven't lived in Hope for a very long time, which means I wasn't here to witness Luke and Emma's love story. But I know love when I see it. It's a palpable thing. Something you feel, like instinct. It's just . . . there. And when it happens between two people, it can't be denied."

She felt Carter's gaze on her, saw him out of the corner of her eye despite her attempt to focus only on the smiling bride and groom. She retrained her attention and concentrated on the simmering tears in her sister's eyes.

"So when Emma brought Luke to meet me, their love hit me instantly, and I knew he was the one for her. She had changed from this focused, driven individual, to someone who was part of a couple. She became a lot less 'me' and a lot more 'us.' And that's what love is, when it becomes less about what's best for the one, and more about what's best for the whole. Because love is not a singular thing, It's not about what's best for me, but about what I can do to make you happy."

She raised her glass. "To Emma and Luke. May you spend a lifetime making each other happy. I love you both."

Glasses clinked, and people drank to the couple. Emma got up and wrapped her arms around Molly. "I love you, too. Thank you for that. And you made me cry, dammit."

Molly blinked back the tears that she hadn't wanted to shed. She laughed. "Sorry. And you're welcome. I hope you're both happy forever."

"We will be."

After Emma returned to her seat, Molly looked over to find Carter staring at her. This time, there was no clever wink, no smile.

She saw the hurt, the realization that the speech hadn't been entirely intended for the bride and groom.

She'd spoken from the heart and the words had just spilled from her. And if he'd gathered some truth from them, there wasn't anything she could do about that.

Their love was in the past. They'd had their chance, and they'd blown it.

There was no future for them, no happily-ever-after.

The thought of it made her ache all over.

CARTER WASN'T GOING to let Molly's words ruin his night. Or, rather, Luke and Emma's night. It was a night of fun and partying, not an evening to remember the past and the wreckage that had been in its wake.

But Molly's toast, what she'd said about love, left a big gaping hole of pain in his heart that was hard to ignore.

She was still hurting, he knew it, and there wasn't a

goddamn thing he could do to change what had happened all those years ago. He'd been young and stupid and had thought only about himself. God, it had been so long ago. They'd been so innocent.

He needed to talk to her. They needed to resolve things, so they could put it away, could move on with their lives.

He kept an eye on her while they ate dinner. She focused on talking to Jane, Chelsea, and Des, refusing to look at him.

Avoiding having that conversation wasn't going to give them closure.

After dinner, the deejay played Emma and Luke's song. He liked seeing his good friend dance with his wife.

Luke's wife. God, his best friend was married now. A lot of his friends were getting married and starting families. At thirty and with a well-established career, that was something Carter should be thinking about doing. He'd bought a nice big house with four bedrooms, but he had no one to share it with. He dated a lot. He'd even had a serious relationship or two over the years. But he hadn't managed to pull the trigger yet. He was waiting for that one woman to gut-punch him and then he'd just . . . know.

Watching as Molly sat and laughed at something Chelsea said, he felt that punch in his gut. Her hair was pulled up in some kind of fancy something or other. It was pretty, with pieces of hair framing her face and making her blue eyes stand out even more tonight. Maybe it was the purple dress that hugged her curves, or maybe it was just that she'd always gut-punched him.

No. Just no. She wasn't the one for him. They'd established that a long time ago, and she was hightailing it out of Hope as soon as she could. Then he could go back to doing what he did, and she could do . . . whatever it was she did.

That's why they both needed closure. So they could move on, and he could find that someone to have his forever with. And maybe, so could Molly.

Chapter 6

AVOIDANCE. MOLLY WAS doing a fine job of avoiding being anywhere near Carter, which so far was working well. She had stood by and watched Emma and Luke perform their first dance, and done her obligatory dance with Logan as part of the bridal party before blending into the crowd. Fortunately, Logan was more than happy to go off with Des, and she was free to mingle. Or hide.

She hung out with her parents, happy to spend as much time with them as she could since she'd be leaving the day after tomorrow. Plus, her mom had an intense new project going on and she wanted to hear details about it.

"It's so exciting, Molly," her mom said as they grabbed a spot at the table. "I'm spearheading the revitalization of the Hope town square project, including the fountain."

"Really? Is this something your marketing firm is doing?"

Her mom shook her head. "No. It's a personal project, a labor of love and something I'm very committed to. You know how much we all enjoyed the fountain, how much fun we all used to have in the town square when you and Emma were little."

Molly couldn't help but be captured by her mother's enthusiasm. "Of course. I played in that fountain when I was a kid. I used to love the flying dolphin sculpture. I miss seeing it."

"We all loved it. But that poor dolphin rusted and had to be taken down. That's part of the process, to have another one commissioned. Even the fountain's been closed for years. The revitalization project has been working to reopen it. Bigger and better, so that future generations will be able to enjoy it. It's required the help and generosity of many of the citizens of Hope. We still have a ways to go, but you know me. I'm relentless, and I've been pushing everyone to get involved."

She could see her mother bullying businesses to give money or offer services in order to get this done. "I'm so thrilled you're deeply involved in this, Mom."

"We have an end date in sight, and construction is already underway. Now that we have momentum going, we can't back down. I have to stay on top of everyone, otherwise the project will fizzle and die. I've worked so hard on this, I just want to see it finished."

Molly laid her hand on her mom's. "If anyone can do it, you can." Her mother was a dynamo of energy, and once she got hold of a project, nothing got in her way. That's what had made her so successful in business all these years. She had no doubt her mother would see that project through.

"I hate to disturb the two of you," her father said, holding out his hand toward Molly's mother. "But if you wouldn't mind, I'd like to dance with this beautiful lady."

Molly grinned, and her mom smiled.

"You don't mind, do you?" her mom asked.

"Not in the least. You two go ahead."

Her mom stood, and took her father's hand. They walked off toward the dance floor, and Molly felt butterflies in her stomach as her father pulled her mother into his arms.

Now there was a forever love. Just like her sister and Luke, who sidled up next to her parents, the two couples whispering and laughing.

It made her ache. Not with jealousy, but with a longing that was almost painful. Logan held Des close, Jane was up there with her husband, Will. Even Chelsea was out there with Bash, the two of them laughing together.

She'd never felt more alone.

She felt a hand on her shoulder. "How about we go out there and dance with everyone else?"

Carter. She lifted her gaze to his. "No, thanks. I'm fine sitting this one out."

He grasped her hand and pulled her up. Short of jerking her hand away from his and causing a scene, there wasn't much she could do. "We'll be polite to each other. Smile. Dance like old friends."

The problem was, they weren't old friends, and holding his hand seemed all too . . . familiar. They'd held hands all through high school. They'd done a lot more than that. And as they stepped onto the dance floor and he put his arm around her waist, tugging her close, the years suddenly fell away.

It was the sophomore dance. She'd been a freshman, and she'd had a ridiculous crush on Carter since day one of high school. They'd definitely noticed each other, and when he'd asked her to the dance, it was as if all her dreams had come true.

He'd kissed her for the first time after the dance, and they were inseparable after that.

Now, as she looked into the sea green of his eyes, she remembered every reason she'd fallen in love with him. The scar above his right eyebrow that he'd gotten playing baseball, the way he always held her gaze when they were close, the feel of his body moving against hers. They'd always fit so perfectly together. And when the deejay switched songs, they both stilled.

It was their song. She knew every word. Carter had even sung it to her—off-key—when they were entwined together in his bed above the garage of his parent's house, after they'd made love.

"I Knew I Loved You before I Met You."

She tried to pull away.

"Did you do this?" she asked.

He looked as horrified as she must. "No. God, Molly, no. I would never . . ."

But she'd already fled the dance floor, hurrying her way out of the ballroom, needing to get as far away from that song, away from the memories, as she could.

She went outside, the cool night air settling around her like an icy blanket. Chilled, she wrapped her arms around herself and started walking, not even caring where she was going. She only knew she had to get away from the past, from that damn song and the bitter memories it represented.

"Molly."

She shook her head as Carter came up beside her. "Go away."

"Molly, stop."

She kept walking. Only there was no place to go. They were surrounded by nothing but deserted road for miles on end. Still, she kept walking, until Carter put his hand on her shoulders.

"Stop. Stop running."

"I'm not running," she said as she turned to face him.

"Isn't that what you've been doing for twelve goddamn years? Running? From me, from what happened?"

"No. I've been living my life. Perfectly happy, without you."

She was shaking. It was cold out here. She needed to get back inside. But she just   couldn't.

He took off his jacket and flung it around her shoulders. She wanted to shrug it off, but she was freezing. She might be angry, might be confused and irritated, the past a hazy cloud in her mind right now, but she wasn't stupid. She slid her arms into it, his body warmth and his scent surrounding her, only adding to her confusion.

"Leave me alone, Carter."

"I've done that. For twelve years. Now we need to talk." He dug keys out of his pocket and led her to the parking lot, to one of the cars.

"This isn't your car."

"No, it's Bash's. I borrowed his keys. Slide in."

She got in and he closed the door, then came around to the other side.

Grateful to be inside the vehicle where it was warmer, she snuggled into his jacket, his scent making her even more miserable.

When he turned to her, she stared out the window.

"I'm sorry," he said.

He'd said those same words twelve years ago. They mattered even less now than they had then. The damage had been done. Words wouldn't help.

"Molly. Talk to me."

She shifted to face him, the anger and hurt she'd held inside boiling to the surface. "About what, Carter? About how you and I messed up so badly all those years ago? How I got pregnant, and then we decided we were so in love we'd go ahead and get married and plan a future together? How I lost our baby, the one we both wanted so much we'd already begun to pick out names? And then you decided that maybe me miscarrying hadn't been such a bad thing, because it meant you could go ahead and go to college?"

He took a deep breath. "That's not what I said, and you know goddamn well that's never what I meant."

"Wasn't it? I lost our child, Carter, the baby you and I made together. I was crushed, while all you felt was relief, because your plans for the future wouldn't be waylaid. You got exactly what you wanted, which was your freedom. And you know why? Because you never loved me. You wanted out of the relationship my pregnancy trapped you in. Damn good thing I lost our baby, wasn't it?"

He looked crushed. She wasn't buying it.

"You know that's not how I felt."

He reached out for her but she backed away, pushing herself into the corner of the seat.

"It's exactly how you felt. Because you went to college and you never once looked back. I was nothing but a distant memory."

She stared straight ahead, shaking from the fury she'd unleashed.

"Feel better now that you got that off your chest?"

She shot him a look. "No. I'll never feel better about what

happened. And that's the part you'll never be able to understand."

She shrugged out of his jacket and left it on the seat, then shoved open the door and got out, desperate to get away from him, away from the raw, painful memories she'd kept buried.

Now she'd dredged them up again. Now she had to face the nightmare and the pain all over again.

"Damn you Carter," she whispered into the night as she made her way back to the ballroom.

She didn't even have her car. She couldn't escape, so she was stuck at the reception until the end.

She should have never come home.

CARTER SAT OUT in the parking lot, catching his breath long after Molly went inside. He figured the less she saw of him, the happier she'd be.

Though he doubted she was going to be happy no matter what.

He had no idea she still held so much resentment toward him. He might just sit in Bash's car the rest of the night and think about how fucked up this situation was.

At least Molly would be leaving soon. Not that he wanted her to go, but there were obvious reasons the two of them shouldn't occupy the same space.

He'd made a lot of mistakes when he was younger, and nothing he said was going to make up for them, so he should just stop trying. It was only making things worse.

Now he knew why she'd spent all these years away from Hope.

She'd wanted to stay far away from him, which only made him feel shittier than he'd felt twelve years ago when he'd found out Molly had left town.

He wished there was something he could say, something he could do. Talking to her now only seemed to make it worse.

Although he'd buried his own pain, now even thinking about what happened hurt. He'd been stupid to think they needed to dredge it all up again.

For what reason? To relive that pain again?

It was best to leave the past alone. Molly had run from it, and he'd done his best to forget it. They obviously both had coping mechanisms that worked, and the sooner they were hundreds of miles away from each other, the better.

He finally got out of the car and locked it, then headed back toward the ballroom, intending to stay far away from Molly. But this was Luke's night, and he was going to celebrate it and leave his relationship with Molly out of it.

Taking a deep breath, he put on a smile and opened the door.

Chapter 7

MOLLY HAD STAYED the night at Luke and Emma's watching the dogs, because the newlyweds spent the night at a penthouse suite at one of Tulsa's premiere hotels. She'd gotten up early this morning and driven over to her parents' house so she could help her mom decorate for the brunch. Everything with her mother had to be thematic, and in this case, it was going to be a Hawaiian bon-voyage-slash-luau theme to reflect Emma and Luke's upcoming island honeymoon.

She'd spent the early morning hours drinking copious amounts of coffee to compensate for the lack of sleep she'd endured last night after her embarrassing meltdown with Carter. She'd gone back inside and dashed into the ladies room, repaired her makeup, and put on her brightest smile, because that night had not been all about her and she wasn't going to bring her drama to her sister's wedding. She'd danced and partied with the women, losing herself in the music and the fun, pushing the pain into the furthest recesses of her mind.

But after the festivities she'd climbed into her sister's guest bed and promptly spent the next three hours staring up at the ceiling.

Which meant today she was exhausted, grumpy and generally out of sorts. The complete opposite of her mother, who was filled with energy and enthusiasm, and cheerful as hell.

"Molly, help me hang these lights, will you?" her mom asked.

Lights? Why the hell did they need lights? "Uh, where's Dad?"

"He already hung the lights over the fireplace, but I want some in the kitchen. And your father went to pick up the food."

Oh, sure. He got the easy task. "Okay."

They strung lights and paper lanterns and blew up hideous plastic palm trees. There was Hawaiian music playing, posters of the islands placed around the house, and coconuts on all the tables. There hadn't been time for her mom to cook, otherwise Molly might be elbows deep in some kind of tropical coconut concoction, so she'd been spared that much, at least.

"There," her mom finally said, climbing down from the ladder where she'd hung an Aloha banner along the mantle. "That's festive, isn't it?"

It looked like Hawaii had exploded inside her parents' house. "You bet."

All Molly wanted to do was go lie down in one of the bedrooms and pass out. Especially knowing the wedding party would be partaking of the brunch today, which meant she'd have to face Carter.

But she'd get through it, knowing it would be the last time. After today, she'd be on the road, out of town, and back where she belonged, which was anywhere but Hope—her motto for the past twelve years.

She was already counting down the hours.

When the door opened and her dad came in juggling a box filled with food, her mother hurried over to help and Molly followed. Soon after, people started filing in and she was too busy greeting people to even think.

When Luke and Emma showed up, she hugged her sister. "How does it feel to be married?" she asked.

Emma grinned. "Not all that different, surprisingly. Yet somehow . . . fairly awesome."

"I'm really happy for you and Luke. I know we didn't get a lot of time together yesterday, but I want you to know that I believe in the two of you. I know you're going to make it work."

Emma gave her a curious look. "Well, of course we are. We love each other."

She didn't know why she'd said that. Maybe because she thought couples making it work was all too rare. Or maybe she was simply projecting. She squeezed Emma's hands. "That's right. You do. And it shows."

Carter came in, and Molly excused herself, went to grab her purse, and fished out his keys. "I brought your car back."

He took the keys. "Thanks. I appreciate it."

"No problem."

"Do you need a ride back to Emma's place?"

"No. I'll be staying here at my mom and dad's tonight, then leaving tomorrow. My car's already here." She was having trouble making eye contact with him. Things had been awkward between them before, but now it was simply brutal.

"Okay, then. Well, good luck, Molly. And drive safe."

"Yeah, thanks." She turned and walked away, needing distance. She felt so much being close to him—and not all of it was bad.

That was the problem, wasn't it? She still felt things for him. And she hated that she did. He'd probably moved on the instant she'd lost their baby, and here she was still feeling some ridiculous connection to him.

She intended to sever that connection, once and for all, starting tomorrow.

She was going to move on with her life and forget that Carter Richards had ever existed.

Everyone sat down to eat. The food was really good, surprisingly.

"I love the décor, Mom," Emma said. "Thank you for the sendoff."

"Yes, thanks," Luke added. "We're so ready for Hawaii."

"I can imagine," their mother said. "You've had a lot on your plates, with all the wedding planning and juggling your jobs on top of it. You both deserve to relax."

Emma looked at Luke. "I won't know what to do with myself, taking more than just a few days off. Whatever will we do with ourselves?"

Luke nuzzled her neck. "I'm sure we'll think of something."

Their mother cleared her throat. Emma laughed, then turned to Chelsea. "Are you sure about watching the dogs? I could easily board them at the clinic. Rachel and Leanne would look after them."

Chelsea waved her hand. "Don't be ridiculous. This way, your house won't sit empty while you're gone. The dogs will miss you both as it is, and I get to sit in a big house instead of my condo. It's a win for all of us."

Emma shot a smile to Chelsea. "Thank you for doing this."

"It's not a problem. Just don't expect me to vacuum up your dust bunnies."

Luke laughed. "God forbid."

"What about you, Molly?" Jane asked. "Are you heading back to Austin soon?"

"Tomorrow, actually."

"We're sure sorry to see you go," Will said. "It's been such a pleasure having you here."

Molly did her best to plant a genuine smile on her face. "Thank you. It's been fun to be in Hope again."

"Maybe you can start visiting more often," Chelsea said. "We have wicked fun girls' night out. We'd love to have you join us."

Emma nodded. "This is true. If you come home to visit, we'll schedule one when you're here."

"I travel a lot, too," Des said. "Maybe you can come up sometime when I'm in town and we can do girls' night then."

There was no way in hell Molly was ever coming back here. But she wasn't going to tell her sister—or her parents—in a roomful of people. "I'll definitely think about it. In the meantime, you all are welcome to come see me in Austin."

"Or wherever you end up next," Carter said, his gaze direct.

She didn't flinch, just met his gaze with a shrug. "I don't know. I like Austin. I might stay put for a while."

Carter's response was to arch a brow. That brow with the scar above it, the one she used to run her fingers over.

She shuddered, remembering oh-so-clearly those intimate moments they spent together, when he'd bring her fingertips to his lips, sucking each of them into his mouth until every part of her trembled. When he'd take her mouth in a kiss that made her dizzy. She'd learned so much about sex, about her own body, with him.

It was as if he knew exactly what she was thinking, because his green eyes went stormy dark.

"Excuse me." She pushed back from the table and went into the kitchen, leaned her hands on the sink, and looked out the window.

They were going to have forever together. A stupid teenage dream.

Back then it had felt so real. The looks they'd exchanged just a moment ago had felt just as real, and they weren't teenagers anymore.

Imagination. Just her imagination.

"What were you thinking about in there?"

She whipped around to find him standing just a few inches away from her.

"Nothing." She started to push past him, but he caught her hand.

"Molly."

She lifted her gaze to his. "Don't."

His thumb brushed her inner wrist, and her pulse kicked up. She didn't want to feel anything for him. She hated him.

She hated herself more, because she still did feel. And when he pulled her closer, she couldn't resist the draw.

"About last night. You did all the talking. There are a few things I want to say to you."

"Hey, Moll, I thought we might—"

With Emma's appearance, Carter took a step back, and so did Molly.

Carter took a deep breath. "I'm going to go talk to Luke."

He turned, grasped Emma by the shoulders, and planted a kiss on her cheek. "Really happy for you and Luke, Em." Then he left the room.

Emma frowned. "What was that all about?"

Shaking off the residual heat, she gave her sister an innocent look. "What was what all about?"

Emma crossed her arms. "Come on, Moll. You and Carter."

"There is no me and Carter. That was over a long time ago."

"Not from where I was standing. He had your hand, and you looked like you were about to kiss."

Molly let out a short laugh. "I can guarantee you that was not about to happen. Or ever happen. We don't even like each other."

"You don't have to like each other to still feel that pull of passion."

"That's not it. There was nothing."

At Emma's look of disbelief, Molly added, "Really, Em. There's nothing between Carter and me. We're over."

Emma hugged her. "I've always felt like there's something to your breakup with Carter that you never told me."

She'd never told anyone. Not Emma, not her parents. They would have swarmed her and coddled her and there would have been a giant mess of recriminations and finger-pointing, and they would have ended up hating Carter when it had been no one else's business. She'd dealt with it alone and run like hell, licking her wounds by herself.

"Nothing to tell. We just weren't meant to be. We were kids, you know? It was a big ugly blowup by two teenagers who thought they were in love—and weren't."

"Are you sure? Because it sure seems to me to be more than that."

One of the main reasons she'd gone—and stayed gone—was because her sister, and her mother, were both very insightful and constantly questioned her. "Absolutely sure. There's nothing more than that. It's just one of those situations where we can't be friends, you know?"

Emma frowned. "He didn't cheat on you, did he?"

The one thing she knew for a fact was that Carter had never been with anyone else while they'd been together. "No, he didn't cheat on me, Em. Let it go, okay?"

Emma finally sighed. "Okay. I just, love you, you know? And it seems to me that you're still hurting over it."

"I'm not. I'm fine. I'm just . . . ready to get on the road again."

Emma leaned against the kitchen counter. "You know, I really wish you would come home, Moll. I can't tell you how much I miss having you in my life."

Molly's stomach clenched. "I miss you, too. But I love the travel, the adventure of moving around. It's who I am."

It wasn't really who she was. She'd missed home every day for the past twelve years. It was who she'd had to become, in order to survive.

Emma hugged her. "Think about it. Home is always here for you if you change your mind."

Molly squeezed her sister tight. "I will."

But she wouldn't change her mind.

Tomorrow, she'd be gone.

CARTER PARKED RHONDA in the garage, smoothing his hand over the steering wheel before pulling the keys out. She was in perfect condition.

Not that he was surprised Molly would take such good care of her. She'd taken good care of him that night at the rehearsal dinner.

He hung his keys on the hook just inside the door, then went to the fridge and grabbed a beer before making his way into the living room. He propped his feet up on the coffee table and grabbed the remote, turned on the TV and found the football game, then leaned back and took a long swallow of beer.

It was over. He'd done his part for Luke and Emma's wedding, which had been a success, just as he thought it would be.

He'd said his goodbyes at Emma's folks' house, even saying a polite goodbye to Molly, who'd managed a smile and an awkward hug.

That had been the worst part, knowing he wasn't going to see her again, when he knew damn well so much had been left unsaid between them.

But, really, what more could be left to say? They'd already said it all—twelve years ago. The past should be left there, and they needed to go their separate ways. Trying to repair the damage would only make things worse.

The problem was, he'd wanted to talk to her, to make the hurt go away for both of them.

He took another drink of beer and stared at the TV, hoping for answers, when he knew there weren't any. But he'd spent years thinking about Molly, remembering every smile, every laugh, every curve of her body. She'd been the one woman he compared every other woman to, and they all had come up short.

Sure, she'd been his first love, and an important one. And yeah, things had ended badly between them, which had left a lingering sadness that he'd never quite forgotten. But he should be over her by now. He should have been able to move on.

The problem was, he hadn't. And he didn't know why. Maybe he never would.

Chapter 8

MOLLY HAD PLANNED to sleep in this morning since she had a long drive ahead of her. Then she'd get up, have coffee and breakfast with her parents, and head out.

She was just rolling over to get out of bed when she heard the scream.

She bolted out of bed, threw open the bedroom door, and went running into the living room to see her mother sprawled on the floor, the ladder lying on top her. Her right arm and leg were twisted at a very unnatural angle. Pokey, her parents' dog, was barking and whining by her.

"Mom!" She dashed over to her. "Are you okay?"

Her mother looked up, dazed. "Molly. It hurts."

Oh, God. Her heart raced, panic setting in. "Where's Dad?"

Tears streamed from her mother's eyes. She groaned. "Store. Oh, honey. I'm hurt."

That was it. She'd been so close to the fireplace, she might also have hit her head, though Molly didn't see any blood. She went to the phone and dialed 9-1-1, told them her mother had fallen, and gave the address.

Her dad arrived in the middle of the phone call. He dropped his grocery bag and rushed to her mother's side.

"Georgia. What happened?"

"I've already called for an ambulance, Dad. They're on the way. I think she's hurt her arm and leg. Not sure if she hit her head or not, so don't move her. She's in a lot of pain."

Her dad smoothed her mother's hair. Her mother was crying. She'd never seen her mom in such pain. And poor Pokey was just as upset as everyone else, licking her mom's uninjured hand. Her mom petted the dog, seemingly aware enough to notice Pokey's distress.

"Shh, it's going to be okay, honey," her dad said.

"I'm going outside to wait for the ambulance," Molly said.

Her dad nodded without looking at her. She ran into her bedroom and tossed on a pair of jeans and a sweatshirt, then went outside and waited at the curb.

Within a few minutes the ambulance arrived. The paramedics came in and she and her dad backed away while they took over.

She put her arm around her father.

"You're shaking, Molly."

"I'm okay." She was so not okay.

They immobilized her mother's right arm and leg, as well as her neck, then loaded her onto the stretcher.

One of the paramedics addressed her dad. "Her vital signs are stable and she seems lucid. There's no obvious appearance of a head injury, but until they check her out, we can't be certain. We're taking her to the hospital. You can meet us there."

Her dad nodded. "We'll be right there."

Her mom looked scared.

Molly was scared, too. Her mother was the rock of the family, always in charge. Always healthy. She never even caught colds. To see her like this, so vulnerable, so wounded, was devastating.

Her dad turned to her. "You ready?"

"Let me brush my teeth and put on some shoes. Then I'll be ready to go."

It took her a minute. She brushed her teeth, ran a brush through her hair, shoved a ponytail holder onto her wrist, and pulled on her tennis shoes, then grabbed her phone and purse and they were out the door.

The ride to the hospital was interminable. Molly filled her father in about waking up and hearing her mother's scream, finding the ladder on top of her.

"She was taking down those damn lights over the fireplace. I told her to wait, that I'd do it after breakfast."

"You know Mom. She likes to get things done right away."

Her father gripped the steering wheel. "I should have done it yesterday instead of watching the football game."

She leaned over and rubbed his shoulder. "It's not your fault, Dad."

They parked and went to the emergency room. Her dad filled out forms and gave insurance information, then they were directed to the waiting area.

"Dad, do you want a cup of coffee?"

He shook his head. He looked as miserable as she felt, but she needed some caffeine, so she wandered over to the vending machine and bought a terrible-tasting cup of coffee. The waiting was awful. After an hour, the front desk called her father's name, so they got up and went to the counter.

"Your wife is in room twelve. Through the doors and down the hall, then turn right."

She grabbed her dad's hand and they walked through the doors.

Her mom was in a room with a glass door. Molly pressed a large button and the door opened.

She was asleep, her hair a mess—Mom would hate that. Georgia Burnett was always impeccably groomed in public. She was hooked up to monitors, and her arm and leg were heavily bandaged.

There was a nurse in there.

"Mr. Burnett?"

"Yes."

"The doctor will want to talk to you. Have a seat and I'll go get him."

"Thanks," Molly said, since her dad could only stare at her mom.

Her mother opened her eyes, blinked a few times. "Emmett?"

Dad stood, and Molly did, too. Her dad went over to her uninjured side. "Georgia."

"I'm sorry I didn't wait for you to take down the lights."

"It's okay. How are you feeling?"

She smiled. "Better. They gave me some drugs to numb the pain. But I'm sleepy."

He patted her hand. "Good. You rest."

"They don't have her neck immobilized any longer," Molly said. "That's a good sign, Dad."

The doctor came in, a youngish guy who looked to be in his late thirties.

"Mr. Burnett, I'm Doctor Webb."

They shook hands.

"This is my daughter, Molly."

The doctor nodded.

"Your wife has suffered compound fractures in both her arm and her leg. Paramedics were concerned about the possibility of head or neck injury, but she checked out just fine there."

Thank God.

"She will need surgery on both her arm and her leg, though. We did X rays and the damage is pretty severe. She took a good fall from that ladder."

"Is she going to be all right?" her dad asked.

"She'll need a lot of rest, followed by physical therapy. After surgery, she'll likely be in the hospital about a week, then we'll release her, but she'll need some help until the casts come off. She'll have physical therapy while the casts are on, and then after."

Her dad nodded. "All right. Okay. Whatever she needs."

"We'll do the surgery tomorrow. We'll get her moved to a room in an hour or so."

After the doctor left, Molly sat and let it all soak in. Her father did as well.

"Should we call Emma?" her dad asked.

"No."

Molly looked up at her mother, who was awake again.

"Emma just left for her honeymoon. She's on a plane right now. Don't call her. You know your daughter, Emmett. She'll turn around and come back. I won't ruin her honeymoon."

Her father looked over at Molly, who was at a loss for what to say. Or what to do. Her mother had had an accident and was in pain, with a long recovery process ahead of her.

Calling Emma and bringing her home couldn't change that.

"Mom's right. Don't call Emma. She can't do anything for Mom right now anyway."

"All right," her dad said, then he looked over at Molly. "You were going to leave this morning."

She was. She glanced over at her mother, who was looking at her.

She couldn't leave. Not now. Not with Emma gone and her mom lying there in that bed so . . . vulnerable and her dad so helpless and alone.

There was no way in hell she could go back to Austin today.

Or for the foreseeable future.

So she said the words she never thought she'd hear herself saying.

"I'm staying."

Chapter 9

"GEORGIA BURNETT IS in the hospital."

Carter looked up from his desk to see Bash leaning against his doorframe.

"What? What happened?"

"She took a fall at home a few days ago. Broke her arm and her leg pretty badly."

Carter leaned back in his chair. "Holy shit. Is she okay?"

Bash nodded. "She's going to be okay, but she's going to be laid up for a while."

"Did someone call Molly and let her know?"

"Molly's still here."

"She is?" How could he not know that? "How do you know all this?"

Bash's lips curved. "Dude. I run a bar. I know everything that goes on in this town. Who lives, who dies, who's sleeping with who."

Carter cracked a smile. "Yeah, I forgot about that. Is Georgia home from the hospital yet?"

"No. She had surgery the other day, so she'll be in there for a few more days."

He needed to get to the hospital. "Okay, thanks for letting me know. What are you doing here, by the way?"

"Some brake work on my car. Why? Are you gonna give me a discount?"

"If I gave everybody that I knew a discount, Bash, I'd never make money."

"You're a cruel bastard, Richards."

"Not the first time I've heard that. Come on, let's go look at your brakes."

After work, he drove to the hospital. He knew Georgia liked daisies, so he stopped and bought her some. When he arrived at her room the door was partially closed, but the light was on, so he knocked.

"Come on in."

That was Emmett Burnett's voice, so he nudged the door open. Georgia was sitting up in bed. Her leg was held up by some kind of contraption with wires and slings. Her arm was in a cast, also immobilized by a sling.

"Carter," Georgia said. "How lovely to see you."

She was smiling. He was damned relieved to see her looking so good. He had envisioned a lot worse. Though seeing her in those casts was pretty bad.

"I would have been by sooner, but I just heard about your accident today. I'm so sorry you got hurt." He laid the flowers over on the table near the wall, then came over and kissed her on the cheek. "How are you doing?"

"Better than I was a couple of days ago. Thank you for the flowers."

"You're welcome."

"Take a seat, Carter," Emmett said, motioning to the chair on the other side of the bed. "Awfully nice of you to come by."

Carter rounded the bed and pulled up a chair. "So . . . tell me what happened."

"What happened was my impatient wife couldn't wait for me to take down the lights over the fireplace, and she was wearing slippery shoes." Emmett gave her a glare.

"I . . . well, he's right, of course," Georgia said. "I do like to get things done. And I wasn't so smart about it this time. Now look at me."

"How long are you going to be laid up and casted?" Carter asked.

"Twelve weeks for the casts, with a lot of physical therapy during and after."

She looked miserably unhappy.

"I'm so sorry." He leaned over and laid his hand on top of her uninjured one. "This must be frustrating for you."

"Especially with the Hope town square project at its most critical time."

Carter nodded. "Hey. That's the last thing you should be worried about right now. We'll carry on and figure something out."

"Guess what? I found the cutest thing downstairs in the gift shop, Mom—"

Carter stood as Molly entered the room. She stopped halfway in when she saw him.

"Oh. I didn't realize you had visitors. Hi, Carter."

"Hey, Molly."

"Look, Molly. Carter dropped by," her mother said with a bright smile. "He even brought me some daisies."

Molly frowned at the flowers suspiciously, like they might have a hidden bomb in them. "How . . . nice."

"I'm actually going to head home for a shower and a change of clothes, and to check on Pokey. If you don't mind, Molly."

"Not at all, Dad. You go ahead."

Emmett leaned over and brushed his lips over his wife's. "I'll be back after dinner."

"That's the real reason you're leaving. You want to stop and get a cheeseburger at Bert's."

He grinned. "Maybe."

She sighed. "Tell everyone I said hello."

"I will. And I'll be back later."

"Okay."

After Emmett left, Molly took a seat on the other side of the bed. "I think I'm going to stop at the bookstore and get you an e-reader. It'll be much easier than flipping through magazines or attempting to read a book. And you've been wanting to try one."

"Okay."

"When will you be released?" Carter asked.

"The doctor said probably in a few days. I'm anxious to get out of here and back home. Though that will bring its own set of challenges."

"Nothing you can't handle, Georgia."

She smiled at him. "Thank you, Carter. In the meantime, there's a project meeting coming up in a few days—you'll have to chair for me."

"I can handle it."

Molly frowned and slanted a look at Carter. "You're involved with the town square project?"

"Yeah. But your mother's been the one who got it all off the ground."

"And now I'm going to be stuck at home for the next few months," Georgia said. "I'm worried, Carter. You know we're at a critical point in all of this. And without me to push and shove and make sure everyone's doing their job, I'm concerned things won't move forward. Then there's the marketing aspect of it all as far as the launch, and working with City Council . . ."

He patted her hand. "Georgia, I don't want you to stress about any of this. We'll take care of it."

"I know you'll crunch the numbers and make sure the budget stays on track. But we need an organized genius, someone to run roughshod over everyone else."

"I'll find someone. No one as good as you, Georgia, but I'll find someone. Until you get back on your feet, so you can finish up the project yourself."

Georgia's face lit up. "Molly can help you."

Molly's gaze shot to her mother. "What?"

"You can help Carter with the town square project."

Carter had never seen Molly look so panicked. But in this case, he was staying out of it.

"Uh, Mom, I'm staying here to help you when you get home."

"And you'll have plenty of time to do both. Once I get settled at home, it's not like you'll be working. With you taking a leave of absence from your job in Austin, you and your dad can't just hover over me twenty-four hours a day."

"Yes, I can. That's what I intend to do. Dad has to work, you know."

"Your dad is taking extended vacation, which he can certainly do since he owns the company. Plus I'll have nursing help. And the project isn't a full-time thing, is it, Carter?"

Okay, maybe he was getting involved. "Not really."

"Then it's settled. You'll need to get Molly up to speed with everything that's been going on." She yawned. "Why don't you two grab something to eat and discuss it? I'm going to take a nap."

Carter looked at Molly, who gave him the same kind of helpless look she'd given her mother.

"I guess we're working together," he said.

THE VERY LAST thing Molly had wanted was to stay in Hope, but her mother's accident had changed all that. She had contacted her boss in Austin and told her that she'd have to remain in Hope for an unknown period of time to see to her mother's welfare, and she didn't know when she'd be back. Her boss said she'd have to hire someone to replace Molly.

Molly could accept that, and she could always find another job somewhere else. She was planning to drive down to Austin this weekend to pick up her things and close up her apartment. She'd bring everything back to Hope, and when her mom was well enough, she'd figure out where she was going after that.

Right now, her mother was a priority.

Working with Carter? Now that wasn't something she'd planned on, but she'd make the sacrifice, because she wasn't going to do anything to upset her mom at a time when she needed to concentrate on healing.

"What are you hungry for?" Carter asked as they walked through the front doors of the hospital.

"What?"

"Food, Molly."

"Oh. I'm not really hungry. I've been mostly eating at the cafeteria here the past few days."

"It's time to fix that. You need something else."

"I don't really want to be gone that long."

"You won't be. We'll grab something quick."

"Okay."

She got in his car and he drove them a few short blocks to a Mexican restaurant.

"They serve it up pretty fast here, so we'll be in and out in a hurry," he said as the hostess led them to their table.

She took a quick glance at the menu, deciding on enchiladas. When the waitress came they ordered drinks and their dinner simultaneously.

"I'm sorry about your mom," Carter said.

"Me, too."

"Did you call Luke and Emma?"

She shook her head. "We decided not to, because they'd turn around and come back from their honeymoon, and there's really nothing either of them could do for her right now. It's best they just enjoy themselves. They'll find out when they get home."

"Emma might end up pissed you didn't tell her."

Their waitress brought their drinks, along with chips and salsa. Molly's stomach gnawed with hunger. She hadn't eaten much today, so she dug in. "She might, but Dad and I are happier knowing she can enjoy her honeymoon worry free. She can be mad at me when she comes home."

"It was a good call."

"Thanks. We thought so as well."

She felt his gaze on her, but it was so hard for her to look back. What would they say to each other that hadn't already been said? The night of Emma and Luke's wedding, she'd laid it all out—everything she'd wanted to say to him all these years.

It hadn't made her feel any better. If anything, she'd felt worse than ever before.

"You don't have to work with me, Molly. I know how hard that'll be for you. I can make other arrangements."

Now she did look up. "I'll do it. Because my mom needs me to, and I need her not to feel stressed about anything right now. I think the two of us can figure out how to move around in the same circle without . . ."

"Feeling anything?"

She didn't know if those were the right words. Certainly not for her, because she'd always felt something for Carter. She likely always would. That's why she couldn't live here. Because she felt so much.

"Right," she said.

"I'll do my best not to feel anything when I'm around you."

"Great. Thanks."

"But I'm not going to guarantee it'll work, because I've always felt something for you, Moll."

She was about to object, but their waitress brought the food. And then Carter dug in and ate, as if what he'd just said hadn't meant a thing.

So typical.

"Tell me about the town square thing."

He scooped up a forkful of rice, chewed and swallowed, then followed that up with iced tea before laying down his fork. "Your mom spearheaded the project and got it off the ground, gathering the city council's cooperation and go ahead, then badgering business leaders into donating funds. She's done everything in her power over the past year to revitalize the town square and fountain, Molly. I'm sure you know better than anyone that once your mother gets an idea into her head, she'll do anything to make it happen."

Molly nodded. "She is rather dedicated to a cause."

"The fountain has lain dormant for years. You remember what it was like when we were kids. There was a play area, and all the kids splashed through the fountain. When it rusted and stopped working, no one repaired it and it just sat there, looking ugly. Your mother wanted it fixed and the whole town square revitalized. She organized a volunteer committee."

Molly listened while she ate. She pointed her fork at him. "And you're on said committee."

"Yeah. Georgia asked me to participate. It was something worth doing, so I joined in."

She cocked her head to the side and gave him a look.

"What?" he asked.

"I'm . . . surprised."

"Why?"

"I don't know. You involved in city politics?"

"It's not politics. It's a revitalization project. Trust me, I stay away from politics."

She wiped her mouth with her napkin, then set her plate to the side. "Oh, I don't know about that. It seems to me there's some political maneuvering in getting funding for a project like this."

"Your mother was the one who pressured local businesses—as well as the city—to provide the necessary funding."

"Now that I believe. But still, you're involved."

"I am a local business owner, Molly. It's in my best interest to make Hope as desirable a city as possible. Aesthetically as well as in other areas. You bring more people to Hope, I get more business as well."

"I see your point." She supposed she just couldn't reconcile the boy she'd once known—and loved—with the man he now was. She was going to have to try and wrap her head around who Carter was now, not who he used to be. He'd remained a figure in her head. Sweet, charming, and oh so sexy, in that boyish, teenage way he'd had about him.

The man sitting across the table from her was completely different. There was a confident air about him that hadn't been present when he was younger. Sure, he'd been cocky back then, but that was high school bravado. He'd been popular in school. He'd played baseball and basketball so he'd been one of the jocks, always a favorite with the girls. Why he'd gravitated toward her, she'd had no idea, since she hadn't played sports at all. She'd been more into drama club and music and books, but they'd shared some classes, and he'd started talking to her. And God, she'd fallen hard for his eyes and his mouth and then they'd begun studying together, which had grown into watching movies and generally hanging out, and that had been the end for her.

They'd spent every day together and she learned about baseball and basketball. She'd never liked sports much, but she learned to like it. He claimed not to be into plays and musicals, but he went to every one of her plays and her choir concerts. They meshed. And they fell in love.

He was her first love. She gave him her virginity—so easily, and without regret. He never made silly promises to her about how he was going to love her forever. He just loved her. And she loved him back.

And for three years it had been magical. Until she got pregnant.

That's when it all changed. She panicked, and so did he. They scrambled, hastily figuring out plans. They discussed abortion. She was graduating early. She had a scholarship. She wanted to go to college. So did he. This was going to change everything.

But in the end, she couldn't do it, and he respected her decision. They were determined to make it work. They'd get married. They were in love. He'd put off college and continue to work at the garage. She'd work part-time until the baby was born. Their parents would help out—as soon as both of them got up the nerve to actually tell them.

A week later, she'd miscarried. She was devastated, while Carter seemed . . . relieved.

And that's when her world ended. Because while she mourned the loss of the child she had already begun to love, Carter had started to back away, his mind already on college. When she wanted comfort, Carter had already planned his escape.

"Molly."

She lifted her head. "What?"

"You were somewhere else just now."

"Oh." She took a sip of water, hating herself for revisiting their terrible past. "Did you say something?"

"I was asking what your plans were for this week."

"Check my mom out of the hospital. Then I need to go to Austin and pick up my stuff."

"So you're moving?"

She nodded. "Back here. Temporarily. I have to quit my job, since things here will be in flux for a while."

"I'm sorry about that."

"It is what it is, and my mom needs me right now."

"I'll do what I can to help, at least as far as the town square project, so she doesn't have to stress about that."

"Thanks. And you need me at the meeting this week? I'm not sure I can make that."

"We'll postpone the meeting. You do what you need to do to get your mom settled and your stuff moved back here."

"Thanks. Again."

"It's no problem." He signaled the waitress for their check. "I know you want to get back to your mom."

He was being so accommodating, so nice to her. She supposed she was going to have to deal with Carter being in her life, at least part-time.

And it wasn't like there was anything personal between them.

Her running days were over and so was avoidance. At least temporarily. She had to stop thinking of him as the boy who'd broken her heart all those years ago. It was time to grow up and get past it, at least for now. For the sake of her mother. And when everything was back to normal, she'd leave again.

Just like always.

But for now, Hope was going to be home, for at least the next few months.

Chapter 10

THE LAST PERSON Carter expected to see in his shop on a Saturday morning was Molly.

He'd caught up on his paperwork at the two Tulsa locations, and was going to spend the day there. But Molly drove that clunker of a car into the bay and he happened to notice—how could he not? So he walked out to the garage.

"I thought you'd be heading to Austin by now."

She pursed her lips before answering. "So did I. But George is making an awful sputtering noise. And it took me a half hour to start him up this morning. My dad told me there was no way George was going to make it all the way back to Austin."

"I'm surprised you made it here. He looks—and sounds—like he needs a decent burial, not another road trip."

"Funny. But he's all I have."

"Can't you borrow one of your parents' cars?"

"Dad's truck is in just as bad shape as George. And anyway, in case of an emergency with Mom, he'd need her car since it's lower to the ground and easier to get her in and out of. I'd never leave him without it, even for just a weekend." She sighed.

"Go get yourself a cup of coffee in the office. I'll go check on the status of George and let you know the verdict."

"Okay, thanks."

Carter went into the garage and had a talk with Chad, who was under the hood of the car.

About fifteen minutes later, he washed his hands and found Molly eating a donut in the lounge.

She stood and swiped her hands back and forth. "You were gone awhile. That can't be a good sign."

"George's fuel pump is shot and so is the injector. They both need to be replaced."

"Crap. I don't suppose that's going to happen in, like, the next hour."

"No. It's going to take at least a day, and we need to get parts. So a few days."

"Double crap. I need to figure out what to do. I suppose I could maybe rent a car . . . or a truck." She chewed her bottom lip, then grabbed her checkbook out of her purse and studied it.

He could see that was a problem. And he'd already figured out a solution. "I'll take you to Austin."

She looked up at him, her eyes wide. "That's not necessary."

"It's no big deal. I'm done here for the day."

"I don't think my stuff will fit in Rhonda."

"I also have a truck."

"Oh." She was fidgeting, and he knew it wasn't a good idea, but it wasn't like she had a lot of options at this point.

"Let me help you with this, Molly. Rather than spending several hours trying to figure out a solution, let's just go. The sooner you get there and back, the sooner you get home to your mom."

She closed her checkbook and tucked it back in her purse. "Fine."

"I'll just go tell Chad I'm leaving so he can lock up."

He went into the shop and let Chad know he was going to be gone the rest of the day, then locked up his office and grabbed his keys.

Molly was waiting for him, her purse slung over her shoulder.

"Do we need to stop by your house?"

"No. My bag is in the car."

He nodded and went back inside and grabbed her overnight bag from her car, then put it in his car. "We'll stop by my house so I can switch over to my truck."

"Okay."

It took about ten minutes to get there. He pulled Rhonda into the garage.

"Come on inside. I'll need to pack a few things. It won't take me a minute."

She hesitated, but then followed him in. He hung his keys on the rack and went into the bedroom.

"Make yourself at home. I'll be right back."

Molly didn't want to be here. She wanted to be halfway to Austin by now. She'd intended to get up early and hit the road. Instead, George had been decidedly uncooperative. Her dad had tried to help her get him started, and when they did, he'd insisted she take the car to Carter's shop. She really hadn't wanted to do that, either, but she didn't have much of a choice since she hadn't wanted to end up stranded on the side of the highway.

She couldn't believe Carter was going to drive her to Austin. She'd tried to think up an excuse as to why this wasn't going to work, but in the end, she wanted a quick solution, and he'd offered. They could make this work. They knew each other, and it wasn't like he was some stranger offering up a road trip in his truck, right?

For her mother, she'd endure anything. Besides, it was nice of him to offer. She was certain he had better things to do this weekend than drive her all the way to Austin and back.

So why had he offered? Especially after the way she'd been treating him, the way she'd yelled at him at the wedding.

She wasn't even going to ask, because right now, she needed him. So when he came back with a small duffel bag in his hand, she smiled.

"Thanks for doing this."

"Not a problem. I was going to clean the house this weekend. I'd rather take a road trip."

She looked around. The place was spotless. And nicely

decorated, too. For a guy, he had pretty good taste in furnishing and décor. She almost wished they could take a moment so he could show her his place.

But that would be a really bad idea, and again, there was the lack of time thing.

"You ready to go?" he asked.

She nodded, so he led her out through the garage and to the driveway. He had a nice black Chevy truck she hadn't even noticed when they'd pulled up. "Is this new?"

"I bought it last year. I needed something for hauling and towing. Rhonda's not exactly good for things like that."

She climbed in and settled in the ample seat. "Understandable."

She fished her phone out of her purse. "I'm going to call my dad and let him know you're driving me. He was worried about George's current state."

"I can see why."

Ignoring him, she pushed the button and her dad answered after three rings. "Hey, Dad. How's Mom doing?"

"She's fine. Propped up on multiple pillows in the living room and giving me orders. And a list."

That made her smile because it sounded normal for her mother. "Good."

"How's the car?"

"Really broken. A fuel pump and injector thing that's going to require parts and a few days to repair. But Carter offered to drive me to Austin in his truck."

"I'm glad to hear that. So you're set, then?"

"Yes, I'm set. I should be back sometime tomorrow. I'll give you a call when we're on the way back home."

"Okay, honey. Don't worry about anything here. The nurse has already been by, and your mom's doing fine."

"All right. Love you, Dad."

"Love you, too."

She hung up, feeling a lot better about things. She tucked her phone back in her purse.

"Everything okay at home? How's your mom feeling?"

"She's doing fine. Thanks for asking."

He hit the turnpike and headed south. Now she just had to endure the miles and what she was certain was going to be endless, uncomfortable silence.

"Tell me about your job, Molly."

She turned her head. "My job?"

"The one you have to leave in Austin."

"Oh. I work . . . or I worked . . . for a music company."

"What kind of a music company?"

"It was an independent label."

"Oh, so a record company."

"Yes."

The sun had moved out from behind the clouds, so he grabbed his sunglasses and slid them on. They made him look sexy. If she were honest with herself, Carter always looked sexy. He wore his hair short, except the top was a little long. Her fingers ached to tangle through the thickness of it, to find out if it was still as soft as she remembered.

"What kind of music?"

She pulled out her sunglasses and put them on. "They're a pretty eclectic label. Rock, pop, folk, some R&B. They had some great artists."

"And what did you do for them?"

"A little accounting. A lot of marketing. I was just getting started, really. Delia—that's who I worked for—she's great and gave me a lot of latitude on the marketing side of things. Unfortunately, since I don't know how long I'll be gone, she has to replace me."

"That sucks."

"Yeah. But I'll just find something else when it's time to hit the road again."

She thought he'd say something about her staying in Hope, but he didn't, which was good. Because she wasn't going to.

"By the way," he said, "I talked to the committee and rescheduled the meeting for next week."

"That's great. Thanks."

"The meeting is Wednesday night. Hopefully you'll be able to make it. Several people expressed concern about your mom having to drop out for now." He changed lanes, then gave her a quick look. "She's been the one who's been getting things done."

"I'll be there."

"Okay, good."

He went quiet then, and so did she. He turned on the radio, setting the station.

She shot him a look. "You still listen to the Beach Boys? Really?"

"What's wrong with that?"

"They're a little . . . seventies."

"Again, what's wrong with that?"

She shook her head. "There's been a lot of great music made in the last forty years, you know."

He cranked up the volume and shot her a half smile. "Not like this."

No wonder he named his car Rhonda.

She took out her phone and made a note about the meeting on Wednesday so she wouldn't forget. Emma would be back next weekend, and she'd have to call her as soon as she got back and fill her in about Mom. She wasn't looking forward to that conversation, but she was sleeping better at night knowing Emma and Luke were having a great honeymoon. Besides, there wasn't anything Emma could have done if they'd cut their honeymoon short. Her sister deserved this. Molly had been the one to stay away all these years. Emma had been gone several years as well, attending school and working out of town, but for the past couple of years she'd been home. And if it hadn't been lousy timing, Emma would have been the one at home dealing with this.

Molly wondered if she would have come back from Austin if Emma had called her to tell her Mom had had an accident. She hadn't come home for anything in the past. She'd like to think she would have for this, but every time she'd thought about a visit home, panic had set in.

And now she sat in Carter's truck, about to spend two days with him. She was tolerating it, and so was he.

Actually, she was more than tolerating it. They seemed to have reached a sort of peace between them. Maybe she'd said what needed to be said, and now that it was out of her system, she could move on. It didn't mean she was going to move home or anything, but maybe now that she could be in his company, she didn't have to be so afraid to be around Hope again. Around Carter again.

Though as she took a glance at him out of the corner of her eye, she couldn't help but notice the way his jeans fit to his muscular thighs, how he'd rolled up his long-sleeved shirt to his elbows, and the crisp dark hairs on his forearms. She even noticed the way he gripped the steering wheel, her gaze gravitating toward his hands.

He'd always had great hands. She could still recall the way they'd glided over her naked skin. He had learned every secret to her body, knew how to elicit a response from her.

She let out a sigh.

"Okay over there? You need me to stop?"

She needed to stop remembering what it felt like to be touched by him. "No. I'm fine."

She wasn't fine. She was decidedly un-fine, fantasizing about the last man on earth she should be fantasizing about, and stuck in the car with him for the next—she glanced at the clock in the truck—six and a half hours.

Great.

"Why don't you pick a radio station you like?" he asked.

Finally.

She found them some tunes from this decade and settled back. They made a stop for lunch at a great burger joint, and she discovered Carter didn't seem at all uncomfortable with her. In fact, he was a good conversationalist. He talked about the town square project, which piqued her interest quite a bit. She actually couldn't wait to go to the meeting next week.

But there was still this invisible wall between them, and she was the one who'd put it there by dredging up the nightmare of the past. It was uncomfortable, at least for her. If they were going to endure this trip—and work on the committee together—she had to do something about taking it down.

"About the night of the wedding."

He flexed his fingers on the steering wheel. "We don't have to talk about that, Molly."

"I think we do. Look, about the things I said . . ."

He gave her a quick glance. "Don't."

She stilled, waiting for him to blow up at her.

"You said what you needed to say. You were hurt. I get it. And I wasn't the most supportive person back then. For that, I'm really sorry. There are a lot of things I'd like a chance to do over—do them right the second time, but I can't. And I'm sorry about that, too. You told me how you felt, so you don't have to apologize for that. You never have to apologize for the way you feel, Molly."

The only thing she could do was stare at him, unprepared for what he'd said.

"Okay."

"We're going to be in each other's orbit for the foreseeable future. We're both going to have to learn to live with that. I can if you can," he said.

She felt the wall crack a little. She kept expecting the same Carter she'd known all those years ago, and this wasn't the same guy. There was a maturity to him she'd never known before.

If she could just tuck the past away and live in the now, if she and Carter could somehow learn to become friends, then she could get through this.

"I think we both can," she said.

He gave her a half smile. "Good."

The rest of the trip passed by with some decent music, and she even relaxed enough to take a short nap. She woke when they entered the city limits, and she gave him directions to her apartment. He pulled into the parking area, and she grabbed her keys out of her purse.

She opened the door to her apartment, conscious of the fact Carter was going to see her personal space. She wasn't sure why that idea concerned her.

"This is nice," he said as he walked into the living room.

"It came furnished."

"That'll make it easier to move out then, won't it?"

"Yes."

"Okay, then. Let's get started packing you up."

Chapter 11

IT WAS OBVIOUS from the efficient, orderly way Molly approached this whole packing thing that she was used to moving. She already had boxes folded up in the back of her closet, and several rolls of packing tape. Well-organized, which made it easy, but a little sad, too.

He opened the boxes and she put him in the kitchen to start clearing out cabinets. She kept her inventory small—only a couple of plates and glasses and pots and pans. She didn't seem to have a full set of anything, so it didn't take long to box up everything in there. She didn't keep knickknacks like a lot of women did. In fact, after he did the kitchen he moved into the living room, but there wasn't much other than a couple of photos of her parents and her sister with Luke and their dogs. He packed those up in one of the open kitchen boxes and headed into the bathroom.

Same thing here. Essentials, and nothing more. No plants, no pets, and other than those couple of photos, nothing personal. Nothing that said, "Molly Burnett lives here."

His place was littered with touches of his past. His baseball trophies, photos, pictures on the walls, memorabilia. Everything that was part of his past was in his house. With her place?

Nothing.

They had more or less fully packed her up in a few hours.

Was this what her life was like? When she got tired of living in one place, she could pack up in a day and move her entire life to the next city?

Molly surfaced from the bedroom, where she'd finished packing up boxes. "So, I guess we'll stay here tonight. It's too late to make that drive back to Hope."

"That works." He looked over at the sofa. "This looks comfortable enough to sleep on."

"We should get dinner. There's a great pizza place a couple of blocks away that delivers. I'll give them a call, unless you have something else in mind."

"Actually, I do. Let's go out."

She frowned. "Out? Out where?"

"This is Austin, Molly. Home of great music. We'll grab something to eat, and you can show me around."

She shifted back and forth on the balls of her feet. "Oh . . . uh . . . well, I haven't been here that long so I don't know where everything is as far as entertainment."

Which meant she didn't go out all that often.

"That's okay. We'll just wander around together and figure it out."

"It's kind of late."

"It's not that late. And I'll bet things are open. Let's go check it out."

She hesitated, and for a minute Carter wondered if she was going to insist on staying in. But finally, she nodded.

"I'll go change clothes."

"Great."

He got out his phone while Molly was in her bedroom. When she came back, he had a grin on his face.

"What?" she asked.

"Did you know this was one of the weekends for the Austin City Limits music festival?"

She rubbed her temple with her fingers. "I might have known that."

"But you didn't mention it."

"I've kind of had a few things on my mind."

"Oh, right. Sure you did. Anyway, wanna go?"

She shrugged. "Sure. If you don't think it's too late."

"I'll bet they're rocking late into the night. Besides, it's not that late. Let's check it out."

"All right." She grabbed her jacket and they were out the door.

Carter was going to make her smile and take her mind off her worries, at least for a couple of hours.

Chapter 12

AS MOLLY HAD suspected, the festival closed up at ten p.m., and it was ten thirty by the time they got there.

"Not a problem," Carter said. "I checked my phone and there are some late-night venues continuing on at some of the clubs. We'll go to one of those, grab something to eat, and listen to some music."

"Providing we can get in. Some of those events are sold out in advance."

"Then we'll find one we can get into."

She took a deep breath. "Hang on. Let me make a call."

She grabbed her phone and punched in Delia's number. "Hey, Dee, it's Molly. I'm in Austin to pick up my things, and a friend of mine and I would like to check out the music here for the festival. Do you think you can get us in somewhere?"

She smiled at Delia's rapid-fire voice, then smiled. "You're great. Thanks so much."

She hung up and gave him directions to Lambert's. "We can also eat barbecue there."

"Perfect."

They had to park a couple of blocks away, but it was a nice

night so the walk wasn't bad. There were a lot of people out and about because of the festival. Molly couldn't believe she'd totally blanked on the musical festival this weekend. Then again, her head had been filled with details about her mom, and rushing back here to get her things, not hanging out and listening to music.

She gave her name to the hostess when they got inside.

The woman smiled at her. "Delia said you'd be coming. Head on up to the bar."

"Thanks," Molly said.

They got a table and a waitress came by.

"Drinks only, or do you want food as well?" the woman asked.

"We're starving," Carter said, so the waitress produced a menu.

They ordered and the waitress dashed off.

"It helps to know music people, doesn't it?" Carter asked.

The seats they'd gotten were good. Not so far up front that they'd be blasted by the music and not be able to hear themselves think. Delia knew where to seat them. "I guess so. Delia's a pretty great boss. I'll miss working with her."

The music was outstanding as well, and the food was great. Molly had to admit this was much better than grabbing fast food and hiding out in the apartment the rest of the night.

Carter seemed to enjoy the music, relaxing after he'd consumed his ribs and getting into the band that was playing. Since he wasn't focused entirely on her, she could watch him, the way the corners of his mouth tilted up when he smiled, the easy way he sat back in his chair. He always seemed so comfortable in his own skin, so at ease no matter the situation.

While she was profoundly uncomfortable—especially around him.

She was going to have to get over it.

He finally shifted his gaze toward her, giving her a smile that rocked her all the way to her toes. It wasn't a heated smile, just an enjoying-the-band-together kind of thing. Yet to Molly, the connection between them was still there, and it disturbed her greatly.

She'd really let him have it the night of the wedding, pouring out her anguish and anger. She'd all but slapped him and told him she hated him.

Yet here he was. He'd driven her all the way down here and hadn't expected an apology. And now he was relaxed and smiling.

What kind of guy did that? Most men would have shut her out of their lives completely, left her sitting on the side of the road to fend for herself.

Not Carter though. Yes, he'd dropped the ball all those years ago, but they'd both been so young. Was she wrong to still blame him for that when there were so many other honorable things about him?

"Are you enjoying the band?" he asked over the loud music.

She nodded. "Yes. They're great."

He grinned. "I'm glad we decided to go out."

"Me, too."

He turned away to watch the band again, giving her more time to watch him.

She didn't want to still be attracted to him. She wanted to feel nothing at all for him. Yet, after all these years, there it was. The smoking-hot chemistry she'd felt for him when she was fifteen still lingered. Despite all the baggage and trauma she'd suffered because of her relationship with Carter, the bottom line was, she was still attracted to him and there was no point denying it.

When the band took a break, she stood. "It's getting kind of late, and we have a long drive tomorrow."

He looked up at her. "Are you tired?"

"Kind of." She wasn't tired at all. She was keyed up, confused, all too aware of Carter, and she wanted to go hide in her bedroom.

"Sure. We can leave." He got up and she grabbed her jacket. Carter was right there to hold it for her so she could slip her arms into it.

Why couldn't he be a giant douchebag? Why couldn't he have turned into some arrogant ass she couldn't stand? Instead, he was courteous and nice and, if it was at all possible, he'd become even better-looking with the passage of time.

So unfair.

He drove them back to her apartment. "I'll wait while you use the bathroom first."

"Okay. Thanks."

She went in and washed her face and brushed her teeth, then came out. Carter had a book in his lap and was lounging on the sofa. She went into the bedroom and grabbed a pillow and blanket.

"Here you go."

He took it from her, and their fingers brushed, sending lightning strikes to every part of her. She quickly pulled her hand away, but she could tell from the look he gave her that he must have felt it, too.

"Molly . . ."

"Good night, Carter."

He gave her a long look before nodding. "Night."

She went into her bedroom and shut the door, pondered locking it, but then realized how ridiculous that would be. He wouldn't come in. She took off her clothes and got into bed, staring up at the ceiling in her darkened room.

For some stupid reason, she wanted to go out there and talk to him. But about what? What could they possibly have to say to each other? It would only lead to more pain on her part. She was already in enough emotional trouble just being near him.

By tomorrow she'd be firmly planted in her parents' house and she'd only have to deal with Carter at the committee meetings. It was minimal contact.

She could deal with that.

Right?

CARTER BRUSHED HIS teeth, then lay on the couch, leaving the small lamp lit so he could read. He sure as hell wasn't tired, not with Molly's scent filling the air around him.

He thought they'd had a good time tonight, but she was still tense around him. He didn't know what to do about that, other than let her get used to him. He knew she was uncomfortable, that being with him brought old memories back to the surface. He couldn't change the past. Neither of them could change what was.

But maybe he could show her a better future, and that the town of Hope—and him—weren't things to avoid.

The only way to do that was to constantly be on her radar. Whether she liked it or not, that was going to be his plan. Because now that she was back in his life, he wanted her to stay there.

Chapter 13

AFTER A FEW days back home with her mother, she realized several things. One, her mother didn't understand the concept of the words *rest* and *still*. Two, though Molly thought she'd be bored and idle, she'd been anything but, since three, her mother was a list maker. And since her mom couldn't get out there and fulfill the items on her lists herself, that left Molly and her dad to run errands for her.

One would think that after working nearly thirty-five years, her mom would find this an opportune time to take a breather and enjoy some time off.

Wrong. Mom, though laid up, was still as energetic as ever, and wanted her fingers on the pulse of everything in town. She was on the phone constantly with the people at her job, on her computer and becoming quickly adept at doing that one-handedly, and running Molly ragged by sending her back and forth to the office to do this and that for her.

Her father, albeit reluctantly, had fled back to his own job—at least part-time—since it seemed that her mother wasn't going to have some kind of critical relapse at any moment. A nurse stopped by a few times a week to check her vitals, and home health aides came in to help her with her baths and therapy. The only person she hadn't managed to bully so far was Holly, the nurse from the home health agency, since Holly was just as bullheaded as her mother. If that was even possible.

"Surely you can get me in a walking cast, Holly," her mother implored while Holly listened to her heartbeat.

Holly took the stethoscope out. "That's the doctor's call, Mrs. Burnett. I'm just here to check your vital signs and manage your medication and pain level."

"I don't like those pain pills. They make me tired."

Holly gave her a look. "They're to help you rest."

"I've rested plenty, and I feel just fine. I'm frustrated being confined. I need exercise."

"We have you scheduled for physical therapy this afternoon."

"That's passive and it's boring. I want to walk. I want to go outside and get some fresh air." Her mother affected a pout. There might have even been some tears glittering in her eyes.

Molly would have been sympathetic if they'd been real tears, but she knew her mother. They were all an act to get her way.

Holly wasn't falling for the bait. "Unfortunately, Mrs. Burnett, these injuries are going to take time to heal and you're going to have to be patient."

Her mother heaved a put-upon sigh. "I'm not a patient woman, Holly."

Holly fluffed her mother's pillows. "So I've noticed. Now let's check your catheter."

Molly understood the injustice of being confined to a bed when you were used to being a self-sufficient woman. She was just glad her mother was back to her old fiery self. But she would need to be patient as she healed, because no amount of bullying was going to make her bones heal any faster.

And Molly was going to have to practice an equal amount of patience. After the nurse left, she asked her mom what she wanted for lunch.

"Some of Bert's chicken noodle soup sounds great to me."

"I'm on it. Will you be all right here for a few minutes while I go get it?"

"Of course, honey." She lifted her phone. "I have my lifeline right here."

"Okay. I'll be right back." She kissed her mother's cheek, grabbed the car keys, and drove to Bert's. The place was packed and she grimaced, realizing she should have called ahead. She went inside and straight to the counter where Anita, the waitress, was handing in an order.

She'd been here twice already since she'd gotten home, so she'd renewed her acquaintance with Bert's staff.

"Hi, honey," Anita said. "Are you looking for a seat?"

"No, just a to-go order today. My mom wants some chicken noodle soup and I'll take some of those chicken fingers with fries."

Anita nodded and jotted it down on her order pad, then slid it on the carousel. "Coming right up. How's she doing?"

"Antsy. She wants to get up and walk around."

"I'll bet she does. I can't imagine Georgia laid up for long. She'll push those doctors until they do her bidding."

Molly laughed. Anita knew her mother well. "Yeah, she'll definitely give it a try."

"Order up," Bert said from behind the counter.

"Gotta go. I'll be back with your order as soon as I can."

"Thanks, Anita."

Molly took a seat on one of the stools at the counter and surveyed the people coming and going. Bert's was a busy place, especially at lunchtime. Or anytime, really. Since they were situated on the highway going to and from Tulsa, they served not only locals, but people on their way to the city and hopping on and off the turnpike. They did a steady business. She remembered coming in here a lot when she was in high school.

"Stopping in to grab a bite to eat?"

She swiveled to see Carter pulling up a seat next to her. "Picking up lunch for my mother."

"How is she?"

"Not happy to be immobilized."

"I imagine. How are you doing?"

"I'm doing fine."

"Are you staying busy?"

She lifted her gaze to his. "You have no idea."

His lips lifted. "So your mom has given you one of her infamous lists, huh?"

"You know about the lists?"

"I know about the lists."

"Speaking of things on my mother's list, are we set for the committee meeting?"

"Yeah. Tonight at seven. Are you sure you have time to deal with this?"

"Please. If I don't, my mother will drag herself out of bed and crawl to that meeting. I'll be there."

He laughed. "I understand. Do you want me to pick you up?"

"That might not be a bad idea. Since George is still being worked on, I can leave the car for my dad then, just in case."

"About six forty-five?"

"Perfect. Thanks."

"No problem. I'm going to grab a seat and get myself something to eat. I'll see you tonight."

"Okay. See you later."

She watched him walk away, trying not to stare at his butt, which was difficult since he wore those jeans so well.

But their conversation went well. Easy, no awkward moments.

She breathed a sigh of relief.

CARTER GOT THROUGH what had been a hellish day. A difficult transmission fix, an unhappy customer returning a car that still wasn't running right, and a call from the manager of one of his other shops about an unruly employee they'd been dealing with for a few weeks now. Carter dragged his fingers through his hair, mentally cursing that situation. He was going to have to fire the guy, likely tomorrow. All in all, it had been a shit day. He would have liked to head over to Bash's bar and forget it with a couple of beers, but tonight was the committee meeting, so beers were off the table, at least for now.

Instead, he went to the gym and knocked out a hard workout, getting his aggression out on the punching bag, then the weight room. After an hour and a drenching sweat, he went home and hopped in the shower, then changed clothes and drove over to Molly's parents' house to pick her up. He had gotten out of the car and was about to go to the door when he saw her come outside.

"I was going to come in," he said.

"Oh, you don't want to do that. My mom's in a mood."

He cocked a brow. "About?"

"Anything. Everything. She's cranky and I've had to deal with her all day. It's my dad's turn now. Let's go."

Resisting the urge to smile, he went around and opened the car door for her. She slid inside and he went to his side, got in, and started the engine.

"Bad day?" he asked as he put on his seat belt.

"You could say that. How was yours?"

"Sucked."

Her lips lifted. "We should be a fine pair at the committee meeting tonight."

"If you think your mother is irritating, wait 'til you meet some of the committee members."

She gave him a look. "Really?"

He turned the corner and pulled out on the main highway. "I figured I should give you an advance warning."

"Any people I should know about?"

"I'll let you form your own opinions, but you're pretty smart, Molly. I don't think it'll take you long to grab a clue as to who's who."

City hall was at the heart of downtown Hope. Carter parked in the lot and they made their way inside.

Mavis Turnball was at the door, waiting for them, which didn't surprise Carter at all.

"Molly Burnett. I haven't seen you since you were in high school. How's your mother doing? I've been meaning to get by to see her, but things are so busy in the mayor's office. Oh, you probably don't remember me at all, do you?"

Molly held out her hand. "Mavis Turnball. And you're still working as a secretary in the mayor's office?"

Mavis grinned. "Yes, I am. Mayors may come and go, but they couldn't survive without me."

Mavis was tall and slender, and wore her dark hair short. Her heels clicked on the wood floor as she led Molly away. Carter decided to stick close, so he followed.

"Let's introduce you to the others. Some you might know already. This is Cletus Beaumont. He works for the sewer department. Amanda Flannigan and her father own Flannigan's Auto Sales. And this is Samantha Reasor. She owns a flower shop. Did you two go to high school together? There's also Chelsea Gardner, who's a teacher at Hope High School. A few aren't here yet. Come on in and get acquainted with everyone."

Molly's head was spinning. Fortunately, she'd gone to high school with Samantha Reasor. And of course she knew Chelsea. They went to get coffee.

"Sorry you got stuck with this," Samantha said.

"I don't mind, really."

"How's your mom doing?" Chelsea asked.

"She's doing okay. She's a little cranky about being laid up."

Samantha, who was even prettier now than she'd been in high school, with her long light blond hair and blue eyes, smiled at her. "Who wouldn't be? It has to be frustrating for her."

Chelsea nodded. "I'm sure it is. Poor Georgia. We're really going to miss having her on the committee. She got things done."

Samantha laid her hand on Molly's forearm. "But we're sure glad you're here, Molly. And it's so nice to see you again after all these years."

"Thanks. It's nice to be back."

"And just a heads-up," Chelsea said, "Mavis is champing

at the bit to be in charge now that your mom isn't here. She's disagreed with most of Georgia's suggestions, which were all good ones."

Samantha nodded. "Plus, your mom kept us on budget. Mavis likes to spend money that doesn't need to be spent."

"I've got all the files and I've looked them over," Molly said. "It seems things are running according to plan."

"So far so good. We have Carter and your mom to thank for that," Chelsea said. "And hopefully you'll be able to help us out."

"I'll do what I can."

Molly had studied the files the past few days and had sat down with her mom to discuss the project, shocked at what she had managed to accomplish in the past year. It was obvious this was her heart-and-soul project, and Molly wasn't going to let her down.

"Are you ready for this?" Carter asked as they made their way to the table.

She nodded. "You let me know what you need from me. I'll back you up a hundred percent."

He gave her a smile. "Okay, then. Let's get this ball rolling."

They went to the table and Carter sat at the head. Molly took a seat next to him.

"Let's get started, everyone," he said.

All in all, there were eight people. She'd met them all after wandering around for about fifteen minutes. Some she'd known, like Mavis and Samantha and Chelsea. Others were new faces.

"Old business first," Carter said. "Cement is being poured this week, then the new pavers in front of the fountain are going down. The water department has set the spout system within the ground already. After that work is finished, the fountain itself will be put in the center. If you all look at your packets for confirmation, the schedule should be self-explanatory."

Molly had pored over the graphics for the water play area and fountain. It was gorgeous, would be fun and interactive for kids in the warm-weather months, and a beautiful area in the center of town.

"I'm just wondering about the budget," Mavis said. "We could downscale it some, and still have something aesthetically pleasing."

Molly had also heard from her mother that Mavis liked to disagree about everything, even things that had previously been voted and agreed upon.

"This has been decided on, Mavis," Carter said. "What is it that you think needs to be changed?"

"Well, I was just thinking that if we downsized the scale of the water play area we could put in some other equipment, like benches or a walkway."

"There are two benches on the north and south sides of the fountain, and plenty of walking space already," Samantha said.

"Yes, but . . ." Mavis paged through her notes. "I just think we need to plan for the future and growth of our town. In retrospect, I think maybe we overspent on the fountain."

This was Mavis jockeying for position on the committee now that her mother was out of the picture. Time for Molly to step in. "Mavis, I realize I'm new to the committee, but wasn't this entire plan decided and voted upon, and money allocated for the precise construction over a year ago?"

Mavis smiled at her, but Molly caught the bitterness in her eyes.

"Well, yes, but—"

"Then it makes no financial sense, especially since resources have already been allocated, and materials have already been ordered, to make changes this late in the process, does it?"

She had her, and Mavis knew it.

Mavis gave her a slimy smile. "I suppose not. But you know someone has to play devil's advocate and suggest alternatives."

"Of course. And I know everyone here appreciates it," Molly said. "But we wouldn't be fiscally responsible if we altered the trajectory of the project this late in the game."

"Of course not. You're absolutely right."

Mavis sat, and the meeting continued.

"I was wondering if we should do nice plaques for contributors," Mavis said. "We could put them around the fountain, and really showcase our bigger contributors."

Molly wrinkled her nose. "Now that would definitely not be aesthetically pleasing."

Chelsea shifted through her notes. "Aren't we planning to thank our contributors in the color informational brochure that'll be handed out upon completion of the project?"

"Yes," Samantha said.

"But see, this is a more permanent solution." Mavis had already drawn up a plan and handed it out to everyone. "Each plaque would be in bronze, and mounted at the foot of the fountain. I'm sure every contributor would be so pleased to see their names engraved forever at our town square. Some have given a lot of money."

"Like my father and I," Amanda Flannigan said. "I like this."

"And we really can't thank you enough for your donations," Carter said. "But there's no money in the budget for something extravagant like this."

"And as I previously mentioned," Molly added, "making changes to the project this late in the game could throw a monkey wrench into the entire thing. While I appreciate the desire to give mention to our more than generous contributors, I'm sure they didn't donate for the recognition, but for the revitalization of our town square. Isn't that right, Amanda?"

Molly gave Amanda a pointed look.

"Well, of course. For the betterment of the town."

"And we all know that, and appreciate it so much," Samantha said.

"Then we're good with the mention in the brochure?" Carter asked.

"I suppose." Mavis looked defeated. And irritated.

"What's the timeline for completion, Carter?" Chelsea asked, then gave a grin in Molly and Carter's direction.

"Should be about a month to six weeks to finish up."

"So we should be on track to wind around the new town square for the holiday parade," Mavis said.

Carter nodded. "Hopefully, if there are no delays."

"Fabulous. And Molly, you'll still be in town for the holidays, won't you?"

Molly gave Mavis a blank stare. "I have no idea."

"I'm penciling you in to judge the holiday parade."

"Um. Sure."

Carter gave her a horrified look and a quick shake of his head.

But apparently, it was too late, since she'd already agreed.

They went through some financial stuff, and a few items of new business. Molly went over the marketing plan for the project, then they wrapped up.

All in all, not too bad.

"I hope you and I have a chance to reconnect," Samantha said. "It's been a long time since high school."

"I know. I'm sorry I didn't stay in touch. I move around a lot."

"That's what your mom said. Maybe we could have lunch or dinner sometime?"

"I'd like that."

They traded numbers and Samantha told her she'd call to set something up.

"Ready to go?" Carter asked.

"Okay. Sure."

He led her out the door.

"Have you got a hot date?"

"No. I'm trying to save you from volunteering to be on some other committee. It's bad enough you agreed to judge the holiday parade."

She stopped in the middle of the parking lot. "I saw that look you gave me. What was so bad about that?"

"You don't even wanna know."

"Well, now I do."

"Come on. Let's go get a drink at Bash's bar and I'll tell you about it."

"I really should go home."

"Is your dad there?"

"Yes."

"Then you can have a drink with me. I'll take you home after. Just call your dad and tell him you'll be a little late."

She felt ridiculous that at thirty years old she had to check in with her parents—one of the drawbacks of living at home again. She hadn't had to answer to anyone for years. But she called her dad, who said her mom was asleep, everything was fine, and to go out and enjoy herself.

Not that she was going out—like on a date, going out. She was just going for a drink. With Carter.

Which didn't mean anything.

After a short drive, Carter pulled into the No Hope At All bar.

"Cute," she said after they got out of the car.

"That's Bash's sense of humor."

"So he owns the bar?"

"Yeah. He bought it out from one of his dad's best friends who was retiring, and renamed it. It's a pretty popular place."

"I can tell. The parking lot is pretty full for a weeknight."

"He shows sports on big-screen TVs, and has a couple of pool tables, so there's a lot more to do than just drink."

"And you come here a lot."

He shrugged. "When I don't have anything else to do. Tonight is a night for a drink."

Molly wondered what the "anything else to do" meant. When he had a girlfriend, or a hot date? For all she knew, he might already have a girlfriend.

Not that it mattered to her if he did or didn't, since she wasn't interested in him that way.

The bar was great on the inside, with multiple televisions showing sports of all kinds, tables spread around for ample seating, a pool table at either end, and a beautifully weathered bar top.

"Do you know Bash?" Carter asked.

"Just from the wedding." She smiled at the quite attractive bartender, who grinned as they took a seat at the bar.

Bash arched a brow. "You both look like you need a shot or a double."

"Committee meeting tonight," Carter said.

Bash nodded. "No wonder. What'll it be?"

"I'll have a Grey Goose and cranberry juice," Molly said.

"Crown on the rocks for me."

"Coming right up."

Molly swiveled on the barstool. "So how often do you come here?" she asked Carter.

"Not often enough."

She laughed. "Life couldn't possibly be that bad, could it?"

"Actually, it's not. I just had a rough day. But the meeting tonight wasn't as awful as I thought it would be."

Bash slid their drinks across the bar top toward them.

"Thanks," Molly said, then took a sip, her eyes widening. "Wow. There's a decent amount of vodka in here."

"Bash makes good drinks. He doesn't half-ass anything."

"I can tell." She took another sip. It tasted good. "So you were going to fill me in on the holiday parade."

"Oh yeah." Carter took a long swallow of his drink, then sat the glass on the bar. "You need to steer clear of Mavis."

"Because . . ."

"I was on the parade committee for three years. Until she fired me."

Molly laughed. "She fired you? What for?"

"For not giving Henderson's first place."

"Henderson's, the car dealership on the edge of town?"

"Yeah."

"Isn't it supposed to be based on who has the best float?"

"According to Mavis, it's based on who provides the mayor the most in campaign contributions every election."

"Ouch." Molly grabbed her drink and took a big swallow, then wished she hadn't. She really tasted the vodka in that one. "That seems a bit unethical."

"That's what I told her. After that, I was replaced on the judging committee."

Molly snorted, then finished her drink. "I can promise you,

I'll be a fair and impartial judge. And besides, I likely won't be here anyway."

"Already planning your exit strategy?" Carter signaled Bash for refills.

She shouldn't have another. The first one was strong enough, and she'd already drained it. In a hurry, as a matter of fact.

But Bash laid down a bowl of pretzels along with their refills, so why not?

She took another drink. "I don't know. Maybe."

"You could stay here."

Her hand stilled and she put her drink down. "That's not going to happen."

"Why not? What's here that you're so afraid of?"

"I'm not having this conversation with you, Carter." Instead, she grabbed a handful of pretzels. So did he, popping them into his mouth and finishing off his second drink. He signaled Bash for a third.

"You sure you should be drinking more?"

"Yes. Definitely sure."

He filled his hand with more pretzels, and Bash refilled both their glasses and the snack bowl before disappearing to the other end of the bar.

"You're avoiding my question."

She lifted her gaze to his, wishing there wasn't so much history between them. If he were just some stranger, she'd definitely want to know more about him. He was incredibly good-looking, had an amazing body, and she wanted to put her hands on him. And her mouth on his. And do all kinds of things with him.

Naked.

She blinked and looked down at her glass. Her third glass, which was now empty.

Definitely the alcohol talking, because sensible Molly did not have lascivious thoughts about the man who broke her heart.

Inebriated Molly, on the other hand, was definitely having some.

"Tell me about your life, Carter."

"What do you want to know?"

"I don't know. Everything, I guess. Tell me about your work."

He shrugged. "I started working for the garage when I was still in high school, as you know. I left for college, but every time I was on break I worked there. When I got my business degree, I bought out the original place in Hope and converted it to a full-service garage. Several years later, I bought out a few more auto service companies in and around Tulsa and made them full-service as well."

She sipped at her drink, which had suddenly appeared before her. "You must have been pretty busy."

"It was hard work, but worth it. Each of the facilities is doing well now."

"I like what you've done with the garage in Hope. It caters to a full clientele. You can meet the needs of every resident in town, whether they need a tire rotation or a full transmission replacement."

Carter stared at her in awe. She could tell she'd nailed it in one pretty good tag line. "I like that. I might use it for advertising purposes."

She laughed. "That's what I do. Summarize what a company has to offer. I could probably help you out. Do you do commercials?"

"I've tried to do a couple, but they haven't been very successful."

"It's likely that you're not hitting your target market. You're either not creating the right advertising, or you're advertising at the wrong place, wrong time."

"That's possible. I should have you take a look at what we've tried out before. Maybe you can give me some advice."

"Sure."

"So tell me what you've been doing."

"A lot of marketing for various companies. I'm kind of a jack-of-all-trades. I can advise on marketing plans, create marketing programs, as well as execute them. I can develop advertising, and create a budget for sales and marketing. I've also worked in business management, streamlining systems, from accounting to human resources."

"That's a pretty rich portfolio."

"It's a lot of on-the-job experience. I started out in sales departments of small companies and learned from some very good people. Then I contributed ideas along the way, and figured out I was pretty good at it. I've been like a sponge over the years."

"Best way to learn a job, in my opinion. We bring on a lot of apprentices in our shops. They tend to be focused and eager to learn."

Molly nodded. "I agree. I was a damn fine student of the craft."

He laughed and raised his glass. "And look at you now."

She clinked glasses with him, then set hers down, kind of gingerly.

"So, do you have a girlfriend?" she asked, then realized that had just fallen out of her mouth.

Damn alcohol.

She could tell her question had shocked him, because he stared at her for a few seconds before answering, "Uh, no."

"Dating anyone?"

"No. Are you?"

She shook her head. "We should have another drink."

"Sure."

This was a new side to Molly. She seemed . . . relaxed, likely due to the alcohol. Carter wasn't going to question it, though, because he was enjoying not having to be on guard, and more importantly, her not being on guard, either. He liked talking to her, getting to know her again.

He signaled Bash for another round, realizing he'd have to get them both a ride home tonight. But it was worth it to spend this time with her.

"So what do you do for fun when you're not busy being the king of auto repair?" she asked, grabbing the fresh drink and taking a long swallow.

"I play basketball with the guys. I go to movies. I hang out here at the bar and shoot pool. I go out now and then."

"Dating, you mean."

"Sometimes."

"And what kind of women do you like to go out with?"

"Are you interviewing me, Molly?"

She laughed. "Not really. Why, does it sound like an interrogation?"

"Kind of."

"Sorry. I'm just . . . interested."

"I'm happy to tell you anything you want to know about me." They were face-to-face on the barstools, her left knee wedged in between his. He wondered, if she hadn't had four of those drinks, if she'd let herself get this close to him.

"Now tell me what *you* do for fun," he said, taking the chance to scoot in closer. He waited for her to pull back. She didn't.

"I like to read, and I love old movies. I like music, which made the job I had in Austin kind of perfect for me."

"Would you have stayed?"

She tilted her head to the side. "What do you mean?"

"Emma said you moved around a lot, job-wise. Town-wise."

"Oh. I don't know. Maybe. I liked Delia, and I liked the job. It's hard to say. I get bored easily."

Her hair had come loose from her ponytail, and he took a strand, sifting it through his fingers. Again, he waited for her to balk, but she didn't, her gaze focusing on his face. On his mouth, making him want to lean in and kiss her.

What would she do then? He wished they were alone, so he could take that chance, but as skittish as Molly was around him, he didn't think a public place like the bar would be the right place to attempt it.

Then again, she was still looking at him with invitation in her eyes, so what the hell.

He leaned in and brushed his lips across hers.

Chapter 14

SUCH A FOOLISH, stupid thing to do, but Molly had been staring at Carter's mouth all night. And if he didn't kiss her soon she was going to grab him by the shirt, haul him off the barstool, and assault him.

But then he leaned in and she held her breath as his mouth touched hers.

It was like a lightning strike, a first kiss like no other, and she'd had plenty of first kisses. In fact, Carter had been her very first kiss, when she was fifteen years old. But this was a new first kiss, and it tasted like whiskey and heaven and she wished they weren't in a crowded bar because she wanted him to kiss her harder, to feel his body pressed up against hers. She felt his restraint as she reached out to hold on to his arms, felt the steely strength of his muscles there, and suddenly, more than anything else, she wanted the chance to explore the differences between the boy he'd been and the man he was now.

When Carter cupped his hand on the side of her neck, she forgot all about where they were and leaned into him. She gave a soft whimper as she felt his arm around her waist, tugging her against the rock-hard feel of his body.

Yes, definitely a man's body now. And she wanted so much more.

Until Bash cleared his throat.

In a kiss-induced haze, she drifted away from the delicious taste of Carter's mouth.

Carter looked over at Bash.

"You two should get a room."

Carter's lips lifted, then his gaze returned to Molly. She saw the heat and desire there and it warmed her body.

He tucked her hair behind her ears. "Maybe we should."

Which would be the absolute worst thing to do. She might be drunk, but she wasn't drunk enough.

"Actually, I should get home. I have an early day tomorrow."

She hated the words, even as she said them. She wanted to stay here—with Carter—wrapped up in this warm cocoon of alcohol and him.

"Sure. Let me scrounge us up a ride home."

She also liked that he knew he'd had enough to drink to not drive home.

"I'll give you both a ride," Bash said. "Let me get someone to cover the bar for a few minutes."

"You sure?" Carter asked.

Bash nodded and walked away. Carter turned to her. "Are you okay?"

"I'm fine. Wish we didn't have to leave. Wish I didn't have to go home."

"You don't have to go home. You could come home with me."

She inhaled a deep breath. "So many issues associated with that."

"Like?"

"Like the fact I live with my parents now, and that brings up a lot of questions if I don't show up tonight. Two, you and I have a history."

"A history I hope we can put in the past. Maybe we can start fresh."

She'd never thought about that. Starting over with Carter brought its own set of problems, none of which she was coherent enough to think about tonight.

"I . . . don't know."

"You two ready?" Bash asked, keys dangling from the key ring on his finger.

"Yup." Molly grabbed her purse and her coat.

"I guess we are," Carter said, sliding a regretful look in her direction.

She knew she hadn't given him an answer, and when Bash dropped her off first, she slid out of the backseat with a thanks for the ride home to Bash, and a quick good-night to Carter.

She slipped in her house quietly and made her way to her room, where she got ready for bed and slid under the covers.

Ten minutes later, her phone buzzed. She picked it up to see a message from Carter.

Good night, Molly.

She took a deep breath, figuring it was best to ignore his text.

But her nice buzz lingered, and her lips still tingled from his kiss.

So she typed a return message.

Good night, Carter. Sleep well.

Chapter 15

HE KNEW IT was a mistake, and he was probably going to regret it, but Carter showed up at Molly's doorstep first thing in the morning with two coffees and a box filled with pastries from Megan Lee's shop.

Molly opened the door wearing a pair of sweatpants and a T-shirt. Her hair was in a high ponytail and she wore no makeup.

"What are you doing here?"

He handed her one of the coffees. "I thought you could use an extra kick this morning, so I brought these by."

"Is that Carter?"

He heard Molly's mother's voice.

Molly took the coffee from him. "Is this like a latte or something that has espresso in it?"

"It is."

"I so need this. Thanks. Come on in. I was just filling my mom in about the committee meeting last night."

He stepped in and she shut the door behind him. Molly's mother was sitting on the sofa, her leg and arm propped up by pillows.

"Carter," Georgia said. "It's so nice of you to stop by."

"I brought pastries."

Georgia smiled. "From Megan's place?"

"Yes."

"I hope there's a cream puff in there. She makes the best."

"I had her put in a mix of items since I didn't know what everyone liked."

Molly laid the box down on the coffee table. "I'll go get some plates."

"I hear Molly was introduced to Mavis's manipulative ways last night," Georgia said as Carter took a seat in the chair across from the sofa.

"Yes, she was."

"I held my own," Molly said as she brought paper plates in and set them down. She opened the box. "There's a cream puff in here, Mom. Would you like it?"

"Only if Carter doesn't."

Carter took a sip of his coffee, then shook his head. "I brought those for you and Molly. Help yourselves."

"Oh, you have to eat, too, Carter."

"I can do that." He fished out a bear claw and set it on a plate, then grabbed a napkin. He took a bite and let the sugar melt on his tongue. Good stuff.

"But you got things accomplished, right? No pushback because I wasn't there?"

"Mavis had that gleam in her eye like she wanted to take over, but Molly held her own. Right up until she agreed to judge the holiday parade."

"Oh." Georgia's gaze shifted to Molly. "I forgot to warn you about that. I'm sorry, honey. Mavis can be pushy about that because she chairs the annual Hope holiday parade every year."

"I didn't know anything about it. Carter filled me in, though."

"I have no doubt you're tough enough to stand up to Mavis. In the meantime, things are progressing with the town square project. I knew you could handle it."

"She did good," Carter said, sliding a smile toward Molly.

She smiled back, surprising him.

He stood, taking his plate to the kitchen trash. "I need to head out to work."

"I'll walk you out."

"Have a good day, Carter," Georgia said.

"You, too, Georgia."

Molly shut the door behind her. "Thanks for bringing the pastries. I know my mom appreciated it. And thank you for the latte. I needed the jolt after last night."

He grinned. "Yeah, me, too. That alarm went off way too early this morning."

"So you've already been to work?"

"Yeah. We had a client bringing in a car before work, so I wanted to be there to open up. I took a quick break for a coffee run, so I need to head back."

"Okay. Have a good day."

"You, too."

She didn't turn and walk back to the house, which left him an opening.

"Molly."

"Yeah?"

"Do you want to go out with me this weekend?"

She blinked. "Uh, do you think that's a good idea?"

"I wouldn't have asked if I didn't."

He waited for her to turn him down. He knew last night was a fluke, and he probably shouldn't have asked.

"Emma and Luke are coming home tomorrow. Emma doesn't know about my mom yet, so there'll be that to deal with."

"Okay. So does that mean no?"

"I . . . don't know. Let me get back to you."

He nodded. "All right. I gotta go."

"See you later, Carter."

"Bye, Molly."

Before she had a chance to walk away, he pulled her against him and brushed his lips against hers. A quick kiss, but it reignited what had happened between them last night.

He took a step back. "Yeah, it wasn't just the alcohol last night."

She didn't say anything, just looked at him with those gorgeous blue eyes of hers.

He grinned. "Have a good day, Molly."

MOLLY STOOD ON the front porch and watched Carter drive away.

So many things were wrong about the two of them, the main thing being their history together.

But so many things were right, including the smoking-hot chemistry that still lingered between them.

Maybe she just needed to jump him, get him in bed and get that residual chemistry out of her system. Then she could firmly close the door on the past. And on Carter.

But going out with him? Was that a good idea?

Probably not. She'd have to think about it.

First she'd have to get through Emma's homecoming.

She went back in the house.

Chapter 16

MOLLY'S PARENTS' HOUSE was filled with people, all talking over each other.

Just as she had expected, Emma was livid when she discovered their mom had had a serious accident and no one had told her. She was mad at Molly, and at their dad.

First, though, Emma had spent several hours with their mother, so Molly had stayed out of the way while Emma and Luke had visited with Mom.

Molly had known Emma was going to be unhappy, and she'd prepared herself for the worst of Emma's anger over keeping her in the dark.

When her sister finally took a break, she grabbed Molly's arm. "We need to talk."

She took her out back. It was a cool fall day, so they grabbed their jackets.

"You look nice and tan. How was the honeymoon?" Molly asked as they grabbed chairs on the patio.

"Oh, no. We're not talking about the honeymoon. Why didn't you call me?"

"Because you and Luke were in Hawaii, because you would have hopped the first flight back here."

"Of course we would have." Emma frowned. "She's hurt, Molly. Badly."

"Yes, she is. And Dad and I took care of it. Of her. And now she's beginning to heal."

Emma's eyes filled with tears. "It was my responsibility to be here for her."

"It was her idea not to call you."

"Of course it was. Because she's independent, and she never wants to bother anyone. That's Mom's way of handling everything. That's why she got hurt in the first place. But you know better. Dad knows better. We're a family and we deal with things together."

"Do we? It was lucky I was here. If I'd been gone, you would have been the one to drop everything. You would have had to put your life on hold to handle this, Emma. But you weren't here and I was, so I dealt with it. Isn't it about time I was the one to step up so you and Luke could enjoy your honeymoon?"

Emma was silent for a minute. "You could have at least told me."

"We could have, but we made the best decision we could at the time, Em. For you and for Luke. You had what we hope was an awesome honeymoon, and you got to have it worry free. If there'd been complications and Mom had been in any danger, I would have picked up the phone and called you immediately so you could have come home. But she was okay, and she's going to be fine. It'll take awhile, but she'll get through this and be her old self again."

Emma took a deep breath, then let out a sigh. "Well, I'm here now. Do you want to take off?"

Molly didn't hesitate. "No. I'm here. I'm committed."

"I could step in, you know."

"I know you could. But you've been doing that. You've always been here for them, even when you were away. Now it's my turn, don't you think?"

Emma stared at her. "When did my little sister grow up?"

Molly laughed. "I don't know. I guess when I saw Mom

lying there on the floor, crying and in pain. It scared the shit out of me, Em."

Emma's eyes filled with tears. She nodded. "I can't even imagine how awful that must have been. I'm sorry I wasn't here."

"Stop that. I was here. And you were exactly where you were supposed to be. On your honeymoon with your husband."

"You quit your job in Austin?"

"Yeah."

"I'm sorry, Moll. You didn't have to do that."

"Yes, I did. You know Dad can't handle this alone. And as for me, there's always another job on the horizon. When Mom's back on her feet again, I'll be on my way."

Emma leaned across the table and grasped Molly's hand. "Or maybe you'll decide Hope isn't so bad after all, and you'll stay."

Molly took a deep breath. "I don't know about that. I do like to travel."

"Is that the real reason you've been gone all these years?"

"No." She was shocked she'd said the word.

Emma leaned back. "That's the first time you've ever admitted there's something else."

"I know. But it's cold out here, and now's not the time to talk about it."

"Promise me you'll tell me."

Molly squeezed her sister's hand. "I promise."

"Okay. So I brought like a thousand photos back from Hawaii. Wanna see?"

"You know I do." Molly stood. "Let's go inside and make some hot chocolate and look at your pictures."

They looked at the photos, which were fabulous, and reaffirmed the decision to not notify Luke and Emma about Mom's injury. It was obvious the time they'd spent in Hawaii had been good for both of them. In every photo Emma and Luke looked relaxed. Happy. So much in love.

Emma and Luke stayed for dinner, and after Emma helped her get their mother situated for the night in the hospital bed in the guestroom, Luke and Emma headed home to reunite with their dogs.

Her dad went to bed as well, which left Molly alone and feeling more than a little restless.

It was Saturday night, and still early. She could watch a movie and make some popcorn, but she really wanted to get out of the house.

She grabbed her phone and, on impulse, called Carter, hoping he wasn't out on a date with someone else. If he was, he probably wouldn't answer her call, right? Because if he did and she heard some other female voice, she'd cringe and be so embarrassed.

He answered on the second ring. "Hey, Molly."

"Hi. What are you doing?"

"You're going to laugh."

"I doubt it."

"I'm decorating my house for Halloween."

Her lips tilted upward. "You are not."

"I am. Want to come over and help me?"

She smiled at the invite. "Sure. I'll be right there."

"I'm warning you, I take my Halloween very seriously."

She couldn't even imagine what he meant by that, but now she was curious. "I feel duly warned. I'll be there shortly."

"Okay. See ya."

She hung up and grabbed the keys to George, grateful to have her car back again after having it repaired. She left a note on the kitchen table for her parents in case her dad got up and was looking for her, then rolled her eyes, mentally noting the inconvenience of being someone her age and living at home again. But that's how it was, and she had to deal with it in order to take care of her mom.

She made a stop in the bathroom and checked her appearance. Not too bad. Her hair was up in a ponytail and she had on jeans and a sweatshirt, but whatever. It wasn't a date, anyway. How dressed up did she have to be to help with Halloween decorations?

But she did put on some lip gloss. Then felt stupid for doing it.

Not a date, remember?

She drove over to Carter's house. The front lights were on.

He was outside, unloading bales of hay from the back of his truck. She got out of her car and walked over to him.

"Planning a hayride?"

"Nope." He dragged one of the bales over toward the giant oak tree in the front yard, then settled it next to two other bales. "Come on into the garage with me."

"This sounds serial-killer-esque. I fear for my life."

"Ha. You're safe, though there is a skeleton involved."

"See? My fears are well grounded."

He laughed, and she followed him into the garage, where he had opened a long plastic storage box.

"Jeebus, Carter. You really do take your Halloween seriously." Inside were two skeletons, which looked totally real, a couple of light-up pumpkins, and some orange lights. God only knew what else lurked in the bottom of the box.

"Carry one of the skeletons for me, will you?"

"If a cop drives by, we could get arrested."

"Fortunately, I know all the cops."

"And they let you get away with this? Hope has become such a corrupt town since I've been away."

"Ha ha." He handed one of the oversized skeletons to her. It was heavier than she thought.

"You got it?" he asked.

"Yeah."

She hoisted it over her shoulder, convinced it looked like she was carrying a body across the lawn. But she followed Carter to the tree and laid the skeleton down on one of the bales of hay.

"Wait here. I have to go get the rope."

Rope?

She looked at the skeletons, then the wide branches on the tree, then shook her head.

Oh my.

When he came back with rope, she shook her head. "Seriously?"

He grinned. "Oh, yeah. The kids in the neighborhood love my house."

"I'll just bet they do."

He climbed up on the bales of hay and strung the rope over one of the tree branches, then made a noose and looped it over the neck of one of the skeletons, hoisting it up so it dangled from the ground. There were spotlights on the tree, and he adjusted one of them so it shined on the skeleton. It was highly gruesome, in an awesome, Halloween kind of way.

"What did these poor skeletons ever do to you?" she asked.

He laughed and took a step back. "Does it look high enough to you?"

She walked to the sidewalk. "Looks perfect for a hanging."

"I knew I could count on your support. Now let's do the second one on the other side of the tree."

When he was finished, it really was perfect, especially with the hideous pumpkin faces at the base of the hay bales.

"I'll string up some spider webbing in the trees on Halloween. I don't want to do that too early in case of rain."

"It's gruesome. Congratulations."

"Thanks. I also pipe horror music to the outside."

"I fear for the psyches of small children coming to your house."

"You'll have to be here on Halloween. A bunch of people come over. We dress up and scare the shit out of kids."

She cocked a brow. "Someday you're going to make your own kids so proud."

He gave her a look, then a grin. "Thanks."

It was at that moment she realized their child would have been twelve years old now. She waited for the anguish, but it passed quickly. She was grateful for that, because she was tired of dwelling on it. It was time to put it in the past.

He brushed his knuckles across her cheek. "What are you thinking about?"

She exhaled, refusing to bring it up. They'd rehashed it enough. "I'm thinking you need some headstones in this yard to fully creepify the look."

He turned around, put his hands on his hips, and stared out over the front lawn. "You know what? You're right. I'll get some next week."

She could already imagine the effect this yard was going to have on the kids. They'd be so scared. Then again, she remembered seeking out just this type of house when she and her friends had gone trick-or-treating when she was a kid. The scarier, the better.

Carter was going to be a huge hit.

He put his arm around her. "How about you come inside with me and we get something to drink?"

"Sure."

They picked up the remnants of the decorations and put them away in the garage, then she followed him inside the house.

She'd been here twice already, though the first time had been when she'd dumped him inside the front door, so that didn't really count. The second time she'd been nervous and had taken only a cursory glance—enough to note it was a nice house—but that had been about it.

Now, though, she was more relaxed, and she took the time to note his leather sofas, the dark wood floors, the recently renovated kitchen. The house wasn't new, but the kitchen was. All new appliances, quartz counters, with a newly tiled back-splash as well. She liked the looks of his kitchen, with its roomy island and plenty of space to work.

"Did you renovate the kitchen yourself?"

He handed her a beer. "I did. More or less. My dad helped some, and I had some friends over to help out when I could wrangle them on weekends, but mostly I did it on my own."

She pulled a seat up to the island. "You did a great job."

He took a long swallow of beer, then smiled at her. "Thanks. The place was a fixer-upper when I bought it, which meant I got it for a bargain. It also meant a lot of work, so I've been . . . working on it here and there for the past couple of years."

She swiveled around on her barstool, giving his place the once-over now that she knew he'd been renovating. "Tell me what you've done. What was it like when you moved in?"

He pushed off the counter, and took her by the hand. "Grab your beer. I'll give you the grand tour. I warn you, though.

I'm not finished yet, so you're going to see old house mixed with new house."

Her lips curved as she lifted her gaze to his. "That's what makes it fun. I like a work in progress. If it's all 'after,' I don't get to see how much work you've done."

He laughed. "Okay then." He took her into the living room, which was large, filled with two leather sofas, a modern, sleek fireplace and a really good-sized flat-screen TV. He'd fashioned a quirky-looking coffee table out of some kind of metal, and there was a side table on one end of one of the sofas.

"This room used to be small. There was a dining room on the side, also closed off. And the kitchen had a wall separating it from the living room. I took that out to open the whole thing up."

"I can see how this works now. It's much more open. And you added those French doors. My guess is there used to be a slider instead."

"Yeah. With the most God awful ugly curtains you can imagine."

"Oh, I can imagine. Remember, I move a lot so I've lived in places with what you could call 'unique' décor."

"Is that right?'

"Yes." She gave the room a critical look. "This is great entertainment space now. It's roomy, and with the island in the kitchen and extra seating there, you can fit in a lot of people."

"That was the idea." He led her down the hall. "The guest bathroom is off to the left. I haven't started on it yet."

Which meant she had to check it out. She opened the door to find blanched oak cabinetry, gold fixtures, a shower/tub combination. All very nineties-type décor. It was clean, though, so she gave him props for that.

She turned to Carter. "It's workable, but boring and dated."

"Yeah. It's the next project on the list. The last rooms to get renovated will be the other three bedrooms. I wanted to do the kitchen and living room first, and I finished the master bedroom just a month or so ago."

As soon as he opened the door to his bedroom, her eyes widened.

Now this was a retreat. Wide windows which surely let in a ton of light, making her wish it was daylight so she could see how the sun would spill into the oversized room. He had a king-sized bed and two nightstands, and there was still plenty of space for the two oversized stuffed chairs and table next to the windows. He'd continued the hardwood in this room, but put a comfortable-looking rug in between the bed and the sitting area. She walked in, admiring the furniture and the peaceful earth tone color of the paint in the room. Quietly, she made her way into the bathroom, but there, she gasped.

"Good Lord, Carter. Is this some kind of lure for women?"

He laughed, his warm breath tickling the back of her neck. "Maybe."

The bathroom was an oasis, with a large soaking tub, two deep vessel sinks with plenty of cabinet space, a dressing table, and a shower with multiple jets. There was a pebbled floor in the shower, and she curled her toes inside her sneakers at the thought of how that floor would massage her bare feet.

"It's decadent."

"If you think this is awesome, you should see the closet."

She pivoted to face him. "Don't tease me."

He stepped out of the bathroom, giving her space to open the door leading to the closet.

The light turned on automatically, and it was like she'd stepped into paradise. The closet was as big as some of the bedrooms she'd lived in, with racks and built-ins for shoes, and there was even a dresser in there.

"I love it." She turned to him. "Are you sure there isn't some woman in your life, and you built this for her?"

"No. Not yet, anyway. But I figured I probably wouldn't live here alone forever. Besides, I like a lot of space. I hate feeling confined. You should have seen the closet before. I could barely get my clothes in there, and it's not like I'm some big clothes guy. So I expanded the master a lot, added on to this room to make it larger."

"It shows. You've done an amazing job, Carter. When did you find the time for all this, plus your job, plus committees?"

He shrugged. "I make time for the things that are important to me."

It was then she realized that he'd set down roots in Hope, that this place meant something to him. Whereas she had run like hell and never once looked back. She'd let her pain drive her all these years. It had forced her away from her family, from everything she'd ever known.

But she wasn't going to blame Carter for it. It had been her choice.

She couldn't—wouldn't—have regrets. She lived a full life, an adventurous one, and she'd learned a lot. She supposed Carter had as well. They'd just done things a lot differently.

He led her back into the living room. She took a seat on the oh-so-comfortable leather sofa. He sat next to her. She sipped her beer, realizing he was building an amazing life for himself. "You should be proud of yourself. I can't imagine what this must feel like."

"What?"

"Working so hard on creating something like this. Setting down roots like you have."

"But you've traveled so much. That must be fun."

"It is. I've met a lot of great people, seen some amazing places."

He took a sip of his beer. "I sense a 'but' in there."

"No buts." None that she was going to voice to Carter. Besides, she was happy. At least she'd *been* happy, before she came back home.

"So you're content with the life you've chosen," he said.

"Perfectly."

"Good to know."

"Are you?"

He shrugged. "More or less. I mean, I have a job I love, doing work I've enjoyed doing my whole life. I've found a house I really like, and I'm turning it into something I can envision will make me and my future family happy for a lot of years. I have friends and family that I care about."

"I sense a 'but' in there," she said with a smile.

"You're right. I live a very full life, but there's something missing. A wife. Kids."

Her stomach clenched. She was the wrong person to have this conversation with. "And a dog?"

He laughed. "Yeah. I need to finish the backyard fence so I can at least get the dog."

"At the very least." She grabbed a coaster and put her beer on the table. "And what's holding you back on the wife and kids part? You're not getting any younger, you know."

"Thanks for noticing."

"You're welcome."

"As far as what's holding me back, I guess the answer to that is, the right woman."

The words "If things hadn't gone so wrong, you could have had me" hovered on the tip of her tongue, but she wasn't petty enough to say them. "She'll come along."

He gave her a direct stare. "Yeah, she will."

She got up. "I should go."

Carter stood. "Why?"

"I don't know." But she wasn't moving. Why wasn't she moving? And he wasn't doing anything about it, like asking her to stay. Did she want him to ask her to stay?

What the hell was wrong with her anyway? And with her feet, which weren't moving out the door.

"Come on," he finally said, helping save her from mortal embarrassment. "Let's go for a ride."

"Where to?"

"You'll see."

She arched a brow. "You're not kidnapping me, are you?"

He shot her a look.

"Okay, fine." She grabbed her jacket and he led her out the door. They climbed in his truck. "I'm surprised you're not taking the Mustang."

"The truck has butt heaters. I figured they'd keep you warm. The temperature is supposed to drop into the thirties tonight and the heater in the Mustang sucks."

"Good thinking."

He drove them out onto the highway, then a little ways out of town, eventually pulling down a side road by the river. It was a quiet overlook where people liked to launch their boats to go fishing. There was also an event area and picnic tables. She hadn't been here in years. Then again, there were a lot of places in Hope she hadn't visited in a long time.

He backed into the parking spot so the rear of the truck was facing the river, then left the radio on. Surprisingly, it wasn't Beach Boys music this time, but some nice, soft country tunes.

"Let's go sit on the tailgate. It's a clear night. We can watch the barges go by."

She got out and he opened the tailgate of the truck. She climbed on, and he sat next to her.

She stared out over the water. It was a clear, crisp fall night and the light from the moon sent a silvery sheen over the dark river.

"Remember when we came here for the fall carnival?"

She smiled at the memory. "Yes. All the rides were fun. I ate so much cotton candy I thought I was going to throw up on the Tilt-A-Whirl."

"But you stomached it anyway. You were always so tough."

She liked that he thought of her that way. "I didn't want to be left behind. You and your friends wanted to ride every ride ten times that night, if I recall correctly."

"Yeah." He leaned back and stretched out his legs, propping one boot over the other. "Frank was the one who ended up getting sick."

"That's because he smuggled in beer, trying to look like a hotshot in front of my friends." She shifted, half turning to look at him. "No, wait. He was trying to impress one of them. Laura Dusell, wasn't it?"

"You might be right about that. He wanted to look like a big shot so he stole that six-pack of beer from his dad's fridge, then hid them in his coat, taking swigs all night."

Molly nodded. "He was acting like an ass, trying to grab a kiss from her. She was turned off by his beer breath and his attitude and kept pushing him away. And then he got off one of the rides and puked right in front of her."

"Not a very impressive move, if I recall."

Molly laughed. "Uh, no. She wanted nothing to do with him."

"Some guys have to learn that lesson the hard way. But you girls didn't make it easy for us."

She rolled her eyes at him. "Oh, please. I was like a lovesick puppy around you. I fell for you as soon as you blinked those long, dark lashes of yours."

He turned his head and gave her a slow, thoughtful stare. "Is that right?"

"Yes, and you know it. You didn't even have to try."

"Oh, believe me. I tried. I zeroed in on you the first day you hit the halls of the high school, and no other girl existed for me after that. You were the only one I thought about."

Her heart skipped a beat at his confession. "Do you still say all the right things to women?"

"No." He let out a short laugh and stared out over the river. "Trust me. No."

Then he turned and looked at her. "With you and me, it was like . . . instantaneous. Like a fireball that hit me right between the eyes. It's never been like that with anyone else."

His confession zinged her right in the heart, and hurt at the same time. It had never been like that with anyone else for her, either. But she hadn't expected him to admit that to her. Especially not now, all these years later.

She still felt it, that sizzling crackle of heat that simmered between them. It was as if could she reach between them, she'd see a sparkle of electricity, that invisible, silvery thread that still bound them. She almost expected it. She feared it, because it had consumed her back then.

Walking away from him had been the hardest thing she'd ever done. Severing the bond with Carter had nearly destroyed her. It was what had kept her away from Hope all these years. The pain of losing him—of what they'd had together—had made her heart ache every day of every year.

So what was she doing here with him now? What was she so stupidly contemplating? Reopening that door would only lead to heartbreak. Was she really strong enough to walk away from him again?

He picked up a lock of her hair, turning her attention to him. "Your brain is working so hard over there it's practically spewing out smoke."

Her lips curved. "Maybe."

"Why don't you give it a rest and stop thinking so much."

"Do you have a better idea?"

"Yeah, I definitely have a better idea."

Tempting, but she wasn't sure she was ready to take that next step yet. Sitting here with him and talking was one thing. Doing something about it was entirely different. Once she did, that wall she'd carefully erected would fall. Then what would happen?

"You used that line on me in high school," she said.

"Oh, but I'm much better at so many things now."

"So I've noticed."

"Have you?" He gave her an expectant look. An irresistible smile.

She hopped off the tailgate and took a walk to the river's edge.

Carter followed.

Fog had started to roll in, surrounding them in an eerie blanket of white smoke and sending a hush over the night.

She shivered and wrapped her arms around herself

"Are you cold?"

"A little."

He positioned himself behind her and wrapped his arms around her, cocooning her against his chest. She felt the heat of his body, the hard shock of how much broader he was now than he'd been in high school.

They used to hang out in the park and sit by the pond. He'd pull her onto a bench, snugging her between his thighs, with his arms wound tightly around her. She'd rest her head against his chest. The two of them could sit together for hours and not say a word, just watching the geese. She'd always been so content just being with Carter.

But they were two different people now, and their lives had moved in opposite directions. During her years away from Hope, she'd often wondered what would have happened between the two of them if she hadn't left. Would they have drifted apart anyway, or would they have stayed together?

She'd never know the answer to that, but here she was tonight, in his arms once again. And she had no idea what that meant. She had no illusions about recapturing the magic of the past, only that she wanted a night where she didn't have to think about what once was. She knew there could never be a future for them, but why not have one night? Just the present, with no yesterday, and no tomorrow to think about.

She turned in his arms to face him, and just like the past, she knew she didn't have to say anything. All either of them had to do was touch the other, feel the heat that had always emanated between them.

She was in a hooded sweatshirt but was still cold. Carter only had his button-down shirt on. And God, his body was warm.

"You're not cold," she said.

His hands drifted down her back, pulling her closer. "I'm a hot guy, you know."

She let out a short laugh. She'd forgotten how much he used to make her laugh. She'd spent so much time dwelling on the end of their relationship, focusing only on the negative aspects, that she'd let go of everything good about him.

They had so much fun together. They always spent a lot of time talking to each other. He listened, always managed to center her when her mind was jumbled and flying off in a million places.

His hands lingered, the warmth from his fingers burning into her skin, even through the layers of clothes she wore.

She lifted her gaze to his, and as he lowered his head, she closed her eyes, feeling his breath sail across her lips.

The first touch of his lips was something magic.

Chapter 17

CARTER WENT SLOW, so afraid every movement he made would send Molly running away.

He'd waited for this all night, gauging her mood, every gaze, every turn of her head, figuring that at any moment she'd take off.

But she stayed, and now she sagged against him, her hands reaching out to grasp his arms. He tugged her close and deepened the kiss, feeling the surrender of her body. He read those signs and flicked his tongue against hers, taking in the warmth of her breath, his body tightening with the need for her he'd held in check for so long.

From the first time he'd seen her on the street, everything he'd felt for her all those years ago had been front and center. But it wasn't just the past, it was now. He'd tried to ignore it, but Molly wasn't someone you ignored. She was beautiful and fiercely independent, an attractive package wrapped up in a hot body. And maybe because he knew her so well, he was drawn to her in a way even he couldn't explain.

Maybe he didn't want to. All he knew was he was tired of fighting it.

No more. Now it came rushing forward, and it was all he could do not to pick her up and carry her to his truck, throw her down in the bed, and take her right there.

Instead, he smoothed his hands over her back, and felt her shiver.

He pulled away. "You're cold."

She tilted her head back. "Cold is not what I'm feeling right now."

"You're shivering."

"Maybe a little."

He took her hand. "Come on."

He led her back to the truck, started it up, and got the heater going. Not for him, of course, because he was plenty hot.

"Where to?" she asked.

"Not to your place. It's a little crowded."

She let out a soft laugh. "Yeah. Let's not go there."

He made the drive back to his house a little faster than intended. He didn't want to seem too eager, but he didn't want to destroy the mood between them, either. Things between him and Molly were precarious enough as it was. One wrong word, one look, and he was sure she'd run.

He pulled into the driveway and went around to her side to open the truck door for her, but she had already climbed out. She slid her hand into his hair and lifted up on her toes to press a kiss to his lips. He lingered there for a minute or so, content to feel her body against his.

It had been a long damn time since he'd just . . . felt her there. It was a good feeling, but he was also getting hard, and they were in his driveway.

"Uh, maybe we should take this inside."

She looked down at what was quickly becoming his obvious desire for her. Then she lifted her gaze to his and offered up a wickedly sexy smile.

"Maybe we should."

Okay, so she wasn't going to change her mind this time.

He had to admit he was pretty damn happy about that. Neither a cold shower nor taking his erection problem into his own hand sounded like a good option to him. Not when this beautiful, hot woman nestled her body against his. He wanted her. Just her. And he wanted her to know just how much.

He led her inside the house and shut the door. Molly moved into the living room, shedding her hoodie before rubbing her hands together to ward off the chill from outside.

"Do you want some coffee?" he asked.

She turned to face him and shook her head. "No. I want you to warm me up."

"I can do that." Taking quick strides, he made his way over to her and drew her against him, wrapping his arms around her back. He pulled up her shirt to slide his hands over the warmth of her flesh.

She shivered. "Your hands are cold."

"They'll be warm in a minute." He bent and teased her lips, coaxing her to open for him.

She did, rising up on her toes to fit her body closer to his. He palmed her butt, loving the feel of her curves. His hands might be cold, but the rest of him was hot as Molly moaned against his mouth, sliding her hand around the nape of his neck to hold on to him.

He wanted to lie next to her, to feel her all over, and not with all these damn layers of clothes in the way. He grabbed hold of her thighs and hoisted her, carried her down the hall and into his bedroom and deposited her on the side of his bed. He pulled away from her only long enough to close the shutters, then he came back.

She was sliding out of her shoes, pulling off her socks, and she stood to unbutton her jeans.

"That would be a lot more fun if I was the one doing it."

Her hand stilled. "Okay."

Molly's breath caught and held as Carter took her zipper between his fingers, his knuckles brushing the bare skin of her stomach as he drew it down. She tried to remember if she was wearing decent underwear today, but her mind had gone suddenly blank because she was staring up at his beautiful face and all she could think about was how could he have possibly gotten more good-looking over the past twelve years?

From far away, he was gorgeous. Up close, devastatingly handsome, and as he tugged at her jeans and started to draw them down her legs, she remembered how they used to fumble at this, so in a rush to get at each other that there had never been any finesse.

Now, though, he took his time, gently giving her shoulder a push to sit on the edge of the bed so he could pull off her jeans. He smoothed his palms up her ankles and calves, then spread her thighs, using his fingers to tease her through the silk of her panties. Just a whispered breath of a touch, but enough to make her arch, to want, to need what he offered.

She could barely breathe. Having him touch her so intimately after so long felt so familiar, and yet as if he'd never touched her before.

"You're so beautiful, Molly. Your skin is so soft, I'm almost afraid to touch you."

She took in a deep breath. "I'm not fragile, Carter. And I definitely want your hands on me."

His lips curved, and he swept one finger over her hip bone, before reaching for the hem of her shirt to lift it over her head, leaving her wearing just her bra and panties.

Oh, right. She'd worn the matching red ones today. Good call, since they were kind of hot.

Carter stood and looked down at her, raking his fingers through his hair. "Yeah, definitely beautiful. I mean, you always were. But now. Wow."

Now it was her turn to smile, warmed by his obvious appreciation of her. "Thank you. Now how about we get your clothes off?"

"Good idea." He started to reach for his shirt, but she got up on her knees and laid her palm on his chest.

She leveled a smile at him. "This would be a lot more fun if you let me do that."

His gaze went dark. "Okay."

She unbuttoned his shirt, pulled it off and tossed it to the side, sucking in a breath as she admired his washboard abs and broad shoulders. He'd always been well built, but nothing like this. He'd broadened—she'd discovered that when she leaned against him. He'd filled out in all the right places. Not too muscular, just . . . perfect.

She swept her hands over his exposed skin, taking her time to map her way across his chest, letting her fingers slide down his stomach, feeling every inch of muscle.

She stopped at his jeans, lifted her gaze to his, keeping her focus there as she undid the button, then drew the zipper down, her hand brushing against his sizeable erection. He was breathing hard, but kept his eyes on hers and didn't say a word.

He was communicating plenty with his eyes and with his erection.

She crouched down and pulled his jeans from his hips, letting them drop to the floor. He kicked them aside and she looked up at him, offering a smile.

"Wow, Carter."

He grinned, then pulled her up to sit beside him. He drew the straps of her bra down, bending to kiss her as he undid the clasp. All play was over as her bra disappeared and suddenly his hand was there to cup her breast, his fingers toying with her nipple.

She gasped, arching into his hand, wanting more. And she got more, as he swept her onto her back, then bent and put his mouth on her, sucking her nipple in. He flicked his tongue over her until she was squirming under him, tangling her fingers in his hair to hold him there so the maddeningly delicious sensations wouldn't stop.

He teased her, tormented her with his mouth, and at the same time moved his hand down her rib cage and over her belly, sliding his fingers into her panties to cup her sex.

This was so much more intense than when they were younger. All she could remember from then was fast, furious passion, a frenzied need to be with each other. A manic coupling, then calm after. Back then, besides the desperate need to get in each other's pants, there'd also been a fear of getting caught, so they'd always been in a hurry.

Now, they had all the time in the world to get to know each other's bodies again. She intended to savor every moment.

Instinctively, she lifted into his touch, craving the need he elicited from her. She was primed and ready like a rocket for launch, and the barest touch could send her right off. It had been so long, and this was Carter, who even after all these years knew her body better than any man ever had.

Surprisingly, he remembered how she liked to be touched, softly at first, and then a little harder as she got closer. How could he recall that after twelve years? As she shuddered and tightened he slid a finger inside her, and she exploded, crying out with an orgasm that left her shaken.

"Yeah, I remember how that feels," he said, nuzzling her neck. "Feels so damn good to take you there again."

And then he was there, his mouth covering hers, kissing her until all she could think about was feeling him inside her, connecting with him in a way she hadn't realized she'd missed so much until now.

He pulled his lips from hers, stared down at her, and she wondered if he thought the same thing.

When he rubbed his thumb across her bottom lip, and said, "I've missed you, Molly," tears pricked her eyes.

She blinked back the waterworks. She didn't want to get emotional about this. It would only lead to heartbreak, and she'd never let Carter break her heart again. So instead, she smiled up at him. "I hope you have condoms."

He grinned. "I definitely have condoms."

"I mean, I'm on the pill. I take precautions. I'm not leaving it all up to you or anything, but we should be careful, you know?"

He brushed his thumb over her jaw, his expression suddenly serious. "Yeah. I know."

He reached into the nightstand and pulled out a box of condoms.

Now she felt like she'd done something to break this magical spell that had been cast between them. The room felt colder. She felt colder. Bringing up the past—that big elephant in the room that seemed to wedge between them—would always be a barrier.

She started to sit up, but Carter pushed her down. "Not so fast. I'm not letting you get away from me that easily."

His body, so warm, was just what she needed.

"Unless you need to pee or something. In which case, go ahead."

She laughed, and his lightheartedness pushed away the last of her doubts. "No, I'm good."

He swept his hand over her breast, teasing her nipple until it was hard, until she felt the sensation shoot right to her core.

"Yeah, you definitely are."

He took her nipple into his mouth, and she was once again lost in sensation, in his mouth and his hands until all she could focus on was the way he made her body feel. That's why she was here, the only reason she was here.

Carter knew Molly had felt a moment of panic. He didn't know what had brought it on, and if he hadn't been able to take her out of that moment—if she'd wanted to leave right then, he would have no choice but to let her, because he didn't want a woman in his bed who didn't want to be there.

But whatever second of doubt she had seemed to have disappeared, because she responded to his touch, arching against him, without words begging for what they both needed from each other.

He couldn't wait any longer. He removed her panties, shed his boxer briefs, and grabbed a condom, then parted her legs, staring down at the woman she'd become, even more beautiful than the girl she'd once been.

She looked up at him, her eyes glazed with passion, as he entered her.

It felt like home, like this was where he'd always belonged. Inside her, skin to skin, her heart beating a fast rhythm as he moved within her.

He didn't want to make too much of this, because where Molly was concerned, he knew it was a temporary thing. He planned to enjoy this moment, since it was likely to be a one-time occurrence.

But damn, it was amazing to have her hands roaming down his arms, her nails raking over his skin as he lifted and thrust within her, to feel the way she tightened around him. Everything was familiar, but also like it was the first time he'd ever made love to this woman. He kissed her, and felt like he was being tossed around in a storm, the pleasure so great, the emotions almost more than he could handle. Carter wasn't an emotional kind of guy, but this was Molly, and to him, she'd always been his. At one time he'd wanted to give her everything, and at least, in this, he intended to.

So when she lifted, he ground against her, enjoyed her quiver, and gave her all he had, caught up in every sound she made, every breath she took. Her expressions told him everything, her body even more. He grasped her hands and held tight to her, and when she released, he let go, the two of them shuddering together in one epic climax that left him shaking.

He buried his face in her neck, breathing in her scent, wondering if this was going to be the last time she'd allow him to get this close.

But she didn't seem in any hurry to push him away, and he sure as hell didn't want her to leave, so he rolled to the side and left only long enough to dispose of the condom. Then he was back, tugging her against him and pulling the covers over them both.

For a while he held her, listening to her breathe, content that she was beside him and didn't feel the need to bolt. He wondered if she'd stay tonight.

Finally, she tilted her head back and looked at him.

"I hope you have some stamina, Carter, because it's been kind of a dry spell for me."

Now *that* he hadn't expected. He arched a brow and lifted up on his elbow. "Is that right?"

She smiled slyly. "That's right. And since you're a known quantity and I don't intend to have sex with any random strangers in Hope, I thought you might want to . . . offer your services."

He laughed. "You want me to act as your stud while you're in town?"

"Yes. That pretty much sums it up."

"I'm kind of offended, Molly."

"No, you're not. You're a man with a penis. You're thrilled

about having no-strings sex with a woman you don't have to wine and dine and promise to marry at the end of it all."

"You have a point. Though I never mind the wining and dining part."

She shrugged. "That's negotiable. So . . . we have a deal?"

"A deal for smokin'-hot sex? I'd be a total dumbass to say no."

"You don't strike me as a total dumbass."

Not quite the way he saw spending time with Molly, but she was right. He wasn't stupid, and he enjoyed having sex with her. If that was all she intended to offer, he was going to take it.

At least it was a starting point.

"It's a deal."

"Good. I'll give you ten minutes recovery time, then I'll be ready for round two."

"You're a hard taskmaster, Miss Burnett."

She rolled over on her back and smiled. "You have no idea. We haven't even gotten started yet, Carter."

Chapter 18

THE LAST THING Molly expected to be doing was carving pumpkins. She thought herself long past the age, and she never did it anymore. If she was home on Halloween night, she'd pass out candy to the kids in whatever apartment complex she was living in. Otherwise, no decorations. And definitely no pumpkin carving.

But her mom had insisted that there had to be pumpkins on the porch, so she'd gone to the store and now she stood at the kitchen counter, elbows deep in pumpkin guts.

Her father was keeping Mom company in the living room, swearing he knew nothing about pumpkin carving and that was Mom's area of expertise. She figured that was his way of getting out of this torturous task.

"Molly, have you gotten to the design part yet?" her mom hollered from the other room.

"Uh, not yet. Still cleaning out the pumpkins, Mom." Maybe she could have a small accident and dump both of these hideous things on the floor. Of course, knowing her mother, she'd just send Molly back to the store to buy two more.

She pulled a handful of pumpkin seeds and gunk out of one.

Ick.

The doorbell rang. Great. Someone else to witness her misery. Maybe it was Emma and Molly could force her to help. She was at least a surgeon and could assist with the face carving.

"That looks fun."

She jerked her head up to see Carter leaning against the doorway, a smirk on his oh-so-handsome face.

She hadn't seen him since that night they'd spent together a few days ago. He'd called her several times, and they'd texted, but her mom had a doctor appointment, and he'd had some issues with some of his Tulsa shops, so they hadn't reconnected.

Not that she'd expected they'd see each other every day or anything. Or at all, for that matter.

"Living the dream here."

He laughed, pushed off the doorway, and came into the kitchen. "I can tell. In the Halloween spirit?"

"No." She peeked around him to see her mom and dad were watching something on television. "Forced into it by my mother, who insisted on having carved pumpkins on the front porch for Halloween."

"I see. So you'd rather not."

"I'd rather not have my hands in all this goo."

He rolled up the sleeves of his shirt. "I'll help."

"You don't have to."

"I don't mind. Remember, Halloween is my specialty."

"Oh, right. I forgot. In that case, be my guest. There's another pumpkin over there to annihilate. Knives are on the counter."

He grabbed a knife and the pumpkin and started to gut the inside while she finished hers. After she emptied the contents of her pumpkin, she washed her hands and watched as Carter efficiently dug out the contents of the one he was working on, sliding his hands inside to empty out all the stuff, not once grimacing at the slime like she had.

"You're very brave."

He laughed. "It doesn't bother me. Do you want to save the seeds?"

She made a face, then shook her head. "No, thanks."

"You should come over here and help me."

"Oh, I've already done my own pumpkin. I'm happy to watch you."

"Not your thing, huh?"

She crossed her arms. "Not in the least. In fact, I'm super happy you showed up."

He turned his head to the side and graced her with a sexy smile. "Glad to hear that."

"Why did you show up?"

"I wanted to drop off some paperwork about the town square project. There are a few decisions we need to make."

"Okay."

He lifted his hands, displaying trails of disgusting pumpkin goo. "Maybe after we're done here."

She laughed. "Of course."

Once he was done cleaning out his pumpkin, they spread newspaper on the table.

"Do you have a design in mind for the face?" he asked

She gave her pumpkin the once-over. "I'm going for something silly. How about you?"

"Mine's going to be scary."

"I'm so not surprised."

They got to work on carving, both of them concentrating on their individual pumpkin faces. Molly had to admit that, with Carter working next to her, this task wasn't as tedious as she'd thought it was going to be. He'd occasionally lift his head and smile at her from across the table, and her dad would pop in and check out what they were doing.

This was . . . nice. And a little unexpected.

She laid her knife down and stood, taking a step back to review her work.

"I don't know about this," she said.

Carter looked up. "What about it?"

"I might have gone a little too far on the scary side, instead of funny."

He got up, and came over, his shoulder brushing against hers as he got in front of her pumpkin. "That's really good, Molly."

"You think so?"

"Definitely."

She'd wanted to do a funny, devilish look. Instead, her pumpkin looked demonic. Still, she'd had fun.

"I guess it'll have to do," she said. "And the good news is, I'm finished."

"Me, too."

She walked over to his, her jaw dropping. "You did this freehand?"

"Yeah."

He had carved the Grim Reaper into his pumpkin. It was beautiful.

"I'm so impressed, Carter. You're really artistic."

He shrugged, then grabbed a paper towel to wipe his hands. "It was fun. I could have done better if I'd taken a little more time. I hope your mom likes it."

"She's going to love it. Really love it. Let's show my parents."

They carried the pumpkins into the living room.

"Wow," her mother said. "These are so impressive. I love yours, Molly. It's so scary. And Carter, that's . . . wow. Did you use those stencil sets?"

Molly shook her head. "Carter carved his freehand."

"That's amazing, Carter," her dad said. "I didn't know you were that creative."

He laughed. "Thanks. I've had a lot of practice over the years. I'm a big fan of Halloween."

"So am I," her mom said. "Thank you for taking the time to do this. And Carter, especially you. I know you didn't come over to carve pumpkins tonight."

"Trust me, it was my pleasure."

"How about we light these babies up and see how they look?" Molly asked.

Her mother smiled. "Oh, I'd love to see them."

Molly went into the kitchen to grab two tea light candles.

They set them in the bottom, got them lit, and her dad turned the lights out.

"Oh, my," her mom said. "They're gorgeous."

They were, especially Carter's. And seeing her mom so happy made Molly's heart soar.

They set the pumpkins out on the front porch, then took a step back to admire their work.

"They look good," Molly said.

"Yeah, they do."

She turned to him. "Thanks again for helping out. I would have hated doing both these pumpkins by myself."

"There's no fun in doing it alone."

"Do you have pumpkins on your porch?"

"Of course."

"Did you do them by yourself?"

"Yeah."

"Sorry. I would have gladly helped you."

He laughed and put his arm around her. "Thanks, but I think you're lying."

"You're right. I hated every minute of that mess. And speaking of mess, I need to go clean that up. Would you like some coffee?"

"In other words, you're inviting me to come in and help you clean up pumpkin guts."

"Darnit. My nefarious plan is spoiled. But yes, that's exactly it."

"You're a hard sell, Burnett. But I'm game. After that, we can go over the paperwork."

"Okay."

They went back inside. Her mom was in her wheelchair, both she and her dad getting ready to head off to bed for the night. Molly offered to help get Mom situated in her bedroom, but Dad declined, saying he had it covered, so she and Carter said their good-nights, then went into the kitchen to clean up the pumpkin mess. Carter bagged all the remnants while Molly washed the knives, the kitchen table and counter. It was done in a matter of minutes, then she made coffee for both of them.

They sat at the table and she opened the envelope containing the project papers so she could scan through them while they sipped their drinks.

She scanned the revised blueprints. "What do you think about the landscaping in the park area?"

He stood and came over to her, leaning over the table to point out a couple of areas. "I'm a little concerned about these. I think we should switch out some of the bushes for trees in this area, and put the bushes over here, plus some perennials in this spot. This is the southern exposure, so it makes more sense, plus it'll put the trees over on the west side to provide more shade in the hotter part of the summer."

Molly looked at the plan now, then envisioned Carter's suggestion. She nodded. "I agree. Your way is better. Plus, if we move one of the benches under the trees, it's a shady area for people to sit."

He made some notes. "Good point. Let's bring that up at the next committee meeting on Tuesday."

They discussed a few of the other agenda items. Carter had good insights, and great ideas. She liked talking with him about business. She could see why his auto shops were a success. He had an eye for details and was well organized. She wished she had been here to see him grow his business from the ground up.

But she hadn't, because of circumstances that had directly involved him—circumstances she'd shoved to the back of her mind and refused to rehash. Not now when they were just starting to get along again.

She was enjoying this time with him, probably because she knew it was temporary. As soon as her mother was back on her feet again, she was gone.

Maybe that's why she was getting along so well with Carter. She could put him in this temporary slot where she didn't have to think about living in this town, seeing him every day, having a real relationship with him.

They could just have fun, and this was all pretend. She could live with that, knowing that at some point it was all going to go away, because she was going to go away.

"I guess I should head on out of here and let you get some sleep."

She looked up from the documents she was stuffing back into the envelopes, then picked up her phone. "It's only ten o'clock, Carter."

"Oh."

She cocked a brow. "I had no idea you were the type to go to bed early on a school night."

He laughed. "I think you of all people know me better than that."

She closed the envelope and slid it across the table, then rolled the blueprints and slid the rubber band around them. "However, I understand you have to get to work early in the morning, so you're right. You probably need your beauty rest."

He pinned her with a look. "Now you're baiting me."

"Maybe."

"Do you want to go out somewhere?"

She shook her head. "Not really."

She moved around the table and stopped in front of him, palming his chest. "I thought we'd hang out here for a bit."

"I can do that. Do you want to watch a movie?"

She had zero interest in watching a movie, but if it got him to hang out with her awhile longer, she was game. "Sure."

They went into the living room and grabbed a seat on the sofa. She turned on the TV, surfing a bit.

"That one."

She turned to face him. "Still into horror movies, I see."

"Well, it is Halloween season. You have to get in the spirit."

She rolled her eyes, but clicked on the movie. At least it was a classic and one she'd seen before, so none of the upcoming carnage would come as a surprise to her.

"Popcorn?" she asked.

He smiled at her. "Sure. Want me to help you?"

"No. It's microwave popcorn, so it'll only take a minute. I'll bring drinks for us, too."

She hopped up and went into the kitchen, put the popcorn in the microwave, then poured sodas. She brought the sodas in and went back for the popcorn, retaking her seat next to him.

"You missed two murders while you were gone," he said.

She laughed and grabbed a handful of popcorn. "Imagine that. Good thing I've seen this movie before."

"So, you're a fan of horror movies, too."

"I didn't say that. I said I've seen this one before. More than once."

"Which makes you a fan." He tossed a kernel of popcorn at her.

She picked it up and stuffed it down his shirt.

He grabbed her wrists and gave her a warning glare, laced with amusement. "You don't want to start a fight you can't win."

Now that was a challenge she couldn't back down from. "Good point."

After he released her hands, she took a handful of popcorn, seemingly ready to put it in her mouth. When Carter turned his attention back to the movie, she stuffed the popcorn down the back of his shirt.

He jerked and grabbed the bowl, thrusting his hand in and grasping a bunch of popcorn, then shoving it under her shirt. She squealed, then immediately silenced herself, though by now she was laughing and there was popcorn all over the floor. It was a good thing Pokey, her parents' dog, slept in her mom's room, because he'd be having a feast otherwise.

Carter reached under her shirt and pushed the popcorn higher, making her laugh even more.

"Shh," he said. "You're going to wake your parents."

She tried to stifle her laugh, but she couldn't stop herself. "Then stop shoving popcorn down my bra."

"Okay." Instead, his hand moved, ever higher, cupping her breast over her bra. "Is this better?"

She stilled, her body warming to his touch. "Much."

He pushed her up the sofa so her head rested on the cushioned arm, then covered her body with his. His lips met hers and popcorn wars were forgotten as she wrapped her arms around him and met his kiss with equal fervor.

The last time it was slow and easy, but now, she forgot everything, even the popcorn, as he crushed her lips and took her mouth with a passion that was overwhelming, heating her body to intense levels. She arched against him, feeling desire and Carter's erection pressing against her, heightening her own need.

She wanted him. Right here, right now, and nothing was going to get in her way. She tangled her fingers in his hair, rewarded with his groan. Desire ratcheted up to unbearable levels.

Until Carter rose up and looked down at her, the desire etched across his face matching what she felt.

"You do know we're in your parents' living room."

It took her a few seconds to catch her breath, to realize he had his hand under her shirt, cupping her breast, his thumb still sweeping back and forth across her nipple. Her heart was beating a crazy, out of control rhythm against the palm of his hand.

She swallowed to coat her desert-dry throat. "Well, now I do. I kind of forgot there for a minute."

Carter heaved a sigh, adjusting against her, letting her feel the rock-hard proof of his need rubbing against her hip.

"So did I." He sat up, then grasped her hand and pulled her to a sitting position.

Popcorn fell from her shirt, and several kernels landed in his lap, drawing her attention to his . . . situation.

She snorted out a laugh.

"Hey, now. You started this," he said, scooping up the popcorn and dumping it into the bowl.

"I did. Unfortunately, we can't finish it. Not here, anyway."

"Yeah. That part sucks."

With a reluctant sigh, she stood.

They picked up all the popcorn, including the pieces inside their shirts, which made each of them laugh. She took the bowl into the kitchen and dumped the contents into the trash and washed her hands.

"I think it's time I left," Carter said, placing his hands on either side of her hips where she rested against the kitchen counter. "Before we get in trouble again."

She sighed. "It's like being a teenager again. Living with my parents. Having to be quiet at night after they go to bed."

"Not being able to have sex whenever you want to?" Carter added.

"Yes. Exactly that. Only I'm not seventeen anymore. And I've been independent for years, so this living at home thing is hard for me."

He smoothed his hand over her hair. "I can't even imagine what it must be like for you. I'm sorry."

She shrugged. "I'm here for my mom, and it's temporary. It's not like I'm suffering or anything."

"Well, I'm suffering right now because of you."

He looked down, and so did she. She laughed. "I think you'll survive."

"I don't know. I might die from this."

"Hardly." She pressed on his chest. "Time for you to go."

He cocked a grin, then pushed off the counter. She walked him to the front door, then stepped outside, lightly shutting the door behind her.

"Thanks for stopping by tonight, and helping me with the pumpkins."

"Thanks for the popcorn."

"Yes. I need to take a shower now and wash all the buttered popcorn and kernels off my body."

He grabbed her shirt and pulled her closer. "Think how much more fun that would be if I were in the shower with you?"

"You are not helping my dilemma."

"Hey, if I have to suffer, so do you." He tipped her chin, then brushed his lips across hers.

She sighed into his salty, buttery-tasting kiss, then sagged against him, not wanting him to go, but having no other choice.

When he pulled away, his eyes were filled with the same regret.

"I'm going to think about you tonight when I'm taking my shower."

Her body trembled. "You do that. And I'll do the same."

His lips quirked into a half smile. "Good night, Molly."

"See you later, Carter."

She headed into the house and turned off all the lights, then went into the bathroom. She pulled off her shirt, and there, nestled between her breasts, was a piece of popcorn.

She couldn't help but laugh.

Chapter 19

"I'M SO GLAD we have some time together," Emma said as they strolled through the mall.

"Me, too." Molly had invited Emma to go shopping with her tonight so they could have some sister time. She'd been so wrapped up with Mom and Carter, and with Emma being off on her honeymoon that she hadn't spent enough time with her sister. The only way to do that was to force the time together.

There was a football game on, so Luke brought the dogs over, and he and Molly's dad were spending the evening together watching football—one of Mom's favorite sports—and having pizza, keeping their mother company.

Mom said she was sad not to be able to go shopping with her and Emma, since shopping was another of Mom's favorite sports.

"Maybe we should pick up something for Mom while we're out," Emma said. "Maybe a new pair of pajamas?"

"I like that idea." She linked her arm with Emma's and they headed to one of the stores, bickering with each other over which pair of pajamas their mother would like best. They finally settled on a cute lime green set they both agreed Mom would love. Emma bought a pair of cognac-colored boots, and when they passed the lingerie store, Molly paused at the window as something caught her eye.

"Really?" Emma asked, cocking a brow. "That's uh . . . wow, Molls."

"I know, ridiculous, right? I shouldn't." She started to walk away, but Emma grabbed her arm.

"Oh, I think you should, as long as you tell me all about you and Carter."

"How do you know I want that outfit for a guy? And why would you think it was Carter?"

Emma laughed. "Honey, no woman buys a getup like that just for herself. That's an outfit a man takes off of you. And as far as it being Carter? Please. I'm not blind."

Leave it to her sister to read signals like they were a flashing beacon. "Okay, you're right."

Emma stood there, arms crossed. "So? Are we getting the outfit?"

"We are not getting the outfit. I'm pondering the ridiculousness of why I'm even considering it."

"Why is it ridiculous? It's sexy. He'll go crazy seeing you in it."

"We're not even dating."

"*Dating* is an antiquated word, at least according to Chelsea. And besides, you stopped at the window, and you thought about Carter when you saw the outfit, didn't you?"

She had thought about Carter, about wearing that outfit for him, surprising him. She'd surprised herself, too. But things between the two of them were . . .

What? She didn't know what they were. They had gotten through the uneasiness, had developed a sort of friendship . . . with benefits. She knew she wasn't staying in Hope, but she liked having sex with him. Things could have been complicated, but so far, they weren't. She knew Carter, better than any man she'd ever known.

So why not continue the fun?

"Okay. I'll try it on."

"Great. Let's do that."

She ended up buying the outfit, and then it was off to

dinner at the Cheesecake Factory, where she ordered a magnificent plate of pasta.

"So tell me about you and Carter," Emma said as she dug into her fish. "I know you two dated in high school, then it was just . . . over, I guess?"

"I don't know, Em. It's a difficult situation with him."

"What do you mean by difficult?"

Molly looked around. It wasn't crowded tonight, and only a server or two hustled by now and then. She hadn't wanted to have this conversation with her sister in public, but she didn't want to have it at her parents' house, either, so she supposed now was as good a time as any to just tell her.

"I got pregnant."

Emma laid her fork down on the plate. "What? When?"

"Senior year."

"Oh my God, Molly. Why didn't you tell me? Do Mom and Dad know?"

She shook her head. "It all happened so fast. Carter and I were stunned. We were careful, you know. Or at least we thought we were being careful, but I guess not careful enough. So when it happened, we weren't prepared. We started to make plans for the baby—for the future. Carter was going to delay college. I'd have the baby. We were going to get married. We were figuring things out for our future, you know? Then a week later, I miscarried."

"Oh, honey." Emma reached across the table and squeezed Molly's hand. "I'm so sorry."

"Me, too. I was devastated. It might have been unplanned, and we were so young, but God, Em, I wanted that baby so much."

"I can't even imagine how awful that must have been for you."

"It was a bad time. The worst time. To compound things, Carter seemed to retreat from me. He almost seemed . . . relieved."

"No."

"Yes. He said he knew I was upset about the baby, and he

was, too, but since the miscarriage happened, things could go on the way we had originally planned. He'd go to college, I'd go to college, and we'd have the future we had always wanted together."

"Oh." Emma pursed her lips. "That was so insensitive of him."

"Yeah. I didn't handle it well, I accused him of not wanting our baby, of not wanting me. I was so hurt. He was hurt. I don't know. I was an emotional wreck, and we ended things badly."

Emma studied her for a few seconds. "That's when you left Hope."

"Yes."

"Molly, why didn't you talk to me? Or Mom."

She studied her plate. "I don't know, Em. I was so full of pain and anguish and anger at the time. I bottled it all up inside and just ran like hell. The only thing that made me feel better was getting away."

She lifted her gaze to her sister's. "I spent three years madly in love with a boy who wasn't what I thought he was. And in an instant, everything changed for me. I had to figure out who I was without Carter. Without my family, and without Hope. I had to become my own person. I might not have done it the right way, but I did it the best way I could."

Emma took a long swallow of her tea, then set it down. "I don't think anyone can tell you what's the right way. You had a deep emotional trauma. Something—and someone—hurt you, Molly. I'm sorry you didn't feel like you could share that with me, or with Mom and Dad, but I understand you dealt with it in a way that made sense to you. I know how that is, how you have to figure out who you are without anyone else's help. I just wished I could have been there for you."

Emma understood, and that gave Molly more relief than she'd ever though possible.

"I've missed you all these years, Moll. I wish you had told me sooner."

She felt her sister's pain from across the table. "I've missed you, too. I was just a mess for so long and I had to figure myself out. Plus, I've harbored all this anger and resentment for Carter."

"And now?"

She shrugged. "We talked it out the night of your wedding. Or I yelled at him and told him how I felt. But it just seemed like I was rehashing old hurts. I had to let it go. I can't do over the past and make it turn out differently, and he feels like shit over what happened. Neither of us are the same people we were back then."

"Carter's a good guy, Molly."

"Yeah, so I've noticed since I've been back. I had this image of him in my head all these years—the image was of the boy who hurt me. It's like I froze him in time in that one moment, making him this awful person. That's not who he is and I had to leave that Carter in the past."

Emma pushed her plate to the side, and waited while their waitress came by and refilled their glasses.

"And now?" Emma asked. "It seems like you're spending some time with Carter."

"I am. He's still the fun, romantic, sexy guy I used to know, and I'm getting to know the man he's become."

"You like him."

"Yes."

"And you're obviously having sex with him."

Such a weird conversation to have with her big sister. "Well, yes."

Emma grinned. "So you put the past behind you, and you're enjoying the now."

"That's it exactly," she said, then took a sip of her own iced tea. "I'm living in the moment, having some fun with him."

"Is that's all there is? Just the now?"

"I can't have a future with him, Emma. I'm not staying in Hope. Once Mom is back on her feet, I'm out of here again."

Emma's smile disappeared. "Why?"

She shrugged. "Because I like the travel and the opportunities I can have when I move around."

"That sounds like a line from a brochure, not how you really feel, Moll. Maybe you should listen to your heart, and give Carter—and Hope—another chance. You might fall in love all over again."

That wasn't going to happen. She'd loved Carter once, and he'd broken her heart. She'd never open her heart to him again.

Fun and sex was one thing.

Love? Never again.

Chapter 20

IT WAS HALLOWEEN, one of Carter's favorite days of the year. And even better, it was on a Saturday, so he spent the day prepping the house. He'd e-mailed and texted invites to the party he was having tonight and had shopped for all the booze and food he was going to need. Now all that was left was the prep.

He'd cleaned the house from top to bottom and he'd bought candy for the kid portion of the night, which would take place early. After nine, the adult portion would start, though whoever wanted to come over early and help hand out candy could do that. He hoped people would show up early. The more people around to share Halloween with the kids, the more fun it would be.

Bash wasn't going to be able to make it since he was running the bar tonight. Too bad for him, because Carter could throw one hell of a party. He'd done these every year, and while the weeknight ones were fun, the weekend ones were legendary.

When the doorbell rang, he grabbed a paper towel to wipe his hands, then went to the door.

Molly being there surprised him, since she'd told him earlier in the week she wasn't sure she was going to be able to make it until much later in the evening. Since it was only two in the afternoon, it was a shock to see her on his doorstep.

"Hey," he said. "What are you doing here?"

"I've been given a reprieve. Emma and Luke showed up at the house after Emma got off work. She wants to cook for Mom and Dad tonight and help them hand out candy."

"So you get a night off?"

She gave him a smile. "I do. So I hope you don't mind, but I hightailed it out of there before she changed her mind. Luke said to tell you they'll be over after the candy portion at Mom and Dad's."

"Okay."

"I thought you might need some help for the party tonight."

"I'm glad you're here. I hope you brought your costume with you."

She held up a bag. "Wouldn't leave home without it."

"Care to give me a hint as to what you're wearing?"

She pulled the bag close to her chest. "Not a chance. You'll have to wait for tonight to see it."

He grinned. "All right, then." He eyed the bag. "But now you've got me curious."

"Do I? Good." She came inside. "Where can I set this stuff down?"

"You can have the master bedroom to get ready, so put your things in there."

She was hoping he'd say that, because she had plans for him for later, and it involved his bedroom. She went in there and laid her purse and bag down, then came back to find him in the kitchen making of all things a cheese ball.

"Aren't you all domestic?"

He looked up. "I don't know about that, but I can read a recipe."

She went to the sink to wash her hands, then rolled up her sleeves. "What can I do to help?"

"Slice some celery and carrots, and then make dip?"

"Sounds like a plan."

Positioned side by side, they prepared the snacks for the party. She enjoyed being with him in his kitchen, and he was obviously one of those rare men who didn't mind cooking. He finished an incredible cheese ball, then prepped a few other appetizers. Molly knew a lot of men who would have just propped their feet up and watched football, then presented their guests with bags of chips and some salsa.

Though he did have a game on in the living room, so they watched while they worked.

"That kid who plays quarterback for Texas is killing it," she said while she made artichoke dip.

"Oh, Nathan Riley? Yeah, he's really good. His dad is a pro quarterback for San Francisco. Following in the family footsteps, I guess." Carter paused, then looked at her. "You follow football?"

"Pro and college both. That surprises you?"

"I guess. I don't remember you being all gung ho about it in high school."

She shrugged. "I was interested in the sports you played, but I wasn't a big sports nut back then. Now, though, I like football."

"That's great. We can finish up in here and watch the game."

She put the artichoke dip in the refrigerator, then washed her hands. Carter put his dish in the slow cooker, then they grabbed some drinks and settled on the sofa to watch the game.

"I've heard Riley's stats are good enough this season he could be considered a Heisman candidate his sophomore year," Molly said.

"You do know your football."

"You thought I was bullshitting you?" she asked.

He gave her a shocked look. "And you cuss now, too. It's like I don't even know you."

"A lot of time has passed, Carter. I'm a big girl now."

"Next you'll be telling me you drink alcohol and have sex."

She laughed and took a drink of the beer he'd given her. "Funny."

He nudged her with his leg. "Who've you got for this game? Baylor is tough and their quarterback is a senior. He's going to be good in the pros."

She nodded. "Agreed, but this is Riley's year. Texas is undefeated, and I think they're going to take the Big 12 again this year. They're my pick for this game."

"I think I'm going to have to agree with you."

On the next play, Riley threw a perfect pass to a wide-open receiver, who ran thirty-six yards for a touchdown.

Carter and Molly smiled at each other.

"Yeah, it's going to be that kind of game."

It was, a blowout, with Texas winning forty-three to sixteen over Baylor. After that, they took a break to set a few things up around the house. Carter made sandwiches for them, and they sat down to watch the Missouri game, though Molly kept an eye on the time, because she'd need about an hour to do her hair and makeup for her costume, and she didn't want to be in the middle of that when people started arriving.

So at halftime, with Missouri thankfully ahead, though only by one touchdown, she headed into Carter's bedroom to start getting ready. It would be dark soon, and who knew when kids would start to arrive.

This ensemble was going to take some work, and she wanted it to be perfect, especially since there were several parts to it.

She grinned as she entered the bathroom.

CARTER DECIDED SINCE Molly was going to get dressed, he probably should, too. He'd moved all his stuff into the spare bedroom so he'd be out of her way in the master, so he dashed into the bathroom to do his makeup—something he definitely was not adept at, but he did the best he could. At least he'd read the instructions, and there was glue stuff to do the bolts, plus the hair piece. He inspected himself in the mirror and laughed. Not bad.

He put on the clothes and the clunky shoes, hoping like hell he could walk in these damn things without falling over. When he'd seen the outfit at the costume store, he knew it was perfect, and it went with the whole atmosphere of the house.

He clomped into the kitchen to refresh his beer, then heard the door open to the bedroom. His eyes widened when he saw Molly.

"Oh my God," she said as she entered the kitchen. "You're Frankenstein."

"And you're the Bride of Frankenstein."

She looked amazing, her hair all wavy, with a shock of white on both sides. She wore a white sheath, and her lips were painted dark, dark red. She had painted on stitched scars across her neck and arms in red, with a few blood drops on the white sheath for effect.

It was awesome. She looked ethereal, and gorgeous.

She came over to him. "Your makeup is perfect. And those bolts on your neck." She reached up to touch one, then looked down at his feet. "Those shoes are amazing. You must be four inches taller."

He laughed. "Yeah, I hope I don't trip over anything."

She lifted her gaze to his. "I can't believe we match. I didn't tell anyone about my costume."

"I didn't, either. It's like a psychic connection or something."

"Yeah, or something."

"It's perfect, Moll."

She didn't say anything for a few seconds, then smiled. "Right. We're going to scare all the kids tonight."

She wouldn't scare anyone the way she looked. She took his goddamn breath away. He wanted to close the door, turn out the lights, and kiss those ruby red lips for about twelve hours.

Hell, he was getting hard just thinking about it, but judging from the wary looks she was shooting his way, and the fact he'd actually invited people over tonight for a party, he was just going to have to get his wayward body under control.

So he took a deep breath and mentally squashed his lustful thoughts—at least for now.

"And speaking of the kids, it's starting to get dark, so I should get the show ready to go."

He turned on the lights surrounding the tree and the house, and set the dry ice so smoke would billow around the porch. Then he turned on the scary music. By then, a few people had started to show up, so Molly got to work making drinks and setting the appetizers out on the table and on the bar.

"Decided not to wear a costume tonight, huh?" Logan asked him as he and Des came in.

"Yeah, too much work. And look at you, all dressed up."

"Des made me," Logan said with a grimace.

"Oh, quit complaining." Des rolled her eyes. "You would have thought I asked him to dig me a grave. Though, if we didn't have so much land and so few trick-or-treaters, that might have been funny, especially since he is dressed like an undertaker, and I'm the dead body."

Carter laughed. "That would have been awesome. I might steal that idea for next year. Though digging that hole would be a bitch."

"Not to mention the potential liability," Molly added.

"So true."

A few more people arrived, then the kids started coming to the door. He found Molly right by his side, and man, did she know how to turn on the horror. She had a dead-eyed look about her as she slid her hand in the bowl of candy, her head tilted to the side in a broken fashion while he stiffly walked outside into the smoke to welcome the kids.

Most of the kids screamed with delight. Some just flat out screamed. They had quite the light show going, and with him and Molly shuffling out through the smoke, it was a hell of a scene.

Chelsea and Samantha had shown up, and they'd snuck out through the side door in the garage and were taking pictures.

Several of the parents were, too.

Carter had to admit his was a popular house, because he was certain several of the kids made more than one trip. And it wasn't for more candy, it was to see the lights and the skeletons and smoke and the graveyard.

Awesome.

Once he'd had to run inside and refill the bowl, and his house was filling up, too. Fortunately, his friends knew to make themselves at home, and Logan and Des pitched in as bartenders, since Bash couldn't be there to fulfill his duties.

He had to admit, he enjoyed watching Molly with the kids. She seemed to know which ones she could be scary with, and which ones to tone it down with. One girl—she had to be about four years old—tentatively came to the door, clutching her daddy's hand like a lifeline. And even though her little brown eyes were wide as saucers, she was determined to come to the front door for candy.

So Molly grabbed the bowl, crouched down, and smiled at the little girl, spending a few minutes talking to her, explaining that this was all make-believe, and not to be scared. Then she invited Carter over, and let the little girl see that Carter wasn't a real monster.

After that, the little girl got her candy and happily ran down the street to the next house.

Molly had an instinct about kids. Someday she was going to make a great mother.

His stomach tightened as he thought about what could have been between them. They could have had a kid—maybe more.

He hadn't been ready for that kind of responsibility back then. He'd have totally fucked it up.

Maybe things happened for a reason.

But now? As he watched Molly laughing with a group of adolescents who'd come to the door, he reevaluated his current life.

He wanted a wife. And kids.

He just wasn't sure who he wanted them with.

Or maybe he did know, and he wasn't sure how in hell he could make that happen.

Tonight wasn't the night to be thinking deep thoughts. Especially since he didn't have answers to any of the questions that had suddenly started popping nonstop into his head.

A few hours later, when the kid traffic had slowed to just a few of the older kids, he and Molly took a breather.

"Beer?" he asked as Chelsea, dressed as a vampire vixen, took over door duty with Samantha, who was perfect as Raggedy Ann.

"I think I'll have a glass of wine instead."

They headed into the kitchen to grab drinks and some snacks.

"Hell of a turnout tonight, Carter."

"Thanks, Evan. And you get the night off for Halloween, huh?"

"Yeah. Lucky me."

"Evan, you remember Molly, don't you? She's Emma's sister."

"Oh, right. Nice to see you again, Molly. We met at the wedding. I work with Luke on the police force."

Molly put her plate down and shook Evan's hand. "Of course. Nice to see you again, too. That whole wedding thing was kind of a whirlwind for me, since I'd just gotten back in town."

"Understood. How's your mom doing these days?"

"She's doing okay. Thanks for asking."

Carter turned to Evan. "Did you bring a date?"

"Megan's here with me, but you know how it is. We're just friends who decided not to come alone. Less awkward that way."

Carter nodded. "Yeah, I totally get it."

Molly was trying to keep up with everyone. She had no idea such a crowd was going to be here tonight. She knew a lot of people from high school, even the ones who'd gone to Oakdale, the other school. Growing up in a small town meant you ran into the same people over and over again, or went to a lot of the same parties when you were teenagers. But some were a few years older or younger than her, so tonight was spent reacquainting herself with people she hadn't seen in years.

"Molly, I'm so glad you're here tonight."

She turned and smiled at Samantha Reasor. "Me too, Samantha. Are you having a good time?"

"It's Sam, remember? And who wouldn't? Carter's

Halloween parties are legendary. I wouldn't miss one. Well, there was the one year right after he and I broke up when we weren't exactly speaking to each other, but other than that, I come here every year."

"You . . . broke up. You two dated?"

"For about a year."

"I see. I had no idea." Of course she'd had no idea, because she hadn't been here.

Samantha waved her hand back and forth. "It's no big deal, and that was a long time ago. Carter and I are friends now. That's all water under the bridge."

"Really. So you two can still be friends after being . . . involved?"

Samantha laughed. "Of course. We had a few months of trying to adjust after realizing we just couldn't make it work together as a couple. It was more on my part than his. He'd ended it well, and he's always a gentleman. I was the one who had to drown my sorrows for a couple weeks in several pints of Ben and Jerry's. No woman likes to get dumped, you know."

"Ouch." So now she knew who'd done the breaking up. It had been Carter who'd ended things. Molly wondered why.

"Yeah. But, like I said, we weren't right for each other. I've moved on, and so has he. And as friends, we're great."

"I think you're a much nicer person than I would be, Sam."

"I don't know about that. You and Carter were a big deal back in high school, as I recall. And you're here now, too, aren't you?"

She let out a soft laugh. "I suppose you're right."

Sam looped her arm through Molly's and led her toward the living room where there weren't so many people. "Carter has that way about him. It's just too hard to stay angry with him. He doesn't have a mean bone in his body, and he'd never deliberately hurt anyone."

Her gaze drifted toward the dining area where Carter stood talking to Logan and a few other guys. "No, I don't suppose he would."

"Anyway, we really need to spend some time catching up."

"I know. I did promise I'd call you so we could get together and have lunch. I'm sorry that time seems to have gotten away from me."

"That's okay. I understand you've been busy with your mom. It's hard when there's someone you have to take care of. I do the same with my grandmother. She's eighty-two and I'm the only one left to look out for her, though she doesn't think she needs anyone. She's an independent sort."

"Is that right?"

"Yes. A little too independent. And she's still driving—too fast for my liking, too."

Molly could already see her mother doing that many years from now. Being independent, driving her crazy.

"What are you two whispering about over here?"

Molly looked up to see Chelsea had come over and had Megan with her. Megan was dressed like an angel, and she looked completely ethereal and quite beautiful tonight.

"My grandmother, and her fierce independent streak," Sam said.

Chelsea laughed. "We should all hope to be as independent as your grandmother when we're eighty-two."

"Yes, but you know Grammy Claire. She still wants to keep her fingers in the flower shop, and she has her bridge club, and her eyesight isn't as good as it once was. So I try to cajole her into letting me drive her places."

"I know, and you're trying to have your own life while seeing to hers," Chelsea said. "That's not working out too well for you, is it?"

Sam sighed. "No, but she's taken care of me all these years. It's time I paid her back. And I don't mind, really. Gramps died a few years back, and she's been missing him, so she likes having me around to keep her company."

"Did you talk to her about the new retirement center?" Megan asked.

"There's a new retirement center?"

Sam nodded at Molly. "Just finished up last year, over in the new section of Hope. It's really nice. I took Grammy Claire there for a tour when it opened."

"And?" Chelsea asked. "What did Claire have to say?"

"She said she isn't going to leave her house. She said her children were born there, and she plans to die there. What am I supposed to do? My aunt Cecile lives in Ohio, and while she visits every now and then, she can't really make any of the major decisions where Grammy Claire is concerned."

"Which means you're the one in charge of her," Chelsea said.

Sam lifted her chin. "Like I said, she's mine and I love her. She's pretty much the only family I have left."

Chelsea rubbed her back. "I understand, Sammy. I didn't mean to get you upset."

"I'm not upset, but I sure could use a glass of wine."

Molly lifted her now empty one. "I'm with you on that one."

They all went into to the kitchen for refills, and Molly smiled when Emma and Luke showed up.

"Did you get Mom situated?"

"We did. Well, Dad mostly did, since he shooed us off after all the trick-or-treaters left, so we changed into our costumes and had to hurry over here. We didn't want to miss the party, which I see is going strong."

"You look cute," Molly said, admiring Emma's sexy prisoner garb. "And really, Luke is playing cop tonight? How unoriginal."

Emma laughed. "I know, but he said he has this idea for later about me playing escaped prisoner, and something about the handcuffs." Emma held up one hand where the cuffs dangled from her wrist.

Molly shot her hand up. "That's more than enough details, thanks."

Her sister grinned. "So how's it going here?"

"Good. The kid turnout was phenomenal."

"I heard the music, saw all the smoke and lights all the way from the corner. Carter went all out, though he does every year."

"So I hear. This must be the Halloween place to be, huh?"

"It is. Everyone who can tries to at least swing by. And I really need a drink, so I'm going to grab a glass of wine."

"Okay."

"Refills sound good to me, too," Megan said, and Chelsea and Sam followed her.

Molly remained where she was, and suddenly a pair of arms wrapped around her. She jumped, then turned to see Carter.

"Oh, it's you."

"Who else would be putting their arms around you?" he asked.

"No idea. No one, of course."

"Good to know."

"Why, would you be jealous if I named someone?"

He cocked his head to the side. "Probably."

She smiled at that, then remembered her conversation with Sam from earlier. "So, you had a relationship with Samantha Reasor?"

"Yeah. We went out for about a year. Did she tell you about that?"

"She did. And now you're friends?"

"We are. Why?"

She shrugged, trying to pretend it didn't bother her. Which it didn't, of course. "No reason. I just didn't know about it."

"No reason you would, since you weren't here when we were dating. And that was awhile ago anyway."

"Okay."

She looked around the room, suddenly feeling awkward.

"Molly."

She lifted her gaze to his.

"It's been over for years. And I'm not currently seeing anyone, if you're worried about me and Sam. Or me and anyone else, for that matter."

"I'm not concerned at all. Sam told me about the two of you, that it ended and you two are friends. I get it, really."

Except she realized she'd missed a lot by being gone. She wondered what else she didn't know about.

Life in Hope had passed her by.

And whose fault was that, Molly?

"How about a refill on my wine?" she asked, planting a

smile on her face. She couldn't do anything about the past. No one knew that better than her.

Fortunately, he smiled back at her, and she couldn't help but laugh at the black lipstick on his mouth.

"What?" he asked as he walked with her to the bar area.

"Your face."

"I know. It kind of rocks, doesn't it?"

He pulled the cork out of the chardonnay and refilled her cup.

"Oh, it totally rocks."

"So does your hair." He smoothed his hand over it. "How did you get it to do that?"

"I have a crimper."

He frowned.

"It's a girl thing."

"I'll leave it at that and just say you look amazing."

"Thanks." She took a sip of wine and looked around. "Your party is really something, Carter."

He nodded. "We got a good turnout this year, since Halloween is on a weekend. I'm happy people showed up. And everyone seems to be having a good time."

They definitely were. Though it was cold out, Carter had put heaters in the backyard, so some folks had spilled out onto the patio, no doubt buoyed by alcohol and the heaters. There were a lot of people in the living room dancing to the music, and some in quiet corners talking. With the added open space, there was a lot of room, which was a good thing because Molly had lost count of the number of folks who'd tumbled through the front door once it had gotten late enough that the kids had stopped coming.

Around midnight, the party started to wind down and people began to leave. While Carter was busy saying good night to everyone, and Will, Evan, and Luke made sure everyone was sober enough to drive home okay, Molly picked up random plates and cups and put away whatever food was left over, then did some dishes.

That's where Carter found her a little while later.

"Hey, you should leave that stuff in the sink. I can take care of it tomorrow."

She laid a plate in the rack, then grabbed a towel to dry her hands. "There were only a few things. And besides, it's all done."

"Thanks."

"No problem." She looked around. "Has everyone left?"

"Yeah. Will and Luke were the last to leave. We had a couple of guys they thought seemed a little unsteady, so they're driving them home."

"That's nice of them."

"Yeah. I turned off all the lights and the garage door is shut, so we're locked in for the night."

She offered up a smile. "Is that right?"

"Yeah." He lifted his arms over his head and gave her his best monster growl.

She laughed. "Now I'm really scared."

"As you should be. You're all alone with the monster now."

"Don't forget, so are you. And speaking of that, I'll be right back."

She went into his bedroom and shut the door, then shimmied out of the white toga she'd worn.

That had been her costume for everyone else. Next up was one for Carter's eyes only.

She grinned and headed into the bathroom.

Chapter 21

CARTER GRABBED A beer, then poured a glass of wine for Molly.

"Carter?"

When he heard her call his name, he headed down the hall toward the bedroom. The door was ajar, so he pushed it open, then nearly swallowed his tongue.

Molly stood next to the bed. She'd removed the white toga costume. Now all she had on was a white one-piece corset, red stiletto heels, and white thigh-high stockings.

His dick got hard in an instant.

"Holy shit, Molly."

Her lips curved in a sexy smile. "This is my other costume."

He tried to swallow. It didn't work. His throat had gone dry. "That's some costume."

"So . . . you like it."

"I like it so much that if I'd known you had it on underneath that sheet, I'd have sent everyone home hours ago." He came into the room, took a long swallow of his beer to cool his parched throat, then set the drinks down on the table by the window. "Seriously, Molly, you take my breath away."

"That was what I was hoping for. We haven't had much alone time since that night we spent together. I didn't want you to think it was a one-time thing. I didn't think it was."

He swept his fingers up her arm. "Neither did I. I've been thinking about you a lot."

She lifted her gaze to his, and, as always, her eyes mesmerized him. "Have you?"

"Yeah. And just so you know, I'd have tried to seduce you tonight, even in that baggy white sheet you were wearing earlier."

She lifted her hand to his face, using her thumb to tease his lower lip. "Good to know. But isn't this so much better?"

He was so hard right now he was afraid he might bust open the seam of his tight Frankenstein pants. Just looking at her— that white corset making her breasts threaten to spill right out, her hair flowing over her shoulders, her legs—oh, man she had great legs—and those shoes.

He pulled his wig off and dragged his fingers through his hair.

"I should go take a shower and get this green makeup off my face."

"And leave me standing here? I don't think so."

"You really want to . . . be with me looking like this?"

Her lips curved. "Maybe I have a thing for movie monsters."

"Kinky." He grasped her wrist and kissed it, then pulled her arm around his neck, drawing her body closer to his so he could touch her skin and that sexy white thing that encased her curves.

"I like the way you feel against me," he said, sifting his fingers through her wildly curling hair.

"But my hair is graying. Will you still want me when I'm old and gray?"

She was teasing him, but he wasn't in the mood for jokes right now. Not when she was half naked and pressed against him. "Yes. Hell yes."

He tunneled his fingers in her hair and pressed his lips to hers. Her answering whimper made him groan, made him want to strip her out of that flimsy, sexy thing and slide inside her, so the pounding ache in his balls would go away.

But oh, he liked the feel of her when he ran his hand down her back. There were strings back there. How the hell did she get dressed in this?

He made a mental note to ask her later, because right now her lips moved under his, her tongue flicked against his, and he picked her up and carried her to his bed, sitting her down on the edge.

He crouched down and slid his hands up her silk-clad legs. "These are nice."

She smiled down at him. "You like them?"

"Yeah. The shoes, too." He lifted her leg. "How can you walk in these things?"

"Did you see me doing any actual walking in them?"

He laughed. "No." He slipped one shoe off, then the other. "But they're hot as hell."

"I thought so, too."

He took her hands and pulled her up, then turned her around so her back was to him. "I like these laces in the back."

He started undoing them. "But honestly, Molly. I'm going to have to get you out of this thing, because I want to touch your skin."

She inhaled, let out a breath. "That would be nice."

Every touch of Carter's hands along her back was sweet torment. And he took his time undoing the laces, which she'd had to embarrass herself and ask her sister to do up for her while she was getting dressed at her parents' house. Which meant Emma had known what she was planning, but once she'd bought the corset, there was no other way, because she couldn't get into the thing without help.

Or out of it, for that matter.

Emma had been nice enough not to say a word, other than give her a secret smile in the bathroom mirror as she'd laced her up. She owed her sister—big time.

And now, as Carter oh-so-delicately and oh-so-slowly undid the laces, she bit down on her lower lip. She'd had no idea that someone getting her out of this corset could be such a sensual thing, but his knuckles caressed her back, and his breath sailed across her neck and there was his erection she knew he deliberately brushed against her butt, making her incredibly aware that this was taking way too damn long.

Until he separated the back of the corset and turned her around to face him.

"While I like this—a lot—that was some damn torture, Moll."

"For me, too."

He looked down, his fingers grazing the swell of her breasts. "Did it hurt?"

"That's not exactly what I meant."

He lifted his gaze to her face. "What did you mean, then?"

"That while you were back there undoing the laces, I was kind of hoping you'd hurry up."

He pulled the corset from her, tossing it to the chair, then cupped her breasts in his hands, using his thumbs to draw circles around her nipples. "Are you on a timetable, Molly? Do you have a curfew?"

She cocked her head to the side and shot him a look. "No. And you know what I mean."

"I'm sorry. You're right. I was thinking when I first saw you that I wanted you naked and underneath me in an instant, so yeah, I get the impatience, believe me. But we have all night, right?"

"Yes, we do."

"Good. Because I want to take my time so I can put my mouth and my hands on every inch of your body."

If he kept talking to her—and touching her—this way, she was going to explode. She supposed that was the end game, but he was stretching her patience to the limits, especially when he knelt down and peeled her stockings off, every movement way too slow to her liking. Still, she appreciated the way he skimmed his fingers over her calves and back up her legs, pausing to kiss her thighs.

Her breath held, especially when he nudged her legs apart and kissed her inner thighs.

She felt those bolts on his neck slide along her legs, lifted her head . . .

And saw a green Frankenstein face. She expected him to make some kind of *grr* noise.

She burst out laughing.

Carter jerked his head up.

"What?"

"I'm sorry," she said between fits of laughter. "But Frankenstein is going down on me."

He cocked a brow, jerked on the bolts glued to his neck, pulling them off. "I told you."

"I know you did. I just didn't expect . . ." She laughed again.

He stood. "Don't. Move. I'll be right back." He headed toward the bathroom, then stopped, turned to her and pointed. "And don't start without me."

That made her laugh even harder. She rolled onto her side. "I promise to let you do all the work."

She heard the water turn on, then it hit her that she could stand to rinse the white stripes of temporary hair dye out of her own hair and the fake blood off her neck. On the plus side, she'd been dying to try out Carter's oversized shower.

She grinned and pushed the bathroom door open, letting the warm steam envelope her, then opened the shower door.

Carter's back was to her, and she admired the muscle she saw there. He turned to face her.

"Much better," she said, looking at his clean face as she shut the shower door behind her.

"Decided on a shower, or did you just miss me?" he asked, moving out of her way so she could stand under the jets.

"Both." She let the spray wet her hair, then reached for the shampoo bottle. "Plus, if you were going to wash the monster away, I probably should, too."

"Babe, there was nothing monstrous about you. You just looked full-on sex bomb."

She couldn't resist grinning as she shampooed her hair. "Well. Thanks for that compliment. But you know, I'm already in your shower, naked, so you don't have to throw them my way."

"Just stating the truth."

After she rinsed her hair and used some conditioner, he grabbed body wash and poured it into his hands, then soaped her up from her shoulders down to her toes, which felt amazing, especially since he once again took his time touching her body, lingering at her breasts and between her legs, turning her into a quivering pile of turned-on woman. By the time she rinsed, she tingled all over. The pulsing jets and the warm steamy water only added to the sensual allure of being in the shower with him.

Plus, she had to admit, she liked having warm, wet, naked Carter all to herself. His hair stuck up in spikes, his eyes looked a more clear green, and his erection hadn't abated since the moment she'd stepped into the shower with him, a fact she took quite personally in the best possible way.

When he slipped his arm around her waist and pulled her close to kiss her, she moaned against him, needing to feel his body against hers. She wrapped her hand around the nape of his neck, glad to be rid of the makeup and costumes and just feel naked flesh against naked flesh.

And when he cupped her breast and teased her nipple, she sucked on his tongue, urging him on. His cock slid between her legs and if it weren't for the fact they didn't have a condom in the shower, he could be inside her right now, assuaging the ache that beat an incessant rhythm deep in her core.

But soon his hand was there, massaging her, his fingers sliding inside as his thumb found her clit and rubbed back and forth.

"Carter," she murmured against his lips, lost in the rippling sensations of his magic fingers.

"Yeah. Now where was I earlier before that monster reared its ugly head?"

He dropped to his knees, and she took in a deep breath, watching as he spread her legs and put his mouth on her sex.

Delicious sensations rippled through her as his tongue glided over her. She was swollen with need and desire, and he mastered her body until all she could do was tremble and moan.

She was so close to the edge, so primed for his touch, the passionate glide of his lips and tongue over her body, that her climax hit hard, making her entire body shudder in response.

He gripped her hips as she rode out her orgasm, then pressed gentle kisses to her thighs as she settled.

He stood, his mouth taking hers in a deep, passionate kiss that primed her passion all over again. Then she looked into his eyes, smiled at him, and dropped to her knees, wanting to give him the same mind-blowing pleasure he'd just given her.

Carter palmed the walls of the shower, unable to believe this dark-haired goddess was on her knees in front of him. He hadn't expected this from Molly—that she'd be so responsive to his touch, so sexy, so eager to be with him. He wasn't about to question why, he was just damn happy to be with her.

As she took his length between her lips, he thought he might have died and gone to heaven. Or maybe it was hell, because her lips and tongue were torture. He gritted his teeth and held on while she engulfed him, sucking him deep until he knew for certain he wouldn't last long—not when all he'd thought about all night was being alone with her, getting her naked and making love to her.

"Molly," he said, "You're going to make me come."

She hummed, a low, throaty sound along the length of his cock, and he lost it, erupting in deep waves as his orgasm catapulted from him, leaving him shaken. When he could function again, he lifted her off the floor and took her mouth, his fingers diving into her scalp to hold her as he kissed her deeply.

She raked her nails down his shoulders and arms, her passion getting him hard again.

He turned off the shower and stepped out, grabbing a towel for her. She dried off her hair in a hurry, then cast the towel aside, grasping his hands and pulling him toward the bedroom.

Yeah, he wanted that, too, more than he could put into words.

She fell onto the bed, and he grabbed a condom from the nightstand, put it on, then rolled next to her.

She pushed him onto his back and climbed on top of him, her hair loose, wet waves falling over her shoulders and breasts as she slid down over his cock.

He'd never seen anything more beautiful—or hotter. Molly, riding him, her breasts thrust out, her nails digging into his chest, her top teeth biting down on her bottom lip, lost in her own pleasure.

He gripped her hips and thrust into her, and she looked down at him, glassy-eyed, lost in her own desire.

"Take us there," he said, giving her control.

She cast a deep dark smile down at him, then rode right into orgasm. When she tightened around him and moaned with her release, he went with her, driving deep and shuddering as he let go.

She fell against his chest, her heart pumping fast and hard against his. He stroked her back, content to hear the sound of her breathing for a few minutes as they both settled. He wanted to hold her here like this, both of them suspended in that moment of contentment, where there was no conflict, no issues, no past or no future. Nothing to do but just . . . be.

When she finally sat up again, she smiled at him, then slid off.

Yeah. Reality.

He left to attend to the condom, then came back, turned off the light, and pulled the covers over them.

"Can you stay tonight?" he asked.

She hesitated for a few seconds, and he wondered if she wanted to leave.

"Yes. I'd like that."

Now it was his turn to smile. "Me, too."

He closed his eyes and wrapped his arms around Molly. Maybe this was just a "right now" relationship for them. Maybe they had no future together other than just the moments they could carve out together, but dammit, when they did, they were great moments.

And tonight, she was here, in his bed, wrapped around him.

For now, that was good enough.

Chapter 22

AFTER A VISIT to the doctor this morning, Molly's mother was comfortably set up in the living room on the sofa, her leg propped on the recliner.

Molly made them quesadillas for lunch, then did puzzles with her until she said she was tired and wanted to nap. She brought her a blanket and pillow and Pokey settled in next to Mom on the sofa, the two of them snoozing comfortably together while Molly did dishes and worked on some of the paperwork for tonight's committee meeting.

She wasn't sure if she was more excited about getting an update on the progress of the town square, or hanging out with Carter, who she hadn't seen in several days. She'd been busy with a slate of doctor visits for her mom, and he'd been in Tulsa at several of his shops dealing with some personnel and inventory issues. He'd called and texted her every day though, giving her a rundown of his day, asking about hers, and always making sure to inquire about her mom.

After she finished the dishes, Molly peeked in on her mom, who was still napping. That gave Molly time to finish perusing the paperwork, making sure to note some items she wanted to bring up on the agenda tonight. Then she started chopping vegetables for the stew she intended to cook for dinner. By the time her dad came home from work, her mom was awake, so he helped her into the shower and then her pajamas.

Molly served dinner, and they visited about the morning's doctor's visit.

"The doctor thinks I'm healing very well," her mom said.

Her dad looked over at Molly. "It's true. He went over reports from the therapists and the nurses. She's a model patient, recovery wise, even though she's cranky about having to stay home."

"You would be, too, if you had to stare at the living room walls every day."

Her dad squeezed her hand. "It's not forever, Georgia."

"No, it's not. The doctor promised he'd do an X ray next week. If the bones in my leg look good, he said he'd fit me with a walking cast, and we can start walking therapy."

"That's very good news," her dad said. "I know how much you want to get up and move around."

"Like you wouldn't believe, Emmett."

"I want that for you, too, Mom," Molly said. "My fingers are crossed."

"I'm going to work hard on therapy the rest of the week. I want that walking cast."

"We'll be dancing together in no time," her dad said.

Molly smiled. She'd like to see that.

"Oh, by the way, I have a committee meeting tonight," Molly said.

"And will you be going out with Carter afterward?" her mother asked.

"I . . . don't know. I'm not exactly going out with him."

Her mother waved her hand. "Whatever it is you young kids call it these days. Anyway, you two should go out. There's no reason you should be stuck in the house with me all the time. Your dad and I will be fine here. Go out and enjoy yourself. I always liked you and Carter together, Molly. I don't know why the two of you broke up in high school, but I sure am glad you're seeing him again."

"Me, too," her dad said.

Molly blinked. She had no idea her parents were even aware she was seeing Carter. So much for thinking she was doing this under the radar. Pretty soon everyone would know, because while her mother was housebound, she definitely had a phone—and a computer—and she used it a lot to talk to her friends. Who talked to their friends. And so on.

After dinner, she did the dishes and dashed off to take a shower. As she left the house for the committee meeting, she waved goodbye to her parents, who were settled in the living room with a movie.

Her heart skipped a beat when she saw Rhonda parked in the lot of the community center.

Ridiculous. It was just a meeting, not a date.

But when Carter came outside to greet her, she couldn't help but notice his smile, or the way he walked, or the way he'd unbuttoned the sleeves of his shirt and shoved them up his arms. He'd worn jeans today, and damn, he always looked so good in jeans.

"Hi," he said, taking the folders from her hands as she got out of her car.

"Hi. You're here early."

"So are you."

"Yeah, I had a busy day today," he said as they walked side by side toward the community center. "I wanted to get a head start scanning through the agenda."

"I went over it today."

He held the door for her, and she stepped inside. No one else was there yet.

"Yeah? Any ideas?"

"A couple. I also drove by the town square today. The new fountain is in. It looks amazing."

"I saw that, too. Mavis called to complain about the dolphin."

Molly rolled her eyes. "What's wrong with the dolphin?"

"Nothing. It's a replica of what was there before, everyone signed off and agreed to it. But if it was up to Mavis, we'd have a bust of the mayor in the middle of the damn fountain. So she'll find something to complain about."

"Whatever. It looks awesome."

"Oh, and before everyone gets here . . ."

He pulled her into his arms and laid a hot, hard kiss on her. Suddenly, agendas and dolphins and fountains were forgotten as she fell into the kiss, wishing they didn't have this damn meeting tonight and could go somewhere and explore this kiss a lot further.

Even though the kiss was laced with passion, and he ran his hands over her back, it was over all too quickly, and Carter took a step back. But the fire lingered in his eyes. "We'll take that up later."

"I'm making a note at the bottom of my agenda."

His lips quirked. "You do that."

"I just will. In the meantime, I'm going to start making coffee."

"I'm actually surprised Mavis isn't already here doing that. She wouldn't want to miss out on any gossip."

"We beat her to the punch. And we got a kiss in as well."

He moved over to the sink and helped her, filling the large coffeepot while she put the ground coffee in.

"In fact," he said, "since no one's here yet . . ."

He cupped the back of her neck and slid his lips over hers. She put the coffee down and moved into him, grabbing on to his shirt to deepen the kiss.

Until someone cleared their throat and she heard the click of heels on the hardwood floor.

"You two should get a room."

When they broke apart, she smiled at Chelsea. "Why, when it's so spacious here?"

Without breaking stride, Chelsea made it over to the coffee station. "Good point, since you have the table. And the floor. And don't forget the stage."

"I like the way you think, Chelsea," Carter said.

Molly laughed. "I just started the coffee."

"It could have been done already if the two of you weren't engaged in a hot and heavy makeout session."

"Oh, we had just gotten started," Molly said.

"Don't make me smack you upside the head with the coffee

creamer box. Those who are getting some shouldn't lord it over those who aren't."

Since Carter was busy talking to a couple of the others who'd just come in, she walked away with Chelsea. "I find it hard to believe that someone as beautiful and funny and smart as you isn't seeing someone on a regular basis."

Chelsea shrugged, then snatched one of the cookies Mavis had just brought in. "I'm picky. Besides, I know all the men in Hope. I went to high school with most of the guys my age."

"There's always Tulsa. Or online dating."

She snorted. "Tried that last one. Major fail. Men lie on those dating sites. They say they have burgeoning careers when really they're still living with their parents, or they're flat broke and can only afford a night out at the nearest McDonald's. Or they tell you they've been focusing on their careers and that's why they're still single in their thirties, when in reality they've been divorced twice and are paying child support for four children."

Molly sighed. "What's so difficult about being honest?"

"I have no idea. I'm brutally honest." She offered Molly a flat gaze. "Maybe that's why I don't go on a lot of dates."

Molly looped her arm in Chelsea's. "I think you have a lot to offer, and if men can't see that, it's their loss."

"Right. And in the meantime, I'm the only one in town not getting laid, whereas you've been back for a month and you've landed one of the hottest guys in Hope."

"Why didn't you ever date Carter? Or did you?"

"He's not my type. He's too nice."

Molly laughed. "So you don't want a nice guy?"

"I like nice guys just fine."

Molly shook her head. Chelsea was confusing as hell. Maybe Chelsea didn't know what kind of man she wanted. Or maybe her standards were too high.

Because as she looked across the table at Carter, she realized there wasn't much wrong with him. He was hot, sexy, funny, had a great job, and was a good person. Any woman would consider herself lucky to have someone like him to settle down with.

"Ready to get started?" Carter asked.

Everyone took their seats, and Carter began the meeting.

Not that she wanted to settle down with Carter—or any man. But if she was looking for a potential partner in life, she couldn't find much fault with Carter.

He had great leadership abilities. As he led the meeting, she noticed he got things back on track when someone strayed off topic, and he refereed any disagreements like a diplomat.

One day some woman was going to get lucky.

When she had the floor, his gaze met hers and he smiled at her. Her stomach tightened.

She'd be long gone by the time a woman married Carter. Made beautiful, dark-haired, green-eyed babies with him.

It wouldn't matter. He'd be happy, and she'd be content, moving on with her life.

Somewhere.

She almost lost focus just thinking about it, but rallied her brain in time to sound like she knew what she was talking about.

They got through the meeting with a minimum of fuss, which was good. Even Mavis seemed to be in a good mood, and didn't argue with their suggestions, including Molly's idea to erect a playground near the square. The cost would be a minimal addition, and everyone approved. She was happy about that, and could already envision children playing in the square.

The project was moving along, and Molly was excited about the way things were going. Every time she drove through town she saw progress, making her want to see the finished product, especially in the spring and summer when it would really be used by the people of Hope.

Of course, next spring and summer she wouldn't be here to see the new town square in action.

She was going to miss out on a lot, because she was leaving as soon as her mother was capable of taking care of herself again.

That kind of sucked, but it was the life she'd chosen, and

she wasn't going to deviate from it. Staying here in Hope just wasn't an option for her.

If she started caring about everything that was happening around here or about the people—she looked across the table at Carter—she might feel like staying.

And that just wouldn't do.

It was much easier to stick with the plan. Stay only long enough to get Mom right again, then take off.

She liked her life the way it was. That was a life she was used to, one she could manage.

A life that couldn't hurt her.

Right now she was having fun. It was light and easy and she was enjoying spending time with her family again. She was enjoying this newfound sex with no strings with Carter. And as long as she kept it a temporary thing, she could handle it.

Making it any more than that would only lead to heartbreak. She'd faced heartbreak once, and it had nearly brought her to her knees. She'd never do it again.

"That wasn't too painful, was it?" Carter asked as they got out of their seats and grabbed another cup of coffee.

"No, actually, it went better than I expected. Especially the playground part."

Carter lifted the cup to his lips, took a drink, then nodded. "Me, too. I thought for sure Mavis would balk. But she didn't. In fact, she agreed it was a good idea."

Molly turned and leaned against the sink. "I wonder what's up with that."

"I wonder what's up with her. Usually she stays and endlessly gossips 'til everyone does their best to make an escape, but she's already grabbing her coat and leaving."

"Hmm. Maybe she has a boyfriend."

Carter studied Mavis's escape. "She has been divorced for several years, but I can't imagine who'd be willing to put up with her."

Molly laughed. "There's someone for everyone out there, you know. Even for Mavis."

"I guess you're right." He pushed off the wall. "How about we go get something to eat."

"I ate dinner before the meeting."

"Okay, then. How about you come with me and watch me eat something? You can get coffee and dessert?"

"I had all those cookies."

He rolled his eyes. "I'm trying to ask you out, Molly. Are you trying to tell me you'd just like to go home?"

Why was she being so difficult? Maybe she'd spent too much time thinking during the meeting tonight. And too much time pondering her relationship with Carter—and all the things that couldn't happen between them.

But that was the future, and this was the present, and she wasn't going to let anything stand between spending time with him right now.

"No, of course not. I'd love to watch you eat."

He laughed. "All right, then. Let's go.

Chapter 23

ON THE DRIVE over to Bert's, on his own because Molly told him she didn't want to leave her car at the community center, Carter pondered her strange mood.

He chalked it up to her being a woman, and they got moody sometimes. He intended to keep that thought to himself so he didn't get into any trouble. His mother told him if he had a stupid thought about a woman, it was best to just shut up about it.

Good advice. His mom was pretty smart.

He pulled into the lot, Molly right behind him, taking the spot next to his. Though they'd fixed George's immediate problems, he still didn't like the way the car sounded.

"You're frowning," she said as she got out.

"George shudders. Coughs. Sounds like he's in death throes."

"He's old. Cut him some slack." She pocketed her keys and started into the restaurant, giving him no choice but to follow. He gave George a long look, but the car didn't make any more sounds, so he headed inside.

It was late, and the restaurant was nearly empty, which meant they had their pick of seats. Molly chose a booth near the wall, and he slid in across from her.

Heather Stanford headed over, pulling her order pad out of her pocket.

"Hi, Heather."

"Hi, Carter." Heather gave Molly a look. "New girlfriend?"

He laughed. "This is Emma Burnett's—I guess she's Emma McCormack now. I have to get used to that. Anyway, this is Dr. Emma's sister, Molly."

Heather's eyes widened. "Oh. Hi. I'm Heather. I have a pug named Cicero. I take him to see Dr. Emma all the time. Well, my parents and I take him, anyway. I go to Hope High School."

"Nice to meet you, Heather," Molly said.

"You're the sister who lives out of town."

"Yes."

"You must have hung around because Mrs. Burnett got hurt. How's she doing? We sure miss seeing her here at Bert's."

"She's doing a lot better. Thanks for asking."

"You be sure to tell her I said hey."

"I will."

"What would you all like to drink?"

"I'll just have water," Molly said.

"I'll have a Diet Coke," Carter said, then picked up the menu when Heather hustled away to get their drinks.

Molly studied the menu.

"So about the whole 'girlfriend' thing," he said.

She looked up from the menu. "What?"

"Heather asked if you were my girlfriend."

"Oh, that. Typical teenager. They think any man/woman combination is automatically a couple. I didn't think anything of it. Don't worry about it."

She went back to studying the menu, while he worried she'd been offended he hadn't automatically acknowledged her as his girlfriend.

Women were confusing. A lot of women he'd dated would have had their feelings hurt. Molly hadn't.

Maybe because she didn't think of them as a couple. Or in a relationship. Or whatever people called it these days. He had no idea.

When Heather came back, he gave her his order, and Molly

decided to have a cup of soup, which made him feel better, since he didn't want to be the only one eating.

"How are things going at work?" Molly asked.

"Good, actually. I have an interview next week with a body guy. I'm hoping he might be the one."

She arched a brow. "Body guy?"

"Someone to do bodywork on the cars. We've gone through several in the shop here in town, with no luck. It's hard to find a guy who's good with his hands."

Her lips quirked. "Indeed, it is."

He laughed. "Anyway, I've heard this guy has good skills, so I'm hopeful. I'm tired of searching—and replacing."

She nodded, then paused while Heather delivered their food. She took a spoonful of her soup, then a sip of water.

"I know how it is to have to hire good employees," Molly said. "I've been in that position several times over the years when I've been put in charge of hiring at some of the places I've worked. It's never a fun job."

He bit into his cheeseburger, then popped a couple of fries into his mouth, washing them down with his pop. "It's my least favorite part of the job. Unfortunately, it's a necessary evil to keep things running smoothly. If it were up to me, I'd be out there with my head in an engine."

"The price of growth, I'm afraid."

"Tell me about it."

"You have—what—four shops now? Maybe you should hire a business manager to do all that paperwork and hiring and firing for you."

"And then what would I do? Play golf?" He shook his head. "I don't think so. I know the kind of talent required to do all the jobs necessary for the shops. A business manager might know the numbers and paperwork part of the job—and believe me, that takes up a lot of my time—but no one knows the inner workings of a car better than I do—or hiring the right kind of talent to get the job done."

Molly leaned back and wiped her lips with her napkin. "You're so confident in what you do."

"I know my job and what it takes to get it done."

"And you love your work."

He smiled. "Most days."

"Describe your best day to me."

"What is this, an interview?"

"No. Just tell me what you would consider a perfect day."

"First, everyone shows up for work. The bays in every shop are filled. There's no goddamn paperwork on my desk, so I have time to visit all four locations and see that all the operations are running like well-oiled machines. I end up at the shop in Hope, where I have a few minutes to roll up my sleeves and stick my head in a tranny rebuild, or maybe work with the body guy on some cool new paint scheme before quitting time."

"Sounds like a great day. And what keeps you from doing that?"

"That's easy. Paperwork. Inventory. Bills to pay. Taxes. Forms to fill out. Sales and marketing issues. Personnel issues."

"It sounds to me like you're one business manager short of having the ideal job."

He sat back and pondered her suggestion for a few minutes, studying her until an idea popped into his head. "You know what? You're right. You want the job?"

Her eyes widened. "Me? No."

"Why not? You've been managing offices all over the country for years. You've got the accounting, sales, and business skills to tackle the job."

"That's true, but "

"But what? You don't think you're qualified?"

She lifted her chin. "If anything, I'm overqualified. I could get you organized in a matter of months. Then you'd be free to visit each of your shops, hire staff, handle the day-to-day paperwork and any hands-on repair work you wanted."

He liked seeing that fire in her eyes, the confidence in her abilities. She was right for the job. She knew it, and he sure as hell knew it. "Exactly. So what's the problem?"

"You know what the problem is, Carter. Actually, there's more than one problem."

"Your mom, of course. I didn't mean you had to start tomorrow. I'm willing to wait."

"That's not it."

"You mean the fact you're not planning to stay in Hope after your mom is back on her feet?"

Molly hadn't voiced her plans to move on once her mother was better, but obviously Carter—and probably everyone else—just assumed it. And they were right. "Yes."

He shrugged. "I think that's just your standard go-to, because it's what you've always done. Why not deviate from the norm? Or better yet, consider Hope your next stopover point in your trip around the world."

She was at a loss for words. "I don't know what you mean."

"So you still feel like traveling, like picking up and moving every few months, finding that next new place to live and that next new job, right?"

"I . . . guess so."

"Okay, fine. Why not make Hope your next new place to live, and a job with me your next new job?"

"But—"

"Then, when wanderlust strikes again, you can pack up and move on."

He looked so sincere, with a glint in his eye that she read as just a bit of a challenge. As if he expected her to say no, that it wouldn't surprise him in the least if she did.

Well, dammit, maybe she would surprise him. Maybe she'd shock the hell out of all of them and stay. Wouldn't it amaze Carter, and this entire damn town, if she didn't take off as soon as her mom was able to move around without help?

What if she did stay? At least for a few months. God knew Carter could use the help, and who better to organize his work life than her?

It would be a challenge, and she loved a job that presented an opportunity to learn. She'd streamline his operational systems and create a dynamic sales and marketing plan for him that he'd be excited about.

Then, once she was satisfied—or when the itch to move on became too great, she could do just that, move on, like she always did.

Only this time, she'd leave Hope on her own terms. She wouldn't be running. Not like last time.

"You're serious about the job offer," she said.

"I wouldn't have made it if I wasn't."

"Then I'll take it."

His brows rose. "Really?"

"Yes, really. Does that surprise you?"

"Maybe a little."

"Okay, that was honest. But I'll still take it, because I think you'll benefit from my expertise."

"And I like your confidence in your abilities, so I'll hire you."

She studied him, wondering what instigated his job offer. Maybe she was second-guessing his motives, but she figured he'd been baiting her, that he'd never imagined she'd agree.

Too bad. Now he was stuck with her.

She liked the idea of it, though. And she intended to show him that she was damn good at a job. She might not have stayed long at all the other jobs she had, but she left each company in a better place than they were when she'd started.

She'd do the same for Carter's company. She'd swoop in, take over his paperwork headache, organize his systems and develop a sales plan. Then, when she was satisfied everything was in working order, she'd leave.

By then, she'd be easy to replace with someone competent enough to take over for her. She'd done it countless times before. It was easy.

Though as she looked over at Carter, the thought of working closely with him warmed her.

And the thought of leaving him behind left anything but an easy feeling in her stomach.

Better to stay in the here and now and not think about the future. Staying in the present was always best.

She'd worry about tomorrow and the next day . . . later.

Chapter 24

CARTER SPENT EARLY Saturday morning sitting across the desk from a man he never would have thought he'd hire as his next body guy.

Brady Conners was overqualified, had just come back to Hope after a long absence, and he didn't know a whole lot about him other than the family connection. Carter had known Brady's older brother, Kurt, from high school, but they hadn't hung out in the same circles. Brady had left Hope after high school—like Molly. And he hadn't come back.

Until now.

"I was sorry to hear about Kurt," Carter said. "He was a good guy."

Brady nodded. "Thanks. And yeah, he was."

Carter could tell Brady didn't want to talk about his brother. Most guys didn't want to get into the emotional stuff, and what had happened with Kurt had been awful.

"Is that why you're back in Hope?" Carter asked.

"Partly."

The guy didn't have much to say. Then again, his work spoke for itself. And if he wasn't too chatty, that was good.

He'd rather have Brady focused on the work and not on bullshitting in the garage.

"You've mainly done a lot of custom motorcycle body paint."

"Yeah. But I started out doing body jobs and worked my way into the custom work. I can handle what you need."

"I know. I talked to some guys you worked with in Memphis. They said you're the best body guy around."

A smirk was all he got in reply. That showed confidence, though, and Carter appreciated a man who knew he was the best.

"I heard you're interested in starting up your own custom paint place."

"You heard right," Brady said. "But I need cash for that, and I'm strapped at the moment. I figure working for you for a while will give me a head start."

Carter appreciated Brady not hiding that from him. Upfront and honest he could deal with. "Are you intending to leave Hope anytime soon?"

Brady shook his head. "No. I'm gonna plant it here for a while."

He wasn't going to ask why, but that's the answer he needed.

"You got a place to live?"

"I'm looking into it. Not exactly interested in staying with my parents."

Carter smiled. "Imagine that. I might be able to hook you up. There's an apartment above the shop here if you're interested. I could cut you a deal on the rent, and you could work your custom jobs here during your off-hours."

Brady studied him, then frowned, no doubt suspicious about Carter's motives.

Carter could understand that. After all, Brady didn't really know him.

"Why would you do that?" Brady asked.

"Because before you dump and run and start your own business, you'll agree to find and train your replacement here. And I want at least a year out of you."

Brady let out a short laugh. "I can manage that."

They worked out the details, and Carter showed him the vacant apartment upstairs. He'd stayed there himself before he'd bought his house. The apartment was serviceable, had a few pieces of furniture, like a bed, a couch, and a crap table in the small eating area off the kitchen. There were a set of dishes, utensils, towels, and stuff. Enough for Brady to survive. Anything else he needed, he could get for himself.

For a single guy, it would do, which was exactly what Brady said once he'd looked it over. He took it on the spot, and Carter told him rent wouldn't be due until next month.

One major problem resolved. He filed Brady's application and paperwork, and was looking forward to him starting work next week.

After that was finished, he headed home, changed into his old jeans and a T-shirt, and decided to wreck the guest bathroom. He had already ordered the new countertop and bought new fixtures, so instead of spending time at the gym today, he decided to get his workout in by tearing up some things.

He pulled out the sink and faucets, took out the cabinets and tossed them in the back of his truck since they were rotted out and of no further use. Then he got to work chipping away at the hideous tile. He was dripping with sweat when he heard footsteps.

"I can't believe you're having this kind of fun and you didn't call me."

He swiped at his brow, then grinned at Luke. "Shouldn't you be with your wife on your day off?"

"Emma had a couple unexpected surgeries this morning, so she's going to hang out with the furry kids for a while longer this afternoon. I thought I'd drop by here to see if you wanted to have some beer and watch football. This looks like more fun."

"You keep calling it fun. I don't think you know the meaning of the word."

"Come on, man. If Emma had gotten off work on time, we would have been at the mall." Luke grimaced. "Trust me, this is better."

"You asked for it. Go grab a pry-bar and a wrench and start chiseling some tiles."

"Now you're talkin'."

Two hours later, they had the tile down and were taking a beer break in the garage when Molly drove up. She looked good in a pair of skinny jeans and a long-sleeved shirt.

"Lazing the day away drinking beer and watching football?" she asked as she made her way into the garage.

"Would I be sweating like this if we were watching football?"

She gave him a close look. "You are sweaty. And filthy. What are you two up to today?"

"Working on tearing up the guest bathroom."

"Carter promised it would be fun," Luke said.

Carter shot Luke a glare. "I promised no fun. You insisted on helping."

Molly laughed. "I'm going inside to take a peek. Is Emma here?"

"She's still at the clinic, looking after some post-surgery patients."

"Okay."

After Molly disappeared inside, Luke took a long swallow of beer, then turned to him. "How's it going with Molly?"

"Good, I guess. She's skittish, with one foot out of town already. But I offered her a job."

Luke arched a brow. "No shit. Did she accept?"

"Yeah."

"You're going to try and get her to stay."

"I don't think anyone can convince her to stay. If she does, it'll have to be her idea. I just figured she might want to linger for a while. Test the waters of Hope."

"And then you'll get her to stay."

Carter shrugged. "We'll see."

"I like you two together. So does Emma. She thinks the two of you are destined to be together, or some such female bullshit."

Carter liked him and Molly together, too. As far as destiny? He didn't much believe in that. Molly was going to do what Molly decided was best for herself. He knew better than to interfere in that. He was just offering her something to do while she was here.

And hey, it benefited him. She was organized, and he needed that. He refused to think his offer of a job was a way to keep her in town. His heart knew better.

The door opened and Molly came out.

"You've got a great mess going on in there. And you got a lot accomplished."

"Yeah, the demo is pretty much done."

"Too bad. I would have liked to wield a sledgehammer."

He cocked his head to the side. "I'm not sure you can pick up a sledgehammer."

"Oh, now you're challenging me. Give me something to destroy."

Luke nudged him. "Yeah, Carter. Give her something to destroy."

Carter raked his fingers through his hair. "Okay."

They went into the house, and Carter took a look at the bathroom, then at Molly.

"How do you feel about pulling up floor tiles?"

She grinned at him, then rubbed her hands together. "Excited."

He shook his head. "Now you sound like Luke."

"Don't listen to him," Luke said. "It's fun, dirty work."

"That's what I'm thinking. I just need one of your old shirts, since this one is one of my favorites."

"Right side of my closet," Carter said.

"I'll be right back."

Carter shook his head, and in a few minutes Molly came back wearing one of his oldest, paint-stained T-shirts, which was miles too big and too long for her, but he had to admit, she looked damn hot in it.

In fact, he'd like to see her wearing just his T-shirt and nothing else, but that was a thought for some time when Luke wasn't giving him an I-know-exactly-what-you're-thinking look, so he shrugged it off and handed her some tools and work gloves.

It turned out Molly was fairly adept at pulling up floor tiles, and between the three of them they had the floor up in an hour. Then they cleared out the debris and swept the room clean.

"If I'd known it was going to be this easy, I'd have called you both over when I started."

Molly blew a stray hair out of her eyes and leaned against the wall. "Luke's right. That was fun."

"See?" Luke said. "Told you."

"You're only saying that because you haven't had to do an entire house," Carter said.

"Emma wants to redo the guest bathroom at our house, so this was good practice."

"Did I hear my name?"

Luke stuck his head out the bathroom door. "You missed it. There's nothing else to destroy in here, so don't ask."

She laughed as she surveyed the wreckage of what was once a bathroom. "Looks appropriately demolished in there, and I'm not about to volunteer. I'm exhausted after spending the day with a post-op dog and cat."

"How are they doing?" Molly asked.

"They're both fine, and their owners picked them up, so now I'm free."

"You look like you could use a glass of wine," Luke said. "I should take you home."

"Or, we could all get cleaned up and go out to dinner," Carter suggested. "It seems like everyone worked hard today."

"I like that idea," Emma said. "We should probably stop at home and check on the dogs first."

"How about we meet somewhere in an hour?" Molly suggested.

Emma nodded. "That sounds good to me."

They made dinner plans, and Luke and Emma left. Molly scanned the bathroom, then turned to Carter. "Clean slate. Does it give you ideas?"

"Always. I want to do a big shower in here."

She shook her head. "I disagree. You already have a big shower in the master. You have to think about your future, and guests. You need a tub/shower combination in here, so someone can take a bath. Plus . . . future kids will be sharing this bathroom. And you need a bathtub to bathe your babies . . . you know, whenever you have them."

He thought about it for a minute, reconsidered. "You're right. Double sink vanity, a lot of cabinets. One of those rain showerheads."

She smiled. "I like that idea. And deep sinks, but spaced out nicely in case you have more than one girl."

"Yeah." He leaned against the wall, staring at her. "Want to go shopping with me?"

"For bathroom stuff? I'd love to."

"Good. How about tomorrow?"

"That sounds fine to me. I can get away on the weekends when Dad is around." She swiped her hands on his shirt. "I should go home and take a shower."

He pushed off the wall. "Or, you could shower here. You have a toothbrush here now. And some of your shampoo and bath stuff. Plus, you didn't get your shirt dirty."

"I do have another pair of jeans in the car, too."

"Then you're good to go."

She tilted her head back to look up at him. "You just want to see me naked."

"Purely a side benefit."

She laughed, then pushed at his chest. "I'll grab my stuff from the car."

Once she'd retrieved her clean clothes and makeup bag from her car, she headed toward the bathroom, giving Carter an impish grin over her shoulder. "I get the shower first."

Carter shook his head. "The hell with that. The shower is big enough for two."

He was only a minute behind her, shrugging off his clothes while Molly turned the water on. He caught a glimpse of her sweet bare ass as she stepped into the shower. He grabbed a couple of towels and set them on the vanity, then opened the door.

She had the jets primed and the water set at a nice, steamy hot temperature. Since there were jets at both ends, he let the water beat at his sore muscles for a minute or two while he admired the view of Molly washing her hair. Then he grabbed the soap and scrubbed his body clean of the day's grime.

"Thanks for buying my shower gel," she said, pouring some into her hand. "Though I wouldn't want you to read too much into having some of my things here."

"First sign of too much comfort and routine for you, I'll toss those right in the trash."

Her lips lifted. "That's reassuring."

She soaped her body, and that was a visual treat, watching her sweep her hands over her breasts, down her rib cage, and between her legs.

His dick hardened in a hurry, and he moved toward her as she rinsed the soap off.

"Touching you there is my job," he said, pulling her against him and cupping her neck, holding her steady as he took her mouth.

Desire snapped hard like a whip inside him. He had to leash it, but he wanted Molly with a need that always made him feel like he was losing control. When he skimmed his hands down her arms and his fingers bit hard into her hip, she whimpered.

"Sorry. Too hard."

"No. Harder," she said, lifting her leg over his hip. "I want you."

He groaned against her lips, that leash loosening just a little, and he pushed her against the wall of the shower and slid his hand between her legs, delving into the silken softness of her.

She arched into his hand, her body moving in rhythm to the strokes of his fingers. His cock, hard and heavy, rubbed against her hip while he pleasured her, and her fingers wrapped around his length, stroking until he thought he might drop.

He kissed her, lost in the sensation of his fingers inside her, of the movements of her hand, the taste of her. It was damned intoxicating—she was like a drug, and he couldn't get enough.

And when she came, he was the one shuddering, trying to hold back, but she gripped him like a vise, and in the end she was his undoing and he went with her, slamming his hand against the wall as he let go.

His breath came in rasps. He had a death grip around Molly, and he was sure there were spots in front of his eyes. And he knew for damn certain he couldn't move. Not for a minute or so, anyway. But he finally shut off the water and led them out of the shower.

They dried off, both of them sneaking hot glances at each other.

"You keep looking at me like that we'll never make dinner."

"Too bad I'm so hungry."

"Yeah," he said, giving her a hot look. "I'm hungry, too."

But not for food.

Her lips lifted.

As he got dressed and ran a brush through his hair, she gave him a sexy smile in the mirror.

"That was nice as round one," she said, putting on her eye makeup. "I'll expect round two after dinner."

"What? You want me to perform after all the physical labor I did today?"

"Damn straight. And if you can't, I'll be very disappointed."

He came up behind her, letting her feel how very performance ready he was.

She grinned. "I knew I could count on you, Carter."

Chapter 25

AFTER A DOCTOR'S appointment this morning, Molly's mom was in the best mood she'd been in since Emma's wedding.

"You watch, Molly," her mom said. Molly held on to her mother as she practiced walking—albeit extremely slowly—around the living room. "With this new walking cast, I'll be out and about in no time."

Her mother lifted up her arm. "Plus, a shorter arm cast, without all the bells and whistles. I feel so much freer now."

"I know Mom. This is great progress. But you're going to have to be a little more patient, and wait for your physical therapy appointment tomorrow so they can work with you and show you how to manage these new casts."

Her mom waved her off, then lost her balance a little and grabbed Molly's arm for support.

"Careful, Mom."

After about five minutes of very slow ambling, her mother took her spot on the sofa.

"That was shockingly exhausting," her mom said.

"You've been on your butt for six weeks, Mom. It's no surprise you're so weak."

Her mother huffed out a sigh. "I thought I'd be dancing by the end of the day."

Molly grasped her hand. "Knowing you, it won't take much time at all. As long as you don't try to push harder than your body allows."

"I suppose. But I'm so tired of being stuck in the house. This has been frustrating."

"I know it has, Mom. But look at you. Six weeks out from a major injury, and you're already in a walking cast for your leg, and a regular cast for your arm. That's progress, and you have to look at it as being halfway to being completely out of those casts."

"You're right. Of course, you're right. I just want life to get back to the way it was before."

"It will. I'll bet your therapist will be so excited to work with you tomorrow."

"She'll torture me. She loves torturing me."

Molly laughed. "You love every minute of it, too. You enjoy the challenge."

"What I'm going to enjoy is getting out of this house."

A week later, her mother was beside herself with excitement. She'd had daily therapy visits, and was getting around on her own with her walking cast. The therapist had been working on her core balance, plus they were doing work with her arm as well.

It had been grueling. Molly had gone with her mother to her appointments.

Her mom was such a fighter. She knew it was going to get worse before it got better, especially after the casts came off. She had every confidence her mother would completely recover from her injuries, because Georgia Burnett would accept no less.

Her dad was almost as excited as her mom when he came home that day and saw her moving around the house on her own, noting her progress after a week under her new physical therapy regimen. They were going to celebrate with a pot roast Molly had prepared for dinner. Mom had even helped, insisting on slicing carrots at the counter. She'd called it part of her therapy, and though she'd been a little slow at it, she'd done a great job.

But Carter texted her saying the new cabinets had come in for the bathroom, as well as the wall tiles. He was going to do some installation after work. He asked if she wanted to come over to see it.

"Of course you should go," her mother said. "You've already taken me to the therapist today and cooked dinner. You've spent every day with me for the past week. Go enjoy time with your boyfriend."

Molly was about to object that Carter was definitely not her boyfriend, but her mother waved her hand in dismissal.

"Go. Spend some time with Carter."

Anxious to get out of the house and not wanting to argue relationship status with her mom, she texted Carter that she'd be over shortly.

She changed clothes, then drove over to Carter's house. His garage door was open, so she went through that way and knocked on the door.

No answer.

She knocked again, but still no answer, so she tried the knob. The inside door was unlocked. Since Carter was expecting her, she stepped inside.

The sound of hard rock music smacked her ears. No wonder he couldn't hear her. The light in the bathroom was on, so she headed in that direction and found Carter. The shell of the vanity was already in. "That dark wood is going to look so good with the tile we laid on the floor the other day."

With the pale beige tiles and the dark brown cabinets, plus the cream color on the walls, the room was starting to take shape.

He looked up and smiled at her. "Thanks again for helping out with that. And for coming with me to pick out all this stuff."

"Are you kidding? I had fun spending your money."

"Now you sound like a girlfriend. Or a wife."

"Bite your tongue. Would you like something to drink?"

"How about iced tea? I made a fresh pitcher after work."

"Okay."

She slipped off her jacket, then went into the kitchen and fixed them each a glass of tea.

When she handed Carter his drink, he took a couple of deep swallows. "Thanks."

"What do you need me to do?"

He handed her a drill. "Will you screw in these brackets so we can start putting the drawers in?"

She loved that he didn't question her ability to use power tools, though she was glad no saws were involved. In short order, they had the drawers placed.

"We need to finish up the tile work on this wall," he said, pointing to the area above where the tub would go. "Painting's already done, and they're going to deliver the countertop tomorrow and put the sinks in."

It was almost finished. "I'm so surprised how quickly it's all come together."

"Bathrooms don't generally take too long once you have the demo portion complete. You and Luke really helped a lot."

"I can't wait to see it all."

They worked for a few hours on the tile, and took a break while Carter ordered pizza, since he hadn't eaten yet. Molly filled Carter in on her mother's therapy visit earlier in the day and her revised cast situation.

"Your mom's a superstar. I'm not at all surprised she's doing so well. Knowing Georgia, she'll break records in her recovery."

"I figure she'll cut the estimated twelve weeks down to eight."

He laughed, and bit into a slice of pizza. "You're probably right. Speaking of, when do you think you'll be ready to start work?"

She thought about it. "I don't know. She's doing very well, but I'd like to hover over her a few more days to make sure she feels confident enough to hang out by herself. Maybe next week?"

"I don't want to push you. You're here to be with your

mom, so you just let me know when you're ready. And when she's ready."

"Okay." She studied him as he ate. "And why? Are you having a paperwork emergency?"

"Not any more than usual."

"I'm looking forward to digging in and seeing what you've got."

He leaned back in his chair and slanted a sexy look her way. "I'm pretty sure you've already seen what I've got."

"Indeed I have." And it had been awhile since she'd seen it. Touched him, felt him, been with him. She'd been wrapped up with her mom, and Carter with work. Though she'd been able to dash over to help him with the bathroom project, during those occasions Luke and Emma had been over as well, which meant no alone time, and they'd worked late into the night. It had been exhausting work, and she'd wanted to be there for her mom, so she hadn't stayed.

Tonight, though, she had an action plan, and that meant time for her and Carter.

He'd finished his pizza, so she pushed back from the chair in the dining area and came over to him, straddling his lap.

He grasped her hips. "Is this dessert?"

"This is definitely dessert."

She slid her fingers into his hair, loving the thick softness of it, so different from everywhere else on him, which was so incredibly hard. She spread her thumb over his bottom lip, then bent and kissed him, taking in his rush of breath as an exhilarating aphrodisiac, an instant turn-on that sent a thrill of expectation through her. Her entire body tingled with awareness when he swept his hands under her shirt to explore the skin of her back.

Suddenly, her bra was undone, and her nipples tightened in anticipation. She straightened and pulled off her shirt, removing her bra, needing Carter's hands on her. A rush of desperate need coursed through her, a frantic desire that had to be satisfied right now.

She felt his erection pressing ever insistently against her

sex, and she surged against him. His gaze lifted to hers, his eyes half lidded, a storm raging in them.

He cupped her butt and stood, lifting her. She thought he'd carry her down the hall to the bedroom, but he pushed the plates and pizza box to the far end of the table and set her on it.

She smiled at him as he popped open the button of her jeans. She kicked off her tennis shoes and helped him as he pulled her jeans down her legs while he unzipped his. He pulled a condom out of his pocket.

"Ever ready, are you?" she asked.

"Around you? Hell yes."

She liked knowing he was as anxious as she was. It reminded her so much of those frantic, teenage years when they couldn't wait to get at each other. Her heart pounded against her chest as he pulled her panties aside and entered her, his body looming over hers as he thrust, his hand sweeping under her to cushion her butt.

"I'm not fragile, Carter," she said, holding on to his arms. "I won't break."

She felt he was holding back, that he wasn't giving her all the pent-up passion he felt for her. She wanted all of it, and when he unleashed it, taking her mouth in a kiss filled with naked desire and fury, then pushed her back against the table, she took it all in, and gave it back in equal measure. She wrapped her legs around his hips, arched against him, then stretched fully out on her back.

She lifted his shirt, raking her nails across his back as the two of them melded together until she couldn't tell where she ended and he began. This was what she'd craved, this lightning storm of pleasure and pain and need. She cried out as she came, and he groaned as he let go, both of them shuddering, holding on to each other as the storm held them in its fury.

When it passed, Molly still trembled, and Carter stroked her side, his body wet with perspiration.

They were stuck to each other, stem to stern.

"I need a shower," she said.

He lifted, smiling down at her. "I think you're just using me so you can spend time in my shower."

She laughed, and he pulled her up. She hopped off the table. "Maybe."

After a quick shower, Molly cleaned the remnants of dinner—and sex—from the table, threw away the trash, and when Carter emerged from the shower, they took a final look at the bathroom remodel.

"I can't wait to see the counter and sinks in there."

"It'll be even better when there's a toilet, but that'll go in last."

"Then you'll have another room finished. Before long, you won't have any rooms to work on."

"There are still three more bedrooms to knock out. But that's just floors and paint, maybe expanding closet space, and choosing furniture. Nothing too major."

She patted his arm. "It's good to have a project."

He walked down the hall with her and into the kitchen, where they refilled their glasses. "I'm also thinking of building a second garage so I can have a project area."

"A project area for what?"

"Rebuilding old cars. There's a '68 Camaro I'm eyeing that I might want to refurbish. But since I house Rhonda in my current garage, I need some additional space."

"I see. You have plenty of room on the side of the garage to build a third garage space."

"That's what I was thinking."

"In your spare time, of course."

He took a sip of his tea, then smiled at her over the rim of his glass. "Of course."

They ended up snuggled up on the sofa watching an action movie, wrapped under a fleece blanket. It was an okay movie, but her mind drifted, thinking about this house, the way Carter had bought it, bare bones, and completely overhauled it. And even though he was almost finished, he was still coming up with new ideas.

It was a lot like the jobs she did. She'd come into a place, look at the bare bones, and find ways to improve things.

She liked that he was always thinking ahead, of the next step, the next project. He kept busy, didn't just sit around doing nothing but drinking beer and being lazy. Carter definitely wasn't a lazy guy. She admired that about him.

Of course, even back when they were teenagers, he'd had a lot of dreams, had plans for the future. They'd been different plans back then, and his present hadn't quite matched up with what they'd talked about in the past.

But whose life ever did? Hers sure hadn't.

Then again, look at them now, cuddling together on the sofa, much like what they'd used to do when they were younger.

She never thought this would happen again, that she'd feel so comfortable with Carter, or that she and Carter would ever—

So maybe things hadn't changed as much as she thought.

She pushed the blanket off. "I should go."

He gave her a confused look. "You don't want to stay tonight?"

She grabbed her tennis shoes. "I don't think so. I have to be there for Mom in the morning. You know, just in case she's unsteady."

Carter ran his hands through his hair. "Oh, right. Sure."

She grabbed her purse and keys and headed for the door. "I'll talk to you later."

"Molly."

She turned, and he pulled her into his arms, giving her a deep, lasting kiss that only added to her confusion.

"I'll talk to you later, okay?"

She nodded. "Okay. Good night."

She was out the door in a hurry, without once looking behind her.

Her heart pounded the entire way home.

Chapter 26

IT WAS THANKSGIVING week, and Molly had a million things to do. She had sat with Mom going over the menu and been to the grocery store.

Molly and Emma had already decided it was going to take an act of Congress to keep their mother out of the kitchen, especially since everyone was going to come over to their parents' house for Thanksgiving this year. Emma offered to host at her and Luke's place, but having Mom travel too much wasn't a good idea. Plus, if she got tired, it was easier for her to just go to her room so she could rest.

Molly had been invited to Carter's parents' house as well, but there was no way she could juggle it all, which was too bad. She'd always liked Amanda and Robert Richards. They were great people, and she'd spent a lot of time at their house when she'd been dating Carter.

In fact, one of these days she had to stop by and say hello to them again.

Just not this week.

"Are you sure we can't just go to Megan's bakery and buy some pies?"

Her mother gave her a look of horror. "One does not buy pies to serve during Thanksgiving, Molly. One makes them."

"Why not? I buy them all the time. Megan makes great pie."

"Yes, she does. And she'll sell a lot of them this week to people who don't cook. But we can cook."

Molly pored over the list of to-dos. "We can do a lot of things. And you will not be making your homemade crust this week."

As her mother opened her mouth to object, Molly waved her pen in her mom's direction. "No. Too much work, too hard on your arm. No homemade crust. I've already bought ready-made crust. It's in the freezer, and your pies will still be awesome. Emma and I will see to that."

Her mother looked crushed, which made Molly's stomach tighten, but she refused to yield.

"I'm not an invalid, you know."

"No, you're not. But this year, there won't be homemade crust on your pies. And you know what? I'll bet they still taste amazing."

Some of the items had to be made early—like six pies— since her mother had to invite practically the entire town of Hope to Thanksgiving dinner, which was why Molly had to buy a twenty-six-pound turkey, plus a huge ham. They made a pumpkin pie and pecan pie, and tomorrow they'd make several more. Her mother suggested they also make cookies.

"How do you do this?" Molly asked later in the day while her mother sat drinking some hot tea and Molly did dishes.

"Do what?"

"Work a full-time job, and make all this food? You do this every Thanksgiving?"

"I do a little bit every night after work. Your father is very helpful."

Molly shook her head. "You're like Wonder Woman, Mom."

Her mother beamed. "Well, thank you, honey. I just enjoy staying busy."

"Now you sound like Carter."

"Really? How's that?"

"He works a full-time job. He's renovated practically every room in his new house. He works on his cars."

Her mom took a sip of tea, then set the cup down. "He's motivated to stay busy. And he isn't out carousing every night."

Carousing. Molly smiled at the word as she finished scrubbing a pot and put it in the dish rack. "I guess so."

"So what's bothering you about him?"

She grabbed the dish towel to dry her hands, then turned around and leaned against the sink. "Nothing bothers me."

"The two of you have restarted your romance since you've been back home."

"Not really. We're just spending time together. There's no romance going on."

Her mother gave her that look, the one she used to give her when she knew Molly had been lying about something. "I think we can be honest with each other, Molly. I've given you a wide berth all these years when you refused to come home, when you left so suddenly. I've always let you and Emma decide your own fates."

"I appreciate that, Mom."

"But you and Carter—you two were so much in love—so seemingly destined for a future together. And then you suddenly broke up and decided you had to go on this grand adventure without him, and you changed your entire life's direction. I didn't understand it then, and I still don't."

She shrugged. "I just . . . changed my mind, Mom. I was under so much pressure at the time, and I made a choice about what I wanted to do with my life. As far as Carter, well that was a high school romance and it just didn't work out, so we broke up. It really wasn't a Romeo and Juliet kind of tragedy, you know."

Her mother gave her that look again. "He's a good guy, Molly."

She so didn't want to have this conversation with her mother, but saw no way out of it at the moment. She kept her head down, focusing on the extensive list she'd started to make. "Yes. He's a good guy."

"Do you want to tell me what happened? Your breakup was so abrupt."

She shrugged. "We just realized we wanted different things. I wanted to travel, and he wanted to go to college."

"You wanted to go to college, too. So what changed?"

Everything. "I don't know, Mom. Like I said, I changed my mind—my direction."

"I'm not stupid, Molly."

Her head shot up. "Of course you're not."

"You left here a wreck, emotionally. Did that have to do with Carter?"

She wrapped her arms around herself. "Please don't ask me to bring up the past when there's nothing I can do to change it."

"Did he hurt you?"

There was nothing that brought out her mother's protective instincts more than a wounded daughter. Her mother—and her father—had come to her defense on countless occasions, whether it was emotional or physical hurt.

But she was a grown woman now, and she wanted to leave the past behind her. Or at least she was trying to. Dredging it up time and time again wouldn't help.

"No, he didn't hurt me. We had come to a crossroads in our lives. I changed my mind about college. We had made plans for our future that no longer meshed. It was kind of a messy breakup—you know how it is for teenagers. He went one way, and I went another. I was an emotional mess about it."

Her mother studied her for a few minutes, then nodded. "And the last thing you wanted was to come crying to your parents about it, because we might have blamed Carter."

"Exactly. I just needed to get away. From Carter, from Hope, from everything that reminded me of the past. I needed a fresh start. I wanted to shake loose of everything here."

Her mother looked hurt.

"Not you or dad or Emma. I don't know, Mom. It's hard to explain. My independence came at a cost, and I know that. I never meant to hurt you."

Her mom stood, and hobbled over to fold Molly into her

arms. "Oh, honey, you didn't hurt me. All these years, I was just so worried about you."

She hated lying to her mother, but she couldn't—wouldn't—share that part of her past. Knowing what had happened would only hurt her deeply, and she might blame Carter for it. That she wouldn't allow.

So instead, she hugged her. "I know you were, and if I could take back all the years of worry, I would. But I'm doing good, Mom. I'm happy with the life I lead."

Her mother pulled back. "Are you? Are you really happy?"

She gave her mother a genuine smile. "I'm living my dream. I love the travel, the opportunity to meet new people everywhere I go. I've had so many interesting jobs and I've learned so much, not just about the work I do, but about myself. I don't know that I would have become as independent as I am if I hadn't chosen this life."

Her mother grasped her hands. "I'm so proud of you, Molly. I've never told you this before, but I see a lot of myself in you. Our paths are different, but our passion is the same."

That was the first time her mother had ever told her she was proud of her. Tears sprang into her eyes. "Thank you, Mom."

THANKSGIVING DAY DAWNED clear and crisp. Just the way Carter liked it.

He knew his mom would be up early, so he headed over there to help out, and spend the day with his parents.

He didn't get to see them as often as he'd like. Work and other projects kept him busy. But they were busy, too. Now that they were retired, they'd bought an RV and enjoyed traveling the country.

But days like today, when his aunts, uncles, and cousins were over, he could settle in, eat his fill of great food, and catch up on all the family gossip.

Still, his mind lingered on Molly, who he hadn't seen for about a week, not since she'd abruptly fled his house while they were watching a movie.

No idea what was going on there. They'd talked a few

times, but he sensed she needed distance, and he knew to give her the space she needed to figure things out.

But there was only so much he was willing to give her. Her mom had invited him over for Thanksgiving dinner, and once things started winding down at his parents' place, he said his goodbyes and drove over to Molly's parents' house.

He knocked and Molly's dad answered.

"Hey, Carter. Happy Thanksgiving."

"Same to you, Emmett." They shook hands and Emmett led him inside. There was still a houseful of people, so he said his hellos to Luke, Logan, and Bash, and Samantha's grandmother, and a few of Molly's cousins and aunts and uncles that he knew from around town.

Damn, was the entire town here? Leave it to Georgia Burnett to have one hell of a holiday shindig.

Georgia was holding court in the living room, so he came over and kissed her cheek. Martha from the ranch was sitting next to her.

"Hi, Martha."

"Hi, yourself. I haven't seen you for a while. Keeping busy?"

"I have been. Nice to see you off the ranch."

"Georgia invited us all out here today to have lunch, so I'm taking the day off."

"Good for you." He went over to Georgia. "And I hear you're doing cartwheels with your new casts on."

Georgia laughed. "Nearly. I'm feeling pretty good these days."

"You're looking even better."

"And you know exactly what to say to make a woman blush. Go find my daughter. She's in the kitchen."

"Yes, ma'am."

Molly was in there with Emma, Chelsea, Des, and Samantha, and Megan, all of them nestled up at the kitchen table, having what he could only assume was intimate girl talk. Their heads were bowed close, and they were all drinking wine and laughing.

Until he walked in. Then they pushed their chairs back as if they'd been caught saying something they shouldn't.

"Oh, hi, Carter," Molly said. "I didn't expect to see you today."

"Your mom invited me."

Chelsea stood, a little unsteady on her high heels. "What's up, handsome?" She kissed his cheek.

"Not much."

"Beer or wine?" Samantha asked. "Though I already know the answer."

She went to the refrigerator and grabbed a beer, popped off the top, and handed it to him.

"Thanks, Sam."

Des got up, too. "How's it going, Carter?"

"Good, Des. How's the movie business?"

"Busy. How's the auto repair business?"

He grinned. "Busy."

"Let's go find Bash," Chelsea said.

"Bash is here?" Des asked.

"Somewhere. Maybe outside having a cigar with the rest of the guys," Megan said.

"There are cigars?" he asked.

"One of Molly's uncles brought them." Chelsea winked and slipped out the back door with Des, Megan and Sam.

He took a long swallow of beer, then took a seat at the table. "I interrupted. Sorry."

She shrugged. "We were just talking. Trust me, it was nothing important. Just gossiping about Chelsea's date the other night."

"Really."

"Yes." She crooked a smile. "It didn't go so well for him. He was late, obnoxious, checked his phone repeatedly during dinner, then wanted Chelsea to pay her half of the tab. And that was after he'd been relentlessly pursuing her for a month."

Carter shook his head. "The poor guy. I can only imagine how badly Chelsea took him down."

"It wasn't pretty—very loud and very public in a very nice restaurant."

He leaned back in the chair and took another swig of beer. "I actually would have liked to have seen that. Sounds like the sonofabitch deserved what he got."

"That's what I said."

"Someday Chelsea is going to find a man worthy of her."

She graced him with a warm smile. "That's what I said. And it's nice of you to think so."

"I like Chelsea. She's ballsy, and a man would like that. She's also beautiful and smart. What man wouldn't appreciate those qualities in a woman? If I knew any men deserving of her, I'd set her up. Unfortunately, no one immediately comes to mind."

She sighed. "I know. Emma and Jane tell me they're always on the lookout for great men for her. Sadly, few measure up."

"There's someone for everyone. Her day will come."

"So I keep telling her." She emptied her wineglass, then went to the refrigerator and grabbed the bottle.

Carter got up. "Here, let me do that for you."

"Thanks."

He pulled the cork out and poured her refill. "How did your dinner go?"

"It was hectic, but we pulled it off, and everyone seemed to enjoy the meal. How was dinner at your parents?"

"Great. They said to tell you hello."

"I'm sorry I couldn't make it over there. I wanted to see them. I do want to see them."

"Plenty of time for that. And speaking of time, how about starting work with me next week?"

"Yeah, I've been thinking about that. You know, Mom's still hobbling around so I don't know if I can leave her just yet."

"Quit using me as an excuse. Time for you to go back to work, Molly."

Carter turned to see that Georgia had made her way into the kitchen.

"Oh, Mom. I didn't see you there."

"Obviously. Carter offered you a job. It's high time you started it, isn't it?"

Carter folded his arms. He wasn't going to interfere in this conversation, though he had been the one to start it.

"Are you sure you're going to be okay here by yourself?" Molly asked.

"Yes. I'm dying to get you out of here to see if I can fend for myself during the day without you hovering over me waiting for me to fall. If I feel like I can't, you'll be the first person I call. How's that?"

Molly looked from her mother to Carter. "Does that work for you?"

Carter nodded. "Of course. Your mother is your first priority."

With a sigh, Molly nodded. "Then I'll start on Monday."

"Good. Now go enjoy the heaters outside with the rest of the young people. I'm going to get a glass of eggnog."

"I can get that for you, Mom."

Her mother shot a glare across the kitchen, and Molly stepped back. "Okay, you can get it for yourself."

"Good girl. Now out of my way." Georgia made a shooing motion.

Molly shook her head. "Guess we're going out back to play with the other kids."

Carter laughed. "I guess we are."

There were portable heaters set up, though it had turned out to be a pretty nice day today. Bash was out there, along with Luke and Logan and a couple of Molly's uncles, and Ben, Martha's husband.

"About time you showed up," Luke said.

"You're lucky we didn't smoke all the stogies before you got here," Logan said.

"I heard there were cigars."

Fred, Molly's uncle, offered him one.

"Thanks."

Molly had wandered off to sit with the women, so he stuck with the guys, catching up on life at the ranch with Logan and Ben, and listening to Bash complain about some personnel issues he'd been having with a couple of his cocktail waitresses. And Carter talked about how he'd hired Brady, and how he was doing.

Typical guy stuff.

But he kept skirting glances across the patio to Molly, who hadn't once looked in his direction.

She was pretty engaged with her friends. They were all laughing and having a good time talking about God only knew what.

"And then we all had sex with the suspect, but since she was a hooker, she charged us. We got a discount though, since we gave her a get-out-of-jail-free card."

Luke's conversation finally entered his brain. He whipped his head around. "What the hell are you talking about?"

Luke smirked. "Nice to see you finally paying attention."

They all laughed.

"You were so focused on what the women were doing, we could have been talking about anything. Luke asked you a question four times and you didn't answer," Logan said. "Why don't you just go over and sit with Molly? Be sure to hand in your man card on the way over."

"Fuck you, Logan."

"Aww, come on," Bash said, slinging his arm around Carter's shoulders. "My man here has obviously got issues."

"Yeah," Luke said. "Serious ones. A woman's got him by the tail."

"More like by the balls," Logan said.

"You're one to talk." Carter pinned Logan with a glare. "And you, too, Luke."

"I can at least keep track of a conversation," Luke said. "Whatever's going on with you and Molly has your brain scrambled."

Maybe it did. And the only way he could address it was with Molly. In the meantime, he shrugged it off and concentrated—really concentrated this time—on his friends.

After a while, the women headed inside and the guys stayed out, conversation turning to sports. They started debating the football game, so they went inside and joined Emmett in watching it, while the remaining women gathered around the dining room table, drinking coffee and talking, though Megan and Chelsea came over to watch football with them.

Once he got into the game, that's where his concentration stayed, especially when they all argued over which team was going to win. It was halftime before he got up from his spot on the sofa to venture into the kitchen, deciding to switch from beer to coffee.

"Having fun?"

He turned from the counter to see Molly. "Yeah. How about you?"

"I am. Thanks for coming over today. My mom was really happy to see you."

"I was happy for the invite, though I guess you and I aren't going to have any time to talk tonight."

She shrugged. "Too many people hovering around today. Sorry."

"No big deal."

She lingered, so he figured there was something on her mind. Then again, like she said, today wasn't the day to have that talk. So instead, he looked out the doorway. Everyone was busy talking or watching the game.

"Molly." He moved in closer.

"Yeah?"

He slipped his arm around her and pulled her in for a kiss, intending on taking just a brief taste of her.

Then she moaned, and clutched his shirt, dragging him in. He groaned and swept his hand across her back, down, letting his fingers skim over the top of her butt, lost in her, wishing they were alone.

But they weren't, so with great goddamned reluctance, he broke the kiss.

She licked her lips.

"Careful," he whispered.

"I'm not careful when I'm with you. I'm trying for distance."

"Why?"

She lifted her eyes to his, deep pools of blue, filled with the same desire and need that was tearing through him right now, making it hard for him to resist pulling her out of the house, driving her over to his, and throwing her down on his bed so he could sink inside her, satisfying both their needs.

She laid her forehead against his. "I don't know." She put her palms on his chest. "I don't know. I just need . . . a minute. A day. I don't know."

He grasped her hands in his. "Take what you need, Molly. I'm not going anywhere."

She drew in a deep breath. "Thank you for that."

She took a step back, and walked away.

At least she looked reluctant when she left the room.

Chapter 27

MOLLY HADN'T BEEN lying when she'd told Carter she was hesitant to start working for him because she was worried about her mother being alone. But she and her father discussed it, and her mother had been getting around just fine on her own. They made her solemnly promise she wouldn't climb any ladders or do anything foolish.

Her mom promised she would only do normal things and said she'd learned her lesson the hard way. And if she felt uncomfortable about being alone, she'd call either Molly or Molly's dad right away.

That suited her just fine, so following a weekend of holiday decorating at the house and a little holiday shopping, Molly reported for work Monday morning at Carter's shop in Hope.

Admittedly, she was nervous, though she couldn't pinpoint why. She'd started plenty of new jobs, always with anticipation and excitement. This should be no different, right?

Then again, there'd been Thanksgiving, and that kiss. She'd wanted so much more. More of that kiss, more alone time with Carter.

But she was confused about her feelings right now, so some space had been necessary.

Not that she had any more clarity today than she'd had last week.

She waited outside Carter's office while he met with an employee. She fidgeted with the hem of her button-down shirt, then found herself playing with the rings on her fingers, and doing a close examination of her fingernail polish.

Finally, disgusted with herself, she took out her phone to play a word game to pass the time until Carter's office door opened.

"Sorry for the delay, Molly."

She stood and grabbed her purse. "Not a problem."

Time to put on her work face.

She entered his office and took a seat while he closed the door to drown out the sound of engines and power tools.

"You look nice," he said.

"Thanks." He'd told her to dress casual, so she had. She looked down at her dark jeans and navy, button-down shirt, along with her brown, knee-length high-heeled boots. She'd also added a scarf. Not too dressy, but she also wasn't so dressed down that she looked like she could be working in one of the garage bays.

"I have some employment paperwork for you to fill out. I've also cleared out the office next to mine so you'll have a quiet place to work."

She took a quick glance at her new office. Small, but more than she'd expected. "That's great. Thank you."

"There's a laptop in there, and a printer. The system is linked to all four of the shops. Once you fill out your paperwork, I'll walk you through everything and get you acclimated as far as the systems we use here to track sales, payroll, human resources, and accounting."

Other than complimenting her appearance, he was all business, and she was thankful for that. She hadn't had a chance to tell him she wanted to separate their personal relationship from their professional, and it looked like she wouldn't have to.

He handed her a stack of papers. "You can take these to

your office and fill them out. I'm sure you know the drill. Once you're done, come see me."

"Okay."

The morning passed in a blur of paperwork, meeting the employees, and learning the various operations of his company. It wasn't a difficult one, but of course it was still new to her.

He did take her out to lunch, but even then, everything remained centered on business. She asked him a lot of questions, and he gave her pointed, on the mark answers. They talked about ways to increase efficiency, all the while having salad and soup. Then it was back to work for more of the same.

By the end of the day she had a fairly decent handle on how to streamline some of the processes, and a lot more questions, which she'd jotted down in her notes file.

"I'll take you to each of the shops this week. Though the processes are the same, each shop works independently," Carter told her as they met up in his office at the end of the day. "Plus, I want you to meet with management at the other shops and all the employees so they get used to coming to you instead of me with questions."

"Sounds good. It'll likely take me a week or two until I'm comfortable enough to answer some of the questions myself. But I'll be happy to field them, just so they get used to coming to me."

He nodded. "And I'll be doing a lot of redirecting, because my managers at the other shops—and staff at this one—are used to bringing every problem to me. I want that to change."

"Right. Unless it's a question about which carburetor goes in an '03 Tahoe. I don't know the answer to that one. Not off the top of my head, anyway."

"If anyone comes to either of us with that question, they're fired."

She laughed. "Noted."

He picked up his phone. "It's five thirty. Go ahead and take off. I'm sure you'd like to get home and check on your mom."

"I called her several times today. After the fourth phone call, she said I was annoying her."

He cracked a smile. "Is that right? That must mean she's doing well on her own."

"I think she's been dying for me to get out of the house so she can gain back a little of her independence. I can't say I blame her."

"Well, you are a free spirit. So is she. I'm sure you can appreciate how difficult it would be to have someone watching you like a hawk, babysitting your every move."

"I'd hate it. I know she does. In fact, she insisted on making dinner tonight. It's the first time since her accident. I hope she doesn't overdo it."

"I'm sure she won't."

Molly stood. "I'm going to head on out. Thanks for a great first day, and for the job. It's actually been really nice to work again."

"You're welcome. Thanks for offering to help out."

"You have a good company here, Carter. With my help, it'll be even better. I can't wait to dig in."

"So I'll . . . see you tomorrow?"

"Sure. See you tomorrow."

At home, everything was as normal as it could be. Her mom was excited to put dinner on the table, and seemed to be full of energy. She told Molly and her dad that she'd wandered around the house, gotten her exercise, and rested when she was tired. She hadn't overdone, and she felt good.

Molly was relieved.

After dinner, Molly went to her room and went over the notes she'd taken during the day, thinking about some of the upgrades she'd like to make. She wanted to ask Carter a few questions, but didn't want to call him.

Work time was for work and calling him at night was . . .

Something she wouldn't do if it was work related.

Their relationship was in flux right now, and that was her doing. That night a couple of weeks ago they'd been snuggling on the sofa, she'd felt comfortable. A little too comfortable, too familiar, which had dragged her back to the past, a place she never liked going.

The feelings had overwhelmed her. But they hadn't just been feelings from the past. It was the feelings she had now that had caused her to panic, made her pull back from him.

Since then, she'd missed him. Seeing him today, working with him today, but unable to touch him, kiss him, or do anything about the emotional pull she always felt when she was around him somehow felt unnatural to her.

She knew she had to do it to maintain a level of professionalism at work, but she didn't have to put him in that no touch, no contact zone after work.

She picked up the phone, and on impulse, punched his number.

He picked up on the second ring. "Hey, Molly."

"Hi, Carter. What are you doing?"

"Watching some TV."

"What? Not tearing up a room?"

He laughed. "Nah. A new employee started at work today, and she wore me out. I have nothing left to give to the poor house."

She rolled her eyes. "I hardly think so."

"So what's up?"

Now that she'd called him, she didn't have a plan formulated for what she was going to say. So she was just going to have to go with her gut. "I was wondering if you wanted to go do something."

"What? You aren't tired of me?"

"Shockingly, no."

"That new action movie came out last weekend. It even has romance in it. You wanna go see it?"

She relaxed her shoulders, relieved he'd made it so easy on her. "I'd love to."

"Hang on a second. Let me check my phone."

She waited.

"There's a showing at nine. Is that too late for you?"

"No, that works. How about you pick me up about eight thirty?"

"That'll work. I'll see you then."

She took a shower, did her hair and makeup, then got dressed and went downstairs. Her parents were playing a board game at the dining room table, and she smiled at seeing her mother up and about again.

Her dad looked up from the game. "You look pretty."

She looked down at her jeans and sweater, happy that he noticed.

"Thanks. I'm going to a movie."

"With Carter?" her mother asked, with the kind of smile only a woman would give you when she knew you had a date.

"Yes, Mom. With Carter."

She distracted them both by talking about the game they were playing, so she didn't have to endure questions about her relationship with Carter. She'd filled them in over dinner about her workday, but fortunately they'd left the questions business related, which had suited her just fine.

Technically, she could leave Hope. Her mother was fine, her dad more than capable of taking care of her now, with Emma helping out by looking in on her.

But now she had a new job, and maybe she'd give that job a chance.

Which didn't mean she was staying, nor that she had any intention of falling in love with Carter all over again.

Though her heart skipped a beat when she heard him drive up.

She kissed her parents goodbye and went outside where Carter was waiting for her in the driveway. She slid into the passenger seat of his car.

"I was going to come in and say hi to your parents."

"Not necessary, and we don't want to be late for the movie."

"Okay."

He shifted into reverse, and headed down the driveway.

Molly inhaled. She had no idea what he wore—aftershave, maybe, or his soap—but she loved the way he smelled. All she wanted to do right now was bury her face in his neck—maybe her tongue, as well.

"Are you all right?" he asked as he drove down the main highway toward the movie theater.

"Fine," she said, shifting her gaze to him. "Why?"

"You made a sound. Like a groan. Or a moan."

"Did I?" She pulled her mirror out of her purse and checked her lip gloss, smiling at herself.

They got to the movie theater, bought their tickets and purchased a couple of sodas and some popcorn, then grabbed seats. Since it was a Monday night in a small town, the theater wasn't crowded, which was perfect.

"I'm glad you called me," Carter said as they watched previews of upcoming movies.

"I'm glad you suggested a movie. I've actually been looking forward to seeing this one. I've kind of got a thing for Channing Tatum."

Carter arched a brow. "Is that right? Now I'm going to have to watch you closely during the movie."

"For what?"

"Drool."

She laughed. "I think I can control myself with Channing, if you can behave yourself around Mila Kunis."

"I'll try my best. No guarantees. Me and Mila go way back. We're like this." He crossed his fingers.

"So . . . there's another woman."

His lips curved and he put his arm around her. "No one but you, babe."

His words made her tingle. They shouldn't, but they did.

The movie started, and Molly settled in to enjoy the action. But she couldn't help but be distracted by the fact this was the first movie they'd been to together since they were teenagers. Back then, they'd hide in the back, hold hands, and steal kisses.

Now, though, they sat in the middle for a good view, though once they finished their popcorn, Carter grasped her hand.

Some things changed. Some didn't. She was satisfied with that.

The movie was great. Action filled, with a lot of tension and nail-biting scenes where she clenched Carter's hand, hoping the characters would come out of it alive. For a while, she wasn't certain. Finally, right near the end of the movie, she released her breath as the characters made their escape.

And the romance at the end was swoon-worthy, the hero making such a huge gesture to the heroine. The heroine kicked butt as well. She loved this kind of film. She was pumped and excited as the lights came up.

"What did you think?" she asked Carter as they stood and excited the theater.

"It was good."

"That's it? Just good?"

He shrugged as he tossed the empty popcorn bucket and drink cup in the trash. "Yeah. Good."

She shook her head. "I thought it was fantastic. That scene when they were dangling out of the helicopter—oh, my God. My heart was in my throat the entire time. And when she had to shoot right over his head. If he hadn't ducked a quarter of an inch, she would have grazed him. It was like they had telepathy."

"Uh-huh. Yeah, that part was good."

She slid into the car. "Good. That's all you're going to say about the movie."

"I'll leave the superlatives to the critics."

"You're no fun to go to the movies with. Next time I'm going with Emma, Jane, and Chelsea."

He turned to her. "I like action movies. They hold my interest. But I'm not much for dissecting."

Now she remembered this about him. She'd come out of the movie theater having loved or hated a film and wanting to spend the next half hour discussing it, while he either said he liked it or didn't like it, and that was the end of it. She remembered it drove her crazy.

So disappointing, but she couldn't change that about him.

At least he'd held her hand.

When he drove her home, she was even more disappointed.

"What? No hot sex at your place?"

"Sorry, Miss Burnett, but it's a school night. And it's already late."

She laughed. "I can't believe you're giving me a curfew."

"This is what happens when you're dating the boss. I have a big day planned for you tomorrow, and you need your sleep."

She unbuckled her seat belt and grabbed the door handle. "You are no fun, Mr. Richards."

"Wanna bet?"

He grasped her arm and tugged her toward him. Before she knew it, he'd hauled her onto his lap. His hands were in her hair—all over her actually, as he kissed her. A smoking-hot kiss that left no doubt he was as reluctant to let her go as she was to be let go.

It was like being struck by lightning, this feeling she got whenever he kissed her. He had been the first boy to give her this feeling, and no boy, or man, since, had ever made her feel the same way.

When he let her go, she lifted away only a few inches, both of them breathing hard.

"You sure about that smoking-hot sex thing?" she asked.

He rubbed his thumb across her bottom lip. "Am I sure? Hell no. I think you can feel that. But if I take you home with me, Molly, neither of us will get any sleep tonight."

Damn. Mental visuals of that would keep her up tonight. "All right." She climbed off of him and grabbed her purse. She looked over at him and his delicious erection.

"Last chance," she said.

He cocked his head to the side. "Don't tempt me."

Clearly he was the only one practicing restraint tonight, because she had none. "Fine. I'll see you tomorrow."

"Good night, Molly."

She got out of the car and watched him drive away.

She could deny a lot of things about what was going on between her and Carter.

But the chemistry between them? That was undeniable.

She took a deep, shuddering breath, then walked into the house.

CARTER PULLED INTO the garage, parked Rhonda, then got out, straightening his jeans as he did.

His erection still hadn't gone away and it was goddamned uncomfortable.

He had no idea why he'd decided to play the martyr tonight and take Molly home. She'd looked gorgeous in skintight jeans that showcased her fine ass. Her lips had been glossed and kissable, and all he'd thought about during the movie was putting his hands and mouth on her.

Instead, he'd taken her home. And then he'd hauled her onto his lap and kissed the hell out of her, making both of them hot and uncomfortable.

What kind of a glutton for punishment did that make him?

Now he was going to be hard all night, and no doubt lie awake and think about how she could have been in his bed, and the two of them could have gotten the release they both wanted.

He threw his keys on the kitchen counter and grabbed a beer, popped it open and downed a few quick swallows, hoping it would cool his libido.

He took a seat in the living room and turned on the television, flipping through channels as he drank his beer. By the time he'd emptied the can, he realized he was still thinking about Molly, and still wished she was here with him. She'd be naked—and so would he—and he could be tasting her, touching her, sinking inside her.

Fuck.

He got up, crunched the beer can in his hand, and tossed it in the trash.

Since it wasn't likely he was going to be sleeping anytime soon, he might as well do some paperwork, and maybe spend the next hour or so mentally cursing himself for being a moron.

The next time he had Molly on his lap, ready and willing, he wasn't going to be stupid and send her home.

Chapter 28

BETWEEN WORK, THE approaching holidays, and town square committee meetings doubling up because the project was almost finished, Molly had her hands full. Good thing she liked being busy.

After work tonight they'd meet with the town square committee, likely for the final time. She'd been buried in her laptop all day and Carter had been at one of his shops in Tulsa, so they hadn't had a chance to sit down and go over the agenda, but he promised he'd be back in time for them to have a discussion over dinner.

She picked up her phone. It was five thirty. She'd told her parents she'd likely go straight from work to dinner to the meeting, so they shouldn't expect her home until late.

As it was, Carter was already running late since he'd told her he'd be back by four.

She busied herself for another ten minutes with setting up the new accounting system when she heard the front door open. She looked up to see him coming in.

He opened the door to her office, a grim look on his face.

"Bad day?" she asked.

"Jack Peterson gave his notice."

She leaned back in her chair. "That's not good. He's one of your most competent managers. Did he give a reason?"

"His wife's been wanting to move back to Minnesota, where her family lives, so her dad's offered him a job up there in St. Paul with the family business."

"Oh. Well, not much you can do about that."

"They're moving in a month, so at least that gives me time to find a replacement. And Jack said he knows someone that works at Best Auto in one of the Tulsa locations. He's currently an assistant manager and Jack says he's really good, so I'm going to give him a call and see if he can come in for an interview."

"At least you have a start."

"True. Anyway, I'm sorry I'm late. Jack and I spent a lot of time talking. He's not happy about this move, but his wife has been miserable living here. I think their relocating is a matter of saving the marriage. So I had to listen."

"Understood. It's not an easy situation for him, I can imagine."

"No, it's not. I got the idea that his wife issued an ultimatum that he either went with her, or she was going to take their three kids and move without him."

Molly frowned. "Ouch. That's ugly."

"Yeah."

"I hope they can work it out."

"Me, too. I hate losing him, but family has to be a person's number-one priority."

She couldn't imagine doing that to her as yet nonexistent husband. But she knew those kinds of relationships existed. "Would you do that for the woman you loved?"

He frowned. "Do what?"

"Leave Hope."

"Yes."

He didn't even hesitate. She was surprised. "Really. You've built a business here, Carter. Your family is here. Everything you know."

He shrugged. "I can build a business anywhere. You don't just walk away from a relationship."

Which was exactly what she'd done. Only she hadn't walked. She'd run. She started to say something, but then he continued.

"Like Jack. He's got fifteen years invested in his marriage to Eileen. They have three children together. To him, it's more important to stay together as a family than fight over a job. Location? That's nothing."

"I suppose."

"I would think you'd see it his wife's way. Why does it matter where you live? You move around all the time."

"But I don't have children."

"That's true."

"I don't know. I think she emotionally blackmailed him into seeing things her way."

"We're not in their marriage, so it's hard for us, as outsiders, to judge."

She took a deep breath and let it out. "You're right. I'm sorry. I guess I feel bad for Jack, because he has to give up a job and a town he loves in order to keep his marriage together."

He stood. "You don't have to apologize to me. I guess he's content enough to do that because he loves his wife more, ya know?"

"You're right. It's a hard choice, no matter what."

Carter nodded. "I'm hungry. How about we grab a quick bite to eat at Bert's before the meeting?"

"Good idea."

A quick bite was right. Time was ticking, and as they ate they went over the agenda for the meeting. Molly barely had time to finish her soup and salad before they had to dash out the door.

She didn't mind being busy, but this was crazy busy. And she didn't even want to think about all the holiday shopping she had left to do, which meant she was going to be stuck braving the mall soon.

They were the last to arrive for the meeting.

"I was afraid you two were going to be no-shows tonight," Mavis said as they walked in and shed their coats.

"Wouldn't miss it," Carter said, rubbing his hands together.

The wind had picked up outside. It smelled like snow, and Molly couldn't wait. She'd bought new boots, though she worried about George—he wasn't equipped for winter weather.

One of these days she was going to have to buy a new car.

Not this year, though. And probably not next year. George was just going to have to suck it up and deal. They'd weathered a lot of winters together. She was sure—okay, more like hopeful—they'd make it through this one, too.

Shrugging off thoughts of her poor old car, she sat down and they got started.

"The last of the landscaping is in," Carter reported. "The fountain has been tested, and is in working order. The playground equipment is finished, and the Christmas tree was brought in yesterday."

Molly shuffled through her papers. "The tree will be decorated tomorrow, and lights will be strung, so it'll be ready for the tree lighting ceremony Friday night, and the parade on Saturday."

Mavis huffed out a sigh. "That's cutting it really close."

"But still in plenty of time," Chelsea said. "We got it all done in time for the holiday parade. I can't wait for everyone to see it."

"I can't wait for Georgia to see it," Samantha said with a wide smile. "She's put so much work into this."

"So true," Cletus said. "Without her, this renovation wouldn't have happened at all."

"We have vendors scheduled to be in place around town square during the holiday parade." Carter turned to Cletus. "You're picking up the flyers from the printer?"

Cletus nodded. "I'll get those on Friday morning so we can hand them out. I saw the draft and they look good. Plus there will be color boards of the project from start to finish in front of town square. I think folks'll be impressed."

"I'm excited—and proud," Mavis said, then turned her attention to Molly. "Molly, don't forget, you're on the parade judging committee."

"Oh, right. I had forgotten about that."

"You need to be in place at nine a.m. in the judge's booth at the corner of Main and Central."

She was actually kind of excited about the parade—about the entire day, especially the debut of the new town square. "I'll be there."

They finished up business, then everyone milled about having coffee and pastries.

"I can't believe she conned you into judging the parade," Chelsea said.

Molly shrugged. "How bad can it be?"

Samantha was there as well, and her gaze shifted between Molly and Chelsea. "We've all been there. It's not pretty."

Chelsea let out a soft snort. "Sam's right. You just wait 'til she tells you who to vote into first place. Then tell me how bad it'll be."

Molly lifted her chin. "My vote can't be swayed. Besides, what can she do to me? Kick me off the parade committee? I won't be here next year."

Samantha laid her hand on Molly's arm. "Oh, Molly. I wish you'd reconsider leaving Hope. We all love having you here again."

"This is true," Chelsea said. "Did I mention we're having a Christmas shopping and wine extravaganza next week?"

Molly gave her a blank stare. "No."

"That's because I just now came up with the idea. And you're invited. It'll be you and me, Megan, Des, Sam, and Emma and Jane. Okay, like everyone. Everyone who's available, anyway."

"Terrific idea," Samantha said. "My shopping list is a mile long and I haven't had time to get out there yet."

Chelsea had a sparkle in her eyes. "It'll be search and destroy, then we'll all get drunk. It doesn't get much more fun than that. Work first, reward second."

Molly laughed. "Sounds intriguing. And potentially inebriating. Count me in."

"Me, too," Samantha said.

"Great," Chelsea said. "I'll text everyone and we'll figure out a day and time."

Carter came up to them. "You ready to go?"

Molly nodded, so she said her goodbyes and they left. She zipped up her coat, happy to slide into Carter's truck so she could turn on the butt warmers once he fired up the engine.

"It's cold," she said. "And it sure feels like it could snow."

"Yeah. Let's hope it holds off until after the parade on Saturday."

She was looking forward to seeing snow, but she understood it could potentially mess up the roads—and the parade, which she was also looking forward to seeing. Being a part of the town square project had been so much fun. She was excited to see it open, to hear and see people's reactions to it.

As she sat there musing about the parade and the town square, she realized that Carter wasn't going in the direction of her house, but taking her to his.

"Kidnapping me?" she asked as he turned down his street.

"Yes. Got a problem with that?"

"No." They hadn't had a moment alone in a while. She was more than ready to be kidnapped.

He pulled into the driveway and turned off the engine. "You're spending the night, unless you have a strong objection."

"Why don't you quit talking about it and take me inside? It's already getting cold out here."

He shot her a look that was pure sexual desire. "You're the one talking."

She opened the door and slid out of the truck. They hurried inside and Carter punched the button to shut the garage door. Molly dropped her purse on the dining room table, peeled off her coat and threw it on the chair, then started down the hall toward the bedroom.

Carter caught her halfway, pinning her against the wall.

His mouth was on hers before she could catch her breath.

This was what she'd wanted, what she'd thought about every day since that night he'd laid a hot kiss on her in his car. She buried her fingers in his hair and moaned against his lips, taking as much as he gave.

His hands slid under her shirt—cold fingers, but she didn't care, since her body flamed hot with desire. And when he cupped her butt and squeezed, angling her body so she could feel exactly how much he wanted her, all she could do was rub against him, anxious energy sizzling through her.

He lifted her shirt off, then popped the clasp on her bra, filling his hands with her breasts. His mouth soon followed, and she felt the frenzy of desire, the need to touch his skin with her hands and her mouth. She unbuckled his belt, drew his zipper down, shoving at his jeans to draw them over his hips.

She slid her fingers inside his boxers and wrapped them around his cock, loving the sound of his groan.

"I've thought about this every night since I put you on my lap in the car," he said, mirroring her thoughts.

"Me, too. I want this, Carter. I want you."

He kissed his way from her breasts to her neck, taking a moment to run his tongue over her throat before taking her mouth again.

Heady passion had her in its grasp, a roller coaster of fevered need. Carter drew her up and carried her the few remaining steps into the bedroom, dumping her none too gently on the bed.

She didn't want gentle. She wanted him.

She kicked off her shoes while he wrestled with the zipper of her jeans, then drew them down her legs. They shed the rest of their clothes and he grabbed a condom, then climbed on to the bed, spread her legs and slid into her, making her cry out from the delicious pleasure.

As he moved within her, he slowed, his gaze meeting hers in a moment of pure tenderness that nearly broke her. She lifted, wanting the raw passion, the animalistic, mindless need, not this heartbreaking emotion that nearly tore her in two.

She closed her eyes, letting the physical sensations carry her away.

But Carter wouldn't allow it.

"Molly. Look at me."

She ignored him for a few seconds, but his movements made her gasp.

"Molly."

She opened her eyes, and it was like drowning in a sea of mesmerizing green.

She was lost, physically and emotionally, and she had no hopes of keeping herself away from him. Not when he was inside her, moving within her, knowing her body as he did. His fingers laced with hers, and he took her right where she needed to go, his eyes never leaving hers as they both came with a fury that made any control she'd hoped to hang on to explode in a million tiny pieces.

And still, he held on to her, as if he was trying to communicate his thoughts, his emotions, without words.

But she couldn't listen. Maybe she didn't want to acknowledge that it was possible he felt something deeper than just this amazing physical force that drew them both together. She focused on the ever-consuming waves of her orgasm, the physicality of it all, the pure thrill of how this man owned her body so completely.

It was all she could allow. Anything else would be devastating to her heart, and she wasn't ready for that yet.

She might never be.

After, he kissed her neck, rolled to the side, allowing them both to catch their breath. Carter left the bed for a moment, then came back, pulling her against him. She laid her head on his chest, listening to his strong heartbeat.

"Give me ten minutes, then we're going for round two."

She lifted her head to stare up at him. "Is there a prerequisite number of times we're doing it tonight?"

He grinned. "Yeah. Until I pass out or can't get it up anymore. We haven't had a lot of time together lately, and I've missed you."

She laughed. "I've missed you, too. And tomorrow's a workday."

"I'll expect you to be on time, too."

She shook her head and lay down again. "My boss is such a dick."

"So I've heard. Want me to kick the shit out of him for you?"

"Would you?"

"Anything for you, babe."

She smiled, then rolled over on top of him to kiss him, hoping she could cut those ten minutes down to five.

Chapter 29

_____

THE DAY OF the Hope holiday parade dawned cold, but snow free. Molly was both happy and sad. Mainly happy for the town and everyone involved in the parade and the town square project.

But there was snow forecast in a few days, so she could still be excited about that.

She'd had to report to the parade center early that morning to meet with the town square committee. She'd gotten up early to have coffee with her parents. Her mom said she was going to come to the parade today, and her father insisted it was going to be in a wheelchair, because there would be too many people around who could potentially bump into her and knock her down. Plus, walking around the house and at therapy was one thing—fatiguing herself at the parade was another.

Despite her mother's protests, Molly sided with her father, and Mom grudgingly agreed to the wheelchair.

She'd hurried down to the parade route to see the town square.

It was beautiful. The fountain was running, the dolphin

was gorgeous, the tiles were amazing, and the playground was perfect. The giant Christmas tree sitting behind the square was a fabulous touch. She couldn't wait to see it lit up tonight after the festival.

She hoped her mother was proud of the final product, since she'd spearheaded the project from the beginning. Molly planned to meet her parents here after the parade.

Speaking of which, she had to get in place at the judge's grandstand. She hurried down the street and around the corner, the brisk walk in the cold air warming her up. She stopped in Megan's shop along the way to grab a very large latte, and she had that in her hand when she arrived at the grandstand, where Mavis waited.

"Oh, good, you're here, Molly. Here's your judging packet. You know, Henderson's Ford is a big contributor to the mayor's campaign. And they always do the best floats. Do you know they win the grand prize every year?"

And so it begins. "Is that right?" she asked as they made their way up the bleacher stairs to the booth.

"It is. The mayor would consider it a personal favor if you'd give them a high vote."

"If they have the best float, they'll get a high mark. I'm sure there are a lot of great floats. On my way over I saw the one that Hope High's science club put together. It looks pretty amazing, too."

Mavis looked flustered. "Yes, yes, I'm sure that one's nice, too. But you know, the mayor is up for reelection this year, and campaign contributors are hard to come by."

Molly looked up at her. "Mavis, you aren't by some chance trying to persuade me to vote a certain way on the mayor's behalf, are you? Because that would certainly be unethical."

She made sure to say it as loud as she could. And since people were starting to fill the stands around them, it caused Mavis's face to turn beet red.

"Of course not. I would never do such a thing."

A few of the other judges arrived, so Mavis gave her a tight smile. "Larry," Mavis said. "How nice to see you. How's it going over at the hardware store? The mayor was just asking about you the other day."

Molly rolled her eyes and sipped her latte. She smiled when Larry took his seat, and introduced herself to him.

"You're Emmett's girl."

"Yes, sir."

"I heard you were back in town. How's your mama doing?"

"Much better, thank you. She intends to come to the parade today."

"I'll be sure to tell my wife. She'll look for her."

After the other judges arrived, they only had to wait about ten more minutes before the Hope Fire and Police Departments got the parade started by leading off with sirens and flashing lights.

She'd missed this parade, missed seeing all the floats and the clowns and the mayor and his wife waving from their fancy car. Then both the high schools and their marching bands with baton twirlers and cheerleaders in front.

She was right about the science club from Hope High— they had put together an amazing float with kids from the club dressed as different forms of colorful bacteria. She loved it, but then maybe she had a soft spot in her heart for the club, since she used to be a member.

· "What a great float," Larry said with a grin on his face.

Okay, so maybe it wasn't just her.

She wasn't all that impressed with the car dealership's float. It was towed by one of their new trucks and had some hot woman on it and a bunch of car sale signs. It looked like they spent a bundle of money on it, but otherwise, it wasn't all that creative. There were many other floats groups had put a lot more time and creativity into, so she scored them all accordingly.

What the other judges thought, she had no idea.

The parade ended, of course, with Santa Claus riding on a float that held his sleigh. Everyone cheered, and Molly finished up her score sheet, then turned it in to the parade committee. The awards would be given out at town square tonight prior to the tree lighting ceremony.

At least her work here was done. She was off to meet her parents.

CARTER FINISHED WATCHING the parade, then wandered around, talking to a few people. He saw Molly climb down from her spot on the judge's booth, so he excused himself to go find her.

She was headed toward the town square, so he picked up his pace and crossed the street to catch up to her.

"Excuse me, miss, but you look familiar."

She stopped, then smiled at him. "Wasn't it a great parade?"

"It was. And did you vote for the mayor's favorite float?"

She laughed. "Well, I gave it a score. I don't think it was the score Mavis wanted me to give it."

"I'm shocked, Molly. No more judging the parade for you."

She slipped her arm in his. "And to think it's now become my favorite holiday tradition. I'm heartbroken."

"Yeah, I'll bet you are."

She saw her parents near the square. "There's my mom and dad. Are your parents here?"

"Yeah. They're supposed to be somewhere near the square, too."

They greeted her parents. Her mom looked plenty warm in her thick coat, hat, and gloves, and Dad had even thought to put a fleece blanket on her lap.

"Did you enjoy the parade?" Carter asked.

"It was great," Emmett said.

Molly sat on the bench next to her mother, who had parked her wheelchair facing the fountain.

"What do you think, Mom?"

Her mom grasped her hand and squeezed it. "Oh, Molly, it turned out even better than I envisioned. Thank you."

"Don't thank me. This was your doing."

"But you stayed and jumped on the committee. You and Carter made sure it got finished. And the playground—a brilliant idea."

"Thanks, Mom."

Carter took a seat next to Molly.

"Thank you, Carter."

"We did it, didn't we Georgia?"

"We sure as hell did. Isn't it fantastic?"

Carter leaned back and surveyed the finished product. "It's amazing. I'm so glad you came up with the idea, Georgia. It's a hell of a beautiful thing."

Carter liked seeing Molly's mom so happy. The two of them had worked hard on this project, and he'd hated that she hadn't been able to finish it. He was glad Molly had taken on the responsibility. He was sure it had given Georgia some comfort knowing her daughter had been involved.

"We couldn't have done this without Molly's help. She's an ass kicker," Carter said.

Georgia beamed a smile. "Well, she is my daughter."

Carter laughed. "That she is."

"I honestly didn't do much, other than back up Carter and keep the meetings on track."

"That's bull. The playground was your idea."

"And it looks wonderful," Georgia said.

"Oh, Carter, this looks amazing."

Molly stood as Carter's parents, Amanda and Robert, came over. It had been so long since she'd seen them.

Amanda was as pretty as she'd always been, with her dark hair cut shorter than she remembered. Robert's hair was a lot grayer now, but he was still a strikingly handsome man—just like his son.

"Thanks, Mom." Carter hugged his mom.

"And Georgia, how are you?"

Amanda sat next to her on the bench.

"I'm doing so much better, Amanda. So nice to see you again. How are you?"

"Good, thank you. I'm so sorry to hear about your accident. But you look amazing. Leave it to you to have a terrible injury and still look gorgeous as always."

Her mom blushed. "Oh, well, Molly's been taking good care of me."

Molly smiled. "I did nothing. My mother has tons of energy and hates being cooped up in the house."

"I know this about her. And what about you, Molly? It's so wonderful seeing you back here in Hope. Will you be staying permanently?"

Molly shifted on the balls of her feet. "Oh, I don't know . . ."

"Mom," Carter said, directing his mother by the elbow, "what do you think of the Christmas tree? Do you think it's big enough? Are you going to stay for the lighting ceremony tonight?"

Carter moved his parents ever so subtly to the tree, and then over to the playground, giving Molly an out from that question.

"People are going to start asking now that I'm recovering," her mother said. "Eventually you're going to have to give them an answer."

She was surprised her mother hadn't asked. But her mom knew her better than most people.

"I don't have an answer, Mom. I don't know. You know what my life has been like all these years. I've gotten sort of used to it."

"Which doesn't mean you can't stay." Her mother grasped her hand and squeezed it. "I've gotten used to seeing your face all the time. And you have a job here. You could get a nice apartment and give it a try for a while."

"Maybe. We'll see."

Even as she said the words, she felt walls closing in on her, and that familiar sense of needing to flee.

But that was the norm, what typically happened whenever one of her bosses offered her a raise or a promotion. It meant permanence.

And Molly just didn't do permanent.

Chapter 30

"OKAY, WE'RE ON a quest tonight," Chelsea said, a fierce gleam in her eyes. She dug into her purse and pulled out her phone. "In here, I have my list. How about the rest of you?"

They stood just inside the entrance to the mall in Tulsa. Molly, Chelsea, Emma, Jane, Samantha, and Megan. A small band of weary but determined women, armed and ready to shop.

"I'm sorry Des can't be here," Emma said.

"Yeah, but she's not sorry, since she and Logan are off on a two-week cruise in the Caribbean for the holidays," Chelsea said. "It was such a sweet surprise Logan gave to Des as an early Christmas gift. We're all going to take a few seconds to be supremely jealous of them."

Jane sighed. "Can you imagine? Multiple ports of call, lots of sun and sand, and all that time for hot sex every day, with no kids to knock on the door saying, 'Mom? What are you and Dad doing in there with the bedroom door locked?' "

Everyone looked at Jane, who squirmed. "Okay, so maybe Will and I need a vacation without kids."

Emma laughed. "You definitely do. You should make that a priority after the new year."

"I agree," Chelsea said. "Emma and I are going to bug you about it, and we'll even help with the babysitting and dog sitting. Now, everyone ready?"

"I'm as ready as I'm ever going to be," Jane said. "I've gotten stuff for the kids, but I haven't shopped for Will yet. Why are men so hard to buy for?"

"Because whatever they want, they go out and get for themselves," Emma said, wrinkling her nose. "I asked Luke for a list. Do you know what he told me he wanted?"

"A new gun?" Samantha offered.

Emma laughed. "No. Socks. The one thing he doesn't buy for himself. Does he honestly think the only thing I'm buying him for Christmas is socks? The man is delusional."

"You could buy him some sexy and slinky lingerie and put yourself under the tree," Chelsea said as they made their way past the food court and toward the first store they'd targeted.

"I like the way Chelsea thinks," Megan said. "But that's probably because neither of us is having sex with anyone."

"Hey," Chelsea said. "Speak for yourself."

Megan stopped. "Okay. Who are you currently having sex with?"

Chelsea lifted her chin, then shrugged. "No one. That's why I have all the sex ideas."

Molly laughed and shook her head. "I have a list. I've bought a few things for my parents. And for my lovely sister over there."

"Yay," Emma said with a grin.

"But I still have a few things to get."

"Like something for your hot boyfriend?" Samantha asked.

"Okay, yeah. Something for Carter might be nice. But he's not my boyfriend."

They stopped at the bath and body store. Everyone looked around. "I could go in there," Chelsea said, "but it would just be for me."

"I could use some body lotion," Megan said.

Samantha nodded. "Me, too."

"I need lip balm," Emma added.

Thirty minutes later, they came out of the bath and body store, with bags filled with non-gifts.

"That was fun, but not very productive," Chelsea said. "Maybe we'll have better luck at the next store."

"I think we should split up," Molly suggested. "Compare lists, and see what stores we all have to go to. Otherwise, we could be here all night. And who wants that?"

She was not a shopper. She liked to pop in, get what she needed, and get the hell out.

"Well, it's probably more productive," Chelsea said, "but not nearly as much fun as it would be if we stayed in a group."

"I'm with Molly," Samantha said. "This is a chore, the mall is crowded, and I need to get this list done."

In the end, they agreed to split up. Molly and Samantha had similar lists, so they headed off to one of the major department stores together. They had two hours before they were all going to meet up again.

"My grandmother needs new pajamas, though if you ask her, she thinks the old raggedy ones are still perfectly suitable."

Molly laughed. "That's because she's stubborn. And from the Depression era, where they used items until they fell apart."

"This is true."

They wandered the nightwear aisle, and Samantha found a really nice pair of warm and pretty mint green pajamas.

"I think she'll love those," Molly said. "I would love those, though I have to admit, I'm fond of these with the dinosaurs on them."

Samantha laughed. "I like those, too. But I think I'll get these green ones. And the purple ones with the daisies on them as well. Now to hunt down some socks for her, and that should take care of Grandma."

While Samantha wandered the sock aisle, Molly found a sweater that would look amazing on Samantha. Since she knew Sam's grandmother couldn't get out much to shop, and since Samantha's parents were gone, there was no one around to buy gifts for her, so Molly bought the sweater and tucked it in her bag. She also found a blouse for her mom, and a sweatshirt she knew her dad would love.

Then it was on to the next store on their lists.

Two hours later they met up at the mall entrance, then headed over to the sushi place and had dinner.

Molly was stuffed by the time they left, so Chelsea suggested they stop at one of the nearby dance clubs and work off dinner.

"Are you kidding?" Megan said as they stood outside the restaurant. "My feet are killing me from wandering around the mall. "How about we go sit somewhere and drink?"

"I'm with Megan," Emma said.

Chelsea sighed. "You all have no stamina. Fine. Where would you like to go?"

"How about Bash's bar?" Jane suggested. "That way we're all closer to home."

"I agree with that," Molly said.

They convoyed over to No Hope At All. It was busy for a Saturday night, to be expected since Bash's place was where everyone gathered to drink, watch sports on the big-screen televisions, and play pool.

Tonight, basketball and hockey were prevalent. Chelsea wrangled them a large table near the back by the wall, which was perfect and out of the line of fire, since it was rowdy tonight.

"I'll get us drinks since the waitresses look slammed," Chelsea said. "I've decided we should all start with a holiday martini. Any objections?"

They all looked at each other.

"None here," Molly said.

"Great. I'll be right back."

"Does Bash even know how to make whatever fancy martini Chelsea has in mind?" Samantha asked.

"If not, I'm sure she'll educate him. Or go behind the bar and do it herself," Megan said with a smirk.

Emma laughed. "This is true."

"I'm so glad you objected to going dancing, Megan," Jane said. "I don't know where Chelsea gets all her energy, but between running after the kids and doing everything to get ready for the holidays, I was exhausted after three hours at the mall."

Emma nodded. "I'm not a shopping person on the best of days. During the holidays? It's the worst."

Molly stayed silent while they all complained of long lists and sore feet. Her feet hurt, too, but if she were honest with herself, this had been the best holiday she'd had in years. Normally, she shopped alone and shipped gifts home, received packages from her family, then spent Christmas Day eating a small turkey breast she'd prepared for herself while she watched all the holiday movies. She'd swear to herself she wasn't lonely and loved her life, but Christmas was always the worst day of the year for her.

She'd spent every Christmas alone for the past twelve years. By her own choice, of course, but still, shopping with all these women had been an absolute blast. Spending time with them over the past months had been wonderful. She'd renewed old friendships and made new ones.

She was going to miss all of them when she left.

At least this year she'd spend Christmas at home, making memories she could cherish for years to come.

"Drinks for everyone." Chelsea balanced a tray, pulling drinks off one by one.

"This looks amazing, Chelsea," Jane said.

Molly had to agree. Whatever was in there was a dark pink and looked delicious.

"Thanks. Well, Bash made them. It turns out there is no drink he hasn't heard of before or can't make. And here I thought he was just a beer and hard liquor guy. Damn him."

Molly laughed, then took a sip. "It's a great martini. Is that pomegranate I taste in this?"

Chelsea put the tray aside, then lifted her glass to take a drink. "Yes. Pomegranate vodka and peach schnapps."

Emma took a sip, then licked her lips. "Oh, yum."

"Yum is right," Megan said. "I love this."

They had their drinks, and then discussion turned to work life as well as personal.

"Settling into married life now, Emma?" Megan asked.

Emma beamed a smile. "Perfectly. Not that much changed, really. We just went from cohabitating with different names, to doing it with the same name. And a lot of paperwork changes to go with it. But honestly, we're more in love every day."

"Nauseatingly romantic, you two," Chelsea said, taking a long swallow of her martini. "You and Jane both. It's all blah blah blah love and sex, all the time."

"I'll drink to that," Samantha said, clinking her glass against Chelsea's. Megan clinked as well.

"You say that now," Jane said. "Only because some hot guy hasn't come into your lives and lit your panties on fire." Jane blinked. "And I can't believe I just said that."

Emma laughed. "I can."

Jane turned to Molly. "Okay, subject change. Molly, how's it going with Carter?"

"It's going good. I've ordered new computer software. That's being installed next week and I think it'll be a much more efficient system. Plus we're moving to a new server that will link all the shops. I think Carter's going to be very happy, once everyone's up to speed on the changes, but it's a user-friendly system, so I don't think the learning curve will be great."

"Awesome," Emma said. "But I think what Jane really meant was how are things going between you and Carter on the personal front."

"Oh. We're fine."

"In other words," Megan said, "Molly doesn't want to share all the dirty details about how Carter lights her panties on fire."

"Aww, come on, Molly," Chelsea said. "You have to share the details with those of us not getting any."

Molly stirred her martini. "Everything's fine. We're just friends, you know."

She caught the look from Emma across the table, and continued to stir her drink. But she was going to stay silent on her relationship with Carter. How could she talk about something she didn't even understand herself?

Besides, they were just friends. And occasional bed partners. Nothing else.

Before long, one martini turned into two, though some of the women moved on to sodas and sparkling water.

Molly had definitely had her fill of alcohol after two drinks, deciding someone had to be the designated driver. She'd noticed Jane had switched to soda as well. Chelsea, however, had decided to challenge Bash on his drink-making skills, eventually moving over to the bar. They all decided to do the same so they could have a front-row seat for the epic challenge.

Bash—such a damn fine-looking man—leaned his forearms across the bar and leveled a sexy, pirate's smile at Chelsea.

"You do realize this is my job, Chelsea. You aren't going to be able to come up with a drink I can't make."

Chelsea shot one across the bow.

"And I've done my share of barhopping, Mr. Know-It-All Bartender," Chelsea said. She drummed her nails on the bar, giving Bash the death stare.

"A Manhattan," she finally said.

Bash pinned her with a glare.

"Isn't that a fairly common drink?" Megan asked.

Bash got out a glass. "Yeah, but it's a tough one, because every customer likes theirs different, and the combination of ingredients can really screw it up if you're not paying close attention."

He fixed the drink, then handed it to Chelsea. She'd been taking at least two good-sized swallows of every drink he made—and paying for them, as well. At least she sipped water in between his trips to take care of other customers.

She was starting to sway a little bit on the barstool, though.

"Are you doing okay, Chelsea?" Molly asked.

She grinned. "I'm great. Getting a little toasted, though, because I'm mixing alcohol. But that's okay. Bash is like every woman's big brother and he'll make sure I'm well taken care of."

Bash, who'd disappeared from behind the bar and into one of the storerooms, showed up just then, spun Chelsea around to face him, pinned her with his hands on either side of the bar, then whispered something in her ear that caused her eyes to go wide and her cheeks to go almost as red as her hair.

Then he pulled back, gave her the kind of slow, sexy smile that had even Molly blushing, and walked back around behind the bar.

"What the hell was that all about?" Emma asked.

Chelsea shuddered in a breath, then turned back around to face the bar. "Oh. Nothing. He just told me to be careful with my alcohol intake, and if I needed a ride home he'd make sure I . . ."

They all waited.

"He'd make sure you what?" Jane asked.

She swallowed, brushed her hair away from her face.

Bash showed up right then.

"I just told her that like the good *big brother* I am to all the ladies, I'd make sure she was well taken care of."

Chelsea cleared her throat. "You know what? I think I've had enough to drink. It's probably time for me to go home."

Bash gave her a smirk. "Is someone driving you home, Chelsea?"

She was still looking at Bash when she nodded. "Yes. Uh . . . Jane will."

Jane blinked. "Of course I will."

Bash started to clear the glasses, but kept his gaze on Chelsea. "Have a good evening ladies. Drive safely."

Molly had no idea what Bash had said to Chelsea, but whatever it was must have been . . . very interesting.

She could still feel the heat that had flamed between them all the way outside into the cold.

Very interesting, indeed.

CARTER WAS IN his garage working on Rhonda when he heard a car pull into the driveway. He swiped his hand across his face, no idea what time it was, except it was late.

He punched the button to lift the garage door and saw Molly getting out of her car. She hurried into the garage and he put the door down. It had snowed the other day, and she lifted her feet to get around the pile he'd shoveled in the driveway.

"This is a nice surprise. I didn't expect to see you tonight," he said as he grabbed a shop rag to wipe his hands.

"I know. I tried calling you and you didn't answer, so I thought I'd drive by to see if you were home. Your lights were on . . ."

He had to admit that he liked that she stopped by. She looked pretty in her skintight jeans, sweater and scarf, and those boots that made her legs look a mile long.

"Yeah, I kind of lost track of time after I started changing fluids out here."

She swiped her fingers across his cheek. "You look sexy covered in motor oil."

He laughed, looking down at his white T-shirt, which was now streaked with black. "Yeah, doing a few tweaks to Rhonda. Wasn't tonight your big night out with all the women?"

"Yes. We went shopping, out to dinner, and finished the night off at Bash's bar."

"I see." He leaned against the front fender. "Did you have fun?"

"I did. And how about you?"

"Rhonda and I are having a great time. Missed you, though."

"I missed you, too. By the way, there were some serious sparks flying between Chelsea and Bash tonight."

He stilled. "Chelsea and Bash? Really? They're not dating."

"I don't think dating was on either of their minds. I think it was just a little drunken flirting on Chelsea's part. Or maybe she wasn't flirting. No idea what was going on, but whoever was in the general vicinity was going up in flames from the hot signals Bash was throwing out."

Carter laughed. "Well, Bash likes the ladies. It doesn't mean anything."

"Either way, it made me wish I was with you, which probably had a lot to do with me showing up here. I hope you don't mind."

"Why would I mind? I said I missed being with you. Though I'm a little too dirty to show my appreciation at the moment."

"Oh, I don't know," she said, moving into him, nestling her body up against his. "Did I mention the smell of motor oil is a huge turn-on for me?"

Unable to resist, he grasped her hips, digging his fingers into the denim of her jeans as his body reacted to her. "Is that right?"

"Yes." She curled her fingers around the nape of his neck, then pressed a kiss to the side of his throat. "A huge turn-on. Like . . . gets me hot instantly."

He was already hard. "I'm going to get you dirty, Molly."

She pulled her scarf off. "That's okay." She pulled up his T-shirt and snaked her fingers over his stomach. "I like dirty."

His tangled his fingers into her hair and gave her a raw, hungry kiss that made him shudder with need.

He'd been thinking about her tonight while he'd worked on the car, had wished she'd been there with him, was damn glad she was here now so he could breathe in her sweet scent, feel the way her lips moved against him, and run his hands over the soft curves of her body.

He turned her around, cupping her neck and pushing her hair to the side so he could kiss the back of her neck, so damn satisfied when she moaned. He swept his hand over her body, needing to touch every part of her, starting with her beautiful back, and ending with squeezing her sweetly shaped ass.

"Are you cold out here?" he asked.

"No. I'm hot."

"Good. Wait right here." He placed her hands, palm down, on the fender of his car. "Don't move."

He dashed into the house, scrubbed the grease off his hands with soap and hot water, grabbed a condom, and came back, stopping at the doorway to see her, watching him, her hair swept over one shoulder, her butt tilted at an upward angle. She gave him a wickedly sexy smile.

She was waiting for him.

And he was ready for her. He came up behind her, smoothing his hand over the curve of her butt. "You have a great ass, Molly. I love to walk behind you and look at it."

"And you have great hands. Why don't you use them on

me?" She straightened and undid the button of her jeans, then unzipped them.

"I'd be more than happy to." He pulled her back against his chest, sliding his hand over her sweater to cup her breasts. Even through the sweater and her bra he could feel the tight buds of her nipples, teased and stroked them until she rubbed her butt against his erection.

It was at times like this he felt it was his God-given right as a man to touch this woman, that they'd been meant for each other. No one had ever made him feel the things Molly made him feel, had ever moved him to want as much as he wanted whenever he was with her.

He shifted his hands lower, lifting her sweater to get at the soft skin of her stomach, then dipped his hand inside her jeans, under her panties.

She was hot, damp, and ready for him, melting all over his fingers as he teased and coaxed her body. He'd known her for what felt like his entire life, knew what she liked and how, and it was a little bit of heaven to feel her arch and tremble as she tightened around him, her entire body tensing with her orgasm.

He held her as she rode it out, then pulled down her jeans and unzipped his and put on the condom. He bent her over his car and took a moment to fully appreciate the beauty of the woman before him, before snugging up against her and easing inside.

She lifted, then said, "Carter," in a soft whisper that tightened his balls and made him thrust deeper. With every plunge he wanted to be so much a part of her he didn't know where he ended and Molly began.

God, she was beautiful like this, pushing back against him, raw and untamed, her cries of completion tearing into him, through him, until a groan tore from his throat and he followed with his own orgasm.

He held on to the car with one hand, his other arm wrapped around Molly. She'd shattered him. She always had.

He closed his eyes, listening to her breathe, feeling the pounding of her pulse and the way their bodies fit together.

It was something he'd never taken time for when they were younger.

Now, it was just goddamned perfect.

They pulled apart and righted their clothes, then went inside to clean up. He took a quick shower and threw on a T-shirt and sweats.

"Do you want something to drink?" he asked as they settled into the living room.

"I'm a little dehydrated from the alcohol I had earlier," she said as she pulled off her boots, wiggling her toes to stretch. "How about some water?"

He fixed them both drinks, then brought them into the living room. Molly had already stretched out on the sofa, pulling a blanket from the back. She held it open for him and he snuggled in beside her.

She grabbed the remote and flipped the television on, found a movie, then inched beside him, resting her head on his chest. He put his arm around her.

Within about ten minutes, she was asleep.

Well, hell. This was even better. A night spent working on his favorite car, followed up by a surprise visit from his woman, and some mind-blowing sex. To top it off, said favorite woman was now asleep in his arms on the sofa.

He loved her. He paused to reflect on that, waiting for the panic and the doubt.

No panic, no doubt, which shouldn't come as a surprise to him. After all these years, she still had his heart, and he didn't know how to tell her without making her run like hell in the other direction.

Even worse, he didn't know how to get her to stay.

Chapter 31

———————

CHRISTMAS DAY WAS a blur of activity for Molly, from having hot chocolate with her parents Christmas morning, to spending time with her mom and Emma.

Emma and Luke—and their dogs, Boomer, Daisy, and Annie, had shown up midmorning for brunch, so they'd all spent time in the kitchen together cooking.

It was so different from the Christmases she'd had over the past twelve years. To be with her mom and sister making homemade cinnamon rolls—a family tradition on Christmas Day—was special. She'd really missed this, maybe more than she'd allowed herself to admit.

When the doorbell rang around eleven and she found Carter there, she was even more surprised.

"I thought we were meeting later."

"Yeah, but I changed my mind. Besides, I have gifts for everyone."

"Oh. That's so nice, Carter." He was constantly surprising her, and warming her heart with the way he treated her family. They had planned to meet at his house later tonight, when it was just the two of them—alone. To know that he'd taken the time to bring gifts for her family was just so . . .

Him.

She didn't know why she was surprised about anything thoughtful he did.

Why did he have to be so damn sweet? Couldn't he be a jerk every now and then? He was making this so hard on her.

And that thought was simply ridiculous and set her off in a way that confused her.

Which was also ridiculous, but there it was.

"Carter," her mother said, greeting him as he walked in and shed his coat. "I'm so glad to see you. Merry Christmas."

"Same to you, Georgia." He kissed her cheek. "Do I smell cinnamon rolls?"

Her mom smiled and slid her arm in his. "You do. And coffee. Are you hungry?"

"Well, my mom did fix breakfast early this morning, but I've had your homemade cinnamon rolls before, and I'm not going to turn them down if you're offering."

"I am."

They headed into the dining room.

"Molly, pour Carter a cup of coffee, will you?"

Molly sighed. "Sure."

Not at all the way she had planned the day, but whatever. He sat at the table downing two cinnamon rolls while he chatted with Luke and her dad, so she busied herself in the kitchen prepping lunch with her sister while her mom rested her leg.

"You seem . . . irritated," Emma said.

"Me? Not at all." She took out her non-irritation on the celery and onions she was slicing for the stuffing.

"Are you mad that Carter showed up?"

"We were going to have a mini-Christmas alone at his place tonight."

"But he's here now, Molly. Isn't it nice that he took time away from his family to be with you?"

"Yes. It's great."

She had *no* idea what was wrong with her.

Then they all opened presents, talking excitedly over each other, looking to see what everyone got. Her mom had snuck out to go shopping and had gotten her a beautiful set of new luggage.

"Not that I want you to use them, mind you," her mom said. "But that stuff you dragged in when you got here had seen better days."

Molly laughed and hugged her parents.

Emma got her a pair of earrings with shiny blue sapphires.

"I love these, Em. Thank you."

"I was going to wait for this until later when we're alone, but I want you to open it now," Carter said, handing her a gift bag.

"Okay. It's not lingerie, is it?" she asked, eyeing her parents.

He laughed. "No. Definitely not lingerie."

She sifted through the tissue paper, and pulled out an envelope, opened it up, then read the contents and looked up at him. "Airline tickets?"

"For New Year's Eve. To Las Vegas. I booked us into the Venetian, and we're going to see a show, then bring in the new year at one of the clubs."

"Oh, Moll, that sounds like so much fun," Emma said.

"What a wonderful gift, Carter," her mom said.

Molly didn't know what to think. New Year's was a week away. But still, a trip? Together?

It was sounding more and more like something a couple would do. A couple in a relationship.

She looked up at him and forced a smile. "It's great. Thank you."

"You've been working really hard. I thought a getaway for both of us was a good idea. And we'll take a couple extra days to hang out and have some fun."

"Sounds . . . awesome."

She brushed her lips against his. "Thank you."

"You're welcome."

"I'll give you your gift later."

He waggled his brows. "It is lingerie, isn't it?" he whispered.

She rolled her eyes. "No."

They ate and talked and cooked, then ate some more. All in all, it was a perfect day. Even better, her mother was completely comfortable moving around the house now, since her casts had been shortened even more. She was doing so well, and Molly couldn't be happier for her. In a couple of weeks she'd be cast free and starting a new form of therapy to work her muscles now that her bones were mostly healed.

While Carter, Luke, her mom, and her dad played cards in the dining room, Molly and Emma sat in the kitchen together.

"A trip to Vegas, Molly. Aren't you excited?"

"Sure. Yes, definitely. I've never been there."

"One of the few places you haven't lived, right?"

She laughed. "This is true." She took a sip of rum-spiced eggnog.

"I like you and Carter together. He's good for you."

Molly's gaze drifted into the dining room, where Carter looked perfectly comfortable with her parents and her brother-in-law. "Yeah. He's a good guy."

"Even with everything that happened in the past, it looks like you and Carter have reconnected. You seem happy."

She shifted her gaze back to Emma. "Do I?"

"Yes. Happier than I've seen you in a long time, Moll."

She hadn't taken the time to think about it, hadn't allowed herself to dwell on how she felt about Carter—or about being back in Hope again. "Things have been going well, and mainly I'm just so relieved about Mom."

Emma's gaze turned to their mother. "Yes. I'm very happy Mom has recovered so well. But I don't think Mom is the sole reason for your happiness, is she?"

Molly shrugged. "I don't know. I haven't given it a lot of thought."

Emma slid her hand across the table and took Molly's. "Maybe it's time you started thinking about it. About you and Carter. Make some decisions about your future."

She gently pulled her hand away. "I don't know, Em. I'm pretty much a live-in-the-moment kind of woman."

Emma frowned. "You're not thinking of leaving, are you?"

"Today? Of course not."

"You know what I mean, Molly. You're happy here. And Carter? It's obvious how he feels about you."

Was it? She didn't know. They'd been having fun together, but they shared a past that had been fraught with difficulties and hurts that Molly couldn't forget about.

She had no crystal ball that could see into the future and guarantee she'd never be hurt again, that Carter would always be there for her.

For right now, everything was fine.

As far as tomorrow? Who knew? She certainly didn't. She'd lived through enough pain and had no desire to go through it ever again. It was much easier to play it safe.

After Emma and Luke took off to spend the rest of the day with Martha and Ben, Molly went upstairs to change clothes, then followed Carter over to his house.

They were barely inside the door when he pulled her against him and gave her a body-warming kiss that sizzled away the cold from outside. Even her toes tingled.

"I've wanted to do that all day," he said.

She couldn't deny the warmth of his kiss, the tender emotion it evoked. "Well. Merry Christmas to you, too.".

He fixed them drinks, then they settled into the living room. Carter had turned on his Christmas tree lights. It looked good. He wasn't going to buy one since he said it was just him, but she'd insisted. Even she owned a tiny Christmas tree that she put up in her apartment. It just wasn't Christmas without one. He'd relented, so then they had to go get decorations. His mother had given him a few of his childhood ornaments as well. Now it sparkled in his front window. Perfect.

"I forgot to ask you how it went at your parents' this morning?" she asked.

"Good. I got socks," he said with a grin.

She rolled her eyes.

"And a new socket wrench set, which I needed."

"Glad to hear that you got guy things."

She pulled the gift she'd gotten for him out of her purse. "I have something for you."

His brows rose as he took the gift from her, then looked over at her. "Is it more socks?"

"You have a thing for socks. I can tell."

"It means doing less laundry."

She laughed. "No. It's not socks. Sorry."

"This is great, Molly. Thank you."

"You haven't opened it yet."

He looked down at the package. "Oh, right. The wrapping is nice."

"God, Carter, there's not a gold bar in there. Just open it already."

He shot her a grin. "Come on, Moll. Where's your sense of anticipation?"

"And why aren't you immediately tearing into the package? Clearly you do it all wrong."

"I like that we're different in so many ways."

She shook her head. "That's great. Now open your present."

"Okay." He slit open the wrapping at one end— carefully, too.

It was all coming back to her now, all the holidays and birthdays where she had to bite her tongue and wait patiently for him to open a present. But he finally got through the wrapping to the box, and opened it, then stared at the framed photograph inside.

He lifted it out and laid it in his lap. "Molly. Where did you find this?"

"I was moving some old photo albums at my parents', and sat down to go through them. One of the albums was mine. I remembered that I took that photo of you."

Carter stared down at the picture of him leaning against his first car, an '87 Honda Civic. The photo was taken of him at the auto shop in Hope, when he'd first started working there when he was sixteen. Back when Mo Bennett still owned the place.

A lifetime ago. His first start.

He ran his fingers across the picture. He'd been so young. Skinny, before he'd gathered up some muscle. He looked like a punk, all smirk and attitude, his arms folded across his chest, his ankles crossed as he looked at Molly.

He lifted his gaze to her. "Thank you for this."

"You're welcome. I had it blown up and framed. I figured you might want to put it in your office at the shop in Hope."

"I will. It means a lot to me to have it." He leaned over and brushed his lips across hers.

"It was either that or socks," she whispered.

He laughed. "Well, this is much better than socks, and you know what a fan I am of those."

He laid the photo down, then went to the tree, grabbing a small box from underneath it.

"This is for you."

"You already gave me a gift." Her eyes widened at the size.

"This is more . . . personal," he said, his eyes glittering with amusement.

She looked down at the box, then at him. "I hope these are earrings or something."

"I guess you'll have to open the box to see."

Carter couldn't wait to see her reaction to the gift.

She unwrapped the package, saw the black velvet jewelry box inside, and lifted her gaze to his.

He saw panic in her eyes. Okay, he'd thought it was funny. Clearly, she didn't.

He tried smiling at her, to ease the tension. She wasn't buying it.

"Carter."

"Just open the box, Molly."

Her hands were shaking as she lifted the lid on the box.

Inside, on the soft black velvet, was a key.

She exhaled, then looked over at him. "What is this?"

"I figured you were tired of standing outside in the cold, so it's a key to my house."

"Oh."

"You know, so anytime you want to pop over, you can just use the key to get inside."

She lifted the key. "This is . . . great. Thanks."

Yeah, he could tell she was underwhelmed. Maybe a little shocked. But he had to take those first steps, go slow, if he was ever going to get anywhere with her.

"You know you already keep some of your things here when you spend the night. And eventually, with your mom getting back on her feet, you're going to want to think about where you want to stay after—she's all better."

She lifted her gaze to his, the key lying like a poisonous snake in the open palm of her hand. "What are you saying?"

All the wrong things, obviously. "That maybe you might want to consider this your secondary home, until you find another place to live."

She held the key in the open palm of her hand like it was something toxic. "Oh."

Okay, maybe this hadn't been a good idea after all.

"Hey, no pressure, ya know? If you don't want to use it, you don't have to. And you can hang out at your parents forever. Or not forever. You're free to do whatever you want, Molly. I just wanted to give you another option."

He wanted to tell her he loved her, that he wanted her to move in with him, stay with him. But the look of stricken panic on her face stopped him, so he reined in the urge.

She finally closed her fingers over the key. "I appreciate this so much, Carter. Thank you for opening your home to me."

She was being so . . . polite, and so quiet, like she was choosing each of her words carefully.

He shrugged. "Hey, no big deal, you know? Since you already had a toothbrush, shampoo, and underwear here, I figured you might want a key."

She finally dropped her shoulders and laughed. "I can see your point." She scooted closer. "And thanks for Las Vegas."

"I'm looking forward to Vegas," he said, trying to jolt her out of whatever shock or funk she'd experienced. "I'm ready to play some blackjack."

"Really. So, you're a gambler. How did I not know this about you?"

"I've taken a few trips to Vegas over the years."

"Have you. And did you win money?"

"Won some, lost some."

"How . . . enlightening. You're like this man of mystery. I can picture you at the blackjack tables."

"And craps tables, too. Wait 'til you see me in Vegas. You might be surprised."

She smiled at him now, and he was relieved.

"I look forward to you surprising me."

He pulled her onto his lap. "Hey, there are still a lot of things you don't know about me, babe."

He pressed his lips to hers and hoped things were on the right track now.

Chapter 32

IT WAS THE day before New Year's Eve, and since Christmas, Molly had dived back into work, keeping her mind occupied, trying not to think about the upcoming trip with Carter.

Her mom was doing great and didn't need her at all anymore. Next week she'd get her casts off and she was talking about going back to work, since she could fit in physical therapy around her job, plus she was already driving again since her casts didn't get in the way.

The new server and computer system installation was flowing smoothly at work, and she'd conducted training for all of the managers. She'd worked out the kinks in the system, and so far, so good. The new system was lightning fast, and she'd linked all of the vital information so Carter could access everything he needed on-the-go on his tablet. It allowed him to be more mobile than in the past, freeing him up to visit all his sites as often as he wanted to. Eventually, he'd even have a little spare time to work in the shop if he wanted.

She'd streamlined his operation, and while there were a lot more things she could do—like work on sales and marketing—he was in much better shape operationally than when she'd started.

Now, she sat on the bed, her shiny new luggage opened as she prepared to pack for Las Vegas.

She'd studied the empty suitcases for about an hour, and couldn't bring herself to put clothes in them, which was kind of a dilemma, because she was due over at Carter's house in a few hours.

She looked up at the knock on her door. Her mom, probably.

"Come in."

She was surprised to see her sister.

"Hey, Emma."

"Can I come in?"

"Sure. What are you doing here?"

"I thought I'd drop by and say goodbye before you left on your trip. I see you're packing." Emma took a seat on the side of the bed.

"Yeah. Or, thinking about packing anyway."

"Do you need some help?"

"No. Not really." She glanced over at all her open drawers, already having made her decision. Now all she had to do was muster up the courage to tell everyone.

Emma looked over at the open drawers as well, then the suitcases before her gaze drifted back to Molly. "You're not going to Vegas with Carter, are you?"

When Molly didn't answer, Emma's shoulders slumped. "Oh, Molls, you're leaving."

She supposed this was a good place to start. "It's time for me to go, Em. Mom's fine and doesn't need me anymore. I've already stayed long enough."

"Why? Did Carter do something?"

"No." She took a step back. "He gave me the key to his house."

Emma gave her a confused look. "And that's a bad thing?"

Molly cocked her head to the side, realizing that sounded a little ridiculous. "You don't understand, Em."

"No, I don't. He loves you. He's always loved you. The two of you are perfect together."

"We aren't perfect. I mean, yeah, it's good right now, but we hurt each other before. It's only a matter of time before it happens again."

"I thought you two talked things through."

She shrugged. "We put the past behind us. Sort of. But is it ever really gone?"

"So you're judging a potential future with Carter based on the past between you?"

She looked down at her hands. "Sometimes you just can't go back."

Emma leaned over, grabbed Molly's hands, forcing her to make eye contact. "And sometimes, my sweet sister, you have to let the past go so you can make a future for yourself. No one knows that better than I do."

"I know what happened to you in your past, and how hard you fought to get through it so you could make a future. But your situation was entirely different from mine. Carter *is* part of my past. I have to let him go."

"You did. For all these years you let him go. You let go of your home, and everyone you knew. Did it help? Did you move forward with your life? With relationships?"

She lifted her chin. "I've been doing fine."

"You've been running away from your memories all these years, Molly, instead of facing down the past and coming to terms with it. That's not growth, that's not putting the past behind you. That's shoving it into a closet and hoping it doesn't throw that door open and scare the shit out of you in the middle of the night. That's not how you deal with it. And this," she said, sweeping her hands over the open suitcases. "Running again isn't how you deal with those feelings, either."

Molly put her hand over her stomach, trying to quell the nausea she felt from her sister's accusations.

She wasn't running, she was simply . . . resuming her life.

"I like moving around. I start to feel unsettled if I stay in one place too long."

"This isn't 'one place,' Moll. This is your home. Where you're surrounded by everyone who loves you. If you ever have any hope of making a future, then you have to stand your ground, confront the past, and demand the future you want."

Tears pricked her eyes. She was going to miss Emma so much. "I love you, Em. But I still have to go."

Emma sighed. "I love you, too, Molly. But sometimes I want to shake you really hard so you'll listen to reason."

Molly stood, unable to continue this conversation. Otherwise, Emma might just be able to get her to change her mind. And that she couldn't do. "Well, I've gotta pack."

Emma stood, too, tears rolling down her cheeks. It was like a knife in Molly's heart to see them there.

"Have you told Mom and Dad yet?"

Molly shook her head. "Not yet."

Emma pulled her into her arms and hugged her tight. "Please don't go. Please rethink this."

Now the tears threatened to fall, but Molly refused to cry. She sniffed, holding it all back. She'd cry later, when she was alone. "I have to."

"I love you so much, Molls. I'm always going to be here for you, no matter what."

Without looking at her, Emma fled the room.

Shaking, Molly turned and faced the luggage again. This time, she went to the drawers and started packing.

Chapter 33

TICKETS, CHECK. MONEY, in wallet.

Carter was packed and ready. Now all he needed was his sexy, beautiful, smart woman to show up at the door.

When he heard the choking, gasping sound of her car, he shook his head and smiled, waiting for her to use her new key to open the door.

He frowned when she rang the doorbell. Maybe she forgot it.

He knew as soon as he opened the door and saw her red-rimmed eyes that she'd been crying. Something inside him told him he knew why.

He stood aside when she walked in. She was wearing old jeans, tennis shoes, and a sweater, her hair pulled up in a ponytail, and he'd wager everything she owned was piled up in George's trunk.

"You're leaving," he said.

She turned around, gave him a clipped nod.

"It's . . . time for me to go."

Her words stabbed like a dagger in his chest.

He crossed his arms. "You're going to have to do better than that, Molly."

She drew in a shuddering breath. "You know it can't work between us, Carter. We have an insurmountable past that I can't see us getting through. It's been fun between us the last few months, but it's not a permanent thing. There's just too much history between us."

He cocked a brow. "History being three years of loving each other in high school, of committing to being together forever?"

"And an unplanned pregnancy, a miscarriage, and an ugly breakup."

"See, that's the difference between you and me. That's the only part of our relationship you chose to remember. The bad. I remembered how great we were together, how much fun we had, how we couldn't wait until we saw each other, how we couldn't get enough of each other. I remembered the plans we made for our future together."

"Plans that were derailed when I got pregnant."

"Right. And that sucked. And your miscarriage was awful. Not just for you, Molly, but for me, too. You were so busy feeling shitty and miserable and devastated and crushed, I wasn't allowed to feel anything because you had to feel and say everything. And then when I got over my shock that you lost our baby, you had already played judge, jury, and executioner on our relationship, and you were already gone."

She blinked, but didn't say anything.

"And now, you've decided this relationship isn't going to work, without discussing it with me. Because God forbid you and I should have an honest discussion about anything, right? All these months I've tiptoed around you, not wanting to do anything to upset the balance of what we had going. I was happy enough just to be with you again, see where things could go between us, let our feelings for each other lead the way.

"But you know what? That's not gonna work for me anymore. I'm not going to let you walk out on me again without you knowing that I love you. Hell, I've always loved you. I don't know about you, Molly, but loving someone isn't something we forget how to do. How I feel about you hasn't changed from the time I was sixteen years old and first laid eyes on you. It's a different love now—it's grown up and a little weathered, but it's still how I feel about you. And it goddamn hurts that you're not willing to put in the effort to build on it. Instead, you're running."

She looked at him, just looked at him, as if his declaration of love had meant nothing.

That hurt. He'd just told her he loved her. Didn't that goddamn mean anything to her?

Finally, she spoke, but it wasn't the words he wanted to hear.

"I'm not running. I just—"

"That's such bullshit. You can't face your own feelings, so you're running like hell away from them. Away from me, because you don't trust me."

"This has nothing to do with trust, Carter."

Her eyes spit fire. Good. At least maybe she felt something. He sure as hell did.

"Doesn't it? Last time you judged me for failing you. And maybe I did. I was a kid back then, and scared as hell about how our lives were about to change. When you lost the baby, for a few minutes, I didn't know what to think or how to feel. And maybe I did feel a few seconds of—I don't know—it wasn't relief, it was numbness. Because all the plans we'd made had been shot to hell—twice—and we'd have to start all over again. You were hurting, I was hurting, and we'd have to figure it all out. I didn't know what to do to make you feel better, so I just shut down and ended up not being there for you when you needed me the most. That was a shitty thing to do, and I regretted it. Unfortunately, you knew me so damn well you picked right up on my reaction, and I'm so sorry for that."

She just sat there, watching him, but at least this time he was going to get to say how he felt. Before she walked away this time, she'd know.

"You know what? I'm not that kid anymore. But you'll never give me the chance to be the man I can be for you, to show you the love you deserve, because, to you, I'll always be the guy who failed you. So as always, you know best, and you're going to end it for both of us before we get any closer—before I have a chance to hurt you again, right?"

She didn't answer, and he hated seeing the tears in her eyes. He'd already hurt her once, and he never intended to do it again. Maybe she was right. Maybe they weren't ever going to be right for each other.

He wanted her to stand up for them. To stand up now and argue with him. He could handle hours of arguments with her, because at least then she'd be present in the relationship. The two of them, fighting for what they both deserved.

But this silent Molly? That he couldn't handle, because it meant she didn't goddamn care enough to try and save what they had.

And if she didn't, then neither did he.

"Have a good trip, Molly, and drive safe."

Carter headed to the fridge and grabbed a beer. He heard the front door close and leaned his head against the refrigerator door, taking in a few deep breaths.

When he came back into the living room, the key he'd given Molly lay on his coffee table.

He picked it up, looked at it in his hand, then heaved it across the room.

Chapter 34

"YOU'VE BEEN ONE hell of a frequent flier here the past week," Bash said as he passed Carter another beer.

"I'm a big fan of basketball. And hockey." He took several swallows of beer, ignoring the hot blonde who took a seat next to him. After she tried to get his attention several times, she shrugged and moved on down the bar.

"You also have satellite and a big-screen TV at home. Plus a fridge filled with beer."

"But I enjoy your company so much." Carter grinned at Bash.

Bash laughed. "Are you flirting with me?"

Carter snorted, then grabbed a couple of pretzels and his beer and made his way over to the pool tables to shoot a couple of games with a few of the guys in the bar.

This had been his second home ever since that night two weeks ago when Molly had shown up at his place and then left. Since he couldn't work twenty-four hours a day, and he figured out after the first few nights that he couldn't sleep, he came here at night and drank for a few hours, then went home and passed out.

He'd missed a few nights at the gym, and Rhonda was feeling a little neglected, but he was getting the job done at work, and that's all that mattered. He intended to focus on his job from now on. Just his job.

"You look like shit."

He looked up from the table to see Luke standing next to him.

"We can't all be pretty like you, my friend."

Luke shook his head. "And you could stand to have a burger and fries at Bert's. Care to join me?"

"You on duty?"

"Just got off and saw your truck in the lot, so I thought I'd drop in and see if you were hungry."

"Not really. How about a beer?"

"From the way you smell, any more beers and I'll have to park in the lot, then pull you over for a DUI when you leave. Come on, man, don't make me do that. Besides, I'm starving. Give me a break."

Heaving a sigh, he hung up the pool cue. "Fine. Let's go get a burger."

Carter waved to Bash, then headed out to his truck.

"How about I drive?" Luke asked. "I'll bring you back to your truck after we eat."

"Okay. Will you run the siren?"

"Funny."

He had to admit, when they walked into Bert's, the smell of food made his stomach rumble. And maybe he hadn't been eating much, but hey, a guy could survive just fine on peanut butter and jelly sandwiches, pretzels, and beer, couldn't he?

"And what are you two fine gentlemen up to tonight?" Anita asked as she came over.

"We're up to two strong cups of coffee, two waters, and two of your best loaded cheeseburgers, with fries," Luke said.

Anita grinned. "Comin' right up."

"How did you know what I wanted?"

Luke shrugged. "I didn't. Told you I was hungry."

They talked work until the food arrived, and by then, Carter was ready to dig in. By the time he'd had two cups of coffee and devoured his cheeseburger, he felt a bit more human again.

"Better?" Luke asked, taking a sip of coffee.

"A lot. Thanks."

"No problem."

"Bash called you, didn't he?"

"Yeah. He said you were starting to resemble a snarling werewolf."

Carter laughed. "That bad, huh?"

"Yeah. So what are you going to do about it?"

"About what?" Carter took another long drink of his coffee.

"You know what. Molly."

He shrugged. "Nothing. I'm not going to go chasing after a woman who's not willing to stand her ground and give us a chance. She's not worth it."

"Isn't she?" Luke gave him a look over the rim of his cup.

"No. She ran back then, and she ran again. Why would I even bother?"

"Because you're obviously in love with her, or you wouldn't look this bad."

"Thanks."

"No problem. And when you're in love with a woman, you chase her down and make her listen to you. You tell her you love her every day until it either sinks in, or you realize it's never going to happen."

"Yeah, I'm not that much of a glutton for punishment, buddy. No thanks."

"How hard did you try to convince her to stay when she told you she was leaving?"

He paused, set the cup down. "Not at all."

Luke rolled his eyes. "And now you're drowning your sorrows because she left you? That makes you a major dumbass, my friend. A woman has to feel like you'd move heaven and earth to have her, you know."

"I do know that. I was just trying to get out of her way." None of what he said made sense. "Well, shit. I didn't try hard enough, did I?"

Luke gave him a clueless look. "How the hell should I know? She's gone, so obviously not."

Carter wiped his mouth with the napkin. "This is bullshit. I need to find her and force her to listen to me. I love her, goddammit and she's going to keep hearing it until it sinks in. She belongs here—with me."

Luke's lips curved. "That sounds more like you. Sad, drunken werewolf is definitely not a good look on you."

"Whatever. Take me back to my truck."

THIS WASN'T WORKING.

Molly could have sworn she'd settle in after two weeks in Oklahoma City.

Typically when she moved to a new city, she was filled with excitement. A new place, a new job, new places to eat and explore.

But this just wasn't her city. It was a great place, but she hadn't found an apartment to rent yet, so she was still living in a convenience hotel, and she hadn't spotted a job she wanted, so she was currently temping.

That's what everything here felt like to her—temporary. Not like home, and after two weeks, it should feel like home.

She supposed she'd just have to up and move again.

The problem was, she didn't want to get out the map and find yet another place.

She was tired of city hopping, tired of traveling around.

She missed Hope. She missed her family and her friends.

She missed Carter. Every night as she lay in bed and stared up at the ceiling, she replayed their last conversation over and over in her head.

The things he'd said to her had been awful and painful and devastating to her heart.

Only this time, he'd been right.

She had judged him, laid all the blame on him, and hadn't allowed herself to forgive him for the past so they could take a shot at having a future together. She hadn't trusted in him, and because of that, she'd cost herself a chance to have a forever with the one and only man she had ever loved.

It had taken that one last ugly blowup for her to see the mistakes she'd made.

And because she hadn't trusted in Carter, and in her own heart, she'd done the only thing she really knew how to do and do well—run.

But running was no longer the solution to her problems.

Now she was afraid that no place was ever going to feel like home again, because home was Hope.

She had to go home.

She had to go home to Carter. And hope and pray that he'd take her back.

Chapter 35

THANK GOD EMMA knew where Molly was, and she was gracious enough to tell him. Otherwise, Carter would have had to start from scratch and travel city to city, because no way in hell was he willing to give her up.

He'd have plenty of time on the drive there to figure out exactly what he was going to say to her, so he grabbed his bag and punched the button to lift his garage door.

He stopped when he saw Molly's car pulling up in the driveway behind his truck.

He walked toward George, still cringing at the sound of the vehicle's coughing and sputtering as it shuddered when she killed the engine.

Molly got out of the car, and his pulse did a NASCAR last-lap race as he watched her. She had on black jeans and boots, her hair loose around her shoulders. She wore a red long-sleeved shirt with a black scarf. It took everything in him not to jerk her into his arms and kiss her until she admitted she felt the same way he did about her. She glanced down at his duffel bag.

"Going somewhere?" she asked.

"Yeah. To Oklahoma City to find you."

"How? Oh . . . Emma."

"Yeah."

"Well, I'm not there anymore."

"I can see that. Come on inside, it's freezing out here."

He turned around and went to the door, opened it and held it for her, taking in that sweet vanilla scent of hers as she breezed past him.

He shut the door and followed her into the living room.

"So . . . you were coming to find me?"

"Hell, yes I was coming to find you. To tell you that leaving was a mistake. And to talk you into coming back."

Her lips curved. "That's . . . nice to hear."

"Why did you come back?"

She took a deep breath. "Because it wasn't home to me. I thought I needed to leave, that my new adventure waited for me in the next city. Turns out I was wrong, Carter. My next adventure is right here."

Now it was his turn to hold his breath.

"Provided you can forgive me. I've been wrong." She stepped closer to him. "All these years, I've been wrong, about everything. You were right. I did hold you accountable for what happened, and I didn't trust in our love. The problem was, I did still love you. Everywhere I tried to run, that love went with me and I couldn't get away from it.

"Now I'm back to face it, to see where we can go with it. If you'll have me. Will you?"

"Yeah. On one condition."

She frowned. "What's that?"

"You need a new goddamned car. Like yesterday."

She let out a soft laugh. "Okay."

"And I like you working with me. I still need you. But only as long as you want to."

"That's more than one condition."

"True. Okay, we'll negotiate that second point."

"Okay." Molly drew in a deep breath. "I love you, Carter. I want that future you've been promising. In this house. With a dog and maybe a few kids."

He arched a brow. "A few?"

She got even closer. "Yeah. A few. Are you okay with that?"

He swept his arm around her waist and pulled her against him, needing to feel that connection he always felt when their bodies touched. "Yeah, I'm okay with that. I love you, Molly. I always have. I always will. Forever."

"Forever."

Molly cupped her hand around Carter's neck, and as soon as their lips connected, she knew at once that she was home. Finally, forever home.

She never intended to leave again.

Dear Reader,

Thank you for reading *Hope Burns*. There will be more romance coming to the town of Hope with the release of *Love After All* in April 2015.

In the meantime, I hope you enjoy the first chapter included here of *Quarterback Draw*, book nine of my Play-by-Play sports romance series. These are stories about sexy, highly successful, hardworking professional athletes and the smart women who are their match in every way.

Happy reading,
Jaci

IF THERE WAS one thing Grant Cassidy hated more than anything, it was PR. Doing commercial shoots was a necessary evil, and some he disliked more than others.

But right now he was in board shorts and bare feet, standing on a beach in Barbados, about to do a shoot for the annual swimsuit edition of a pretty damned famous sports magazine. There were about two dozen barely clad, tanned, gorgeous models who were going to take part in the shoot along with several athletes.

All in all? Not a bad gig.

"This I could get used to."

Grant grinned as one of his best friends, Trevor Shay, stood next to him.

"Don't get too used to it. Your girlfriend will kick your ass if you get too close to any of these models."

Trevor crossed his arms. "Yeah. I really wish Haven could be here in Barbados with me. But she's in school right now and couldn't make it. She did tell me to behave myself. Trust me, none of these women is as beautiful as mine."

Grant laughed. "You're blinded by love, my man."

"It's true. I am. And perfectly happy to go back to my bungalow at night all by myself. How about you? You like dating models. Got one scoped out yet?"

"I wasn't exactly looking. There are a lot of them here, though."

Trevor slapped him on the back as the assistant director motioned for him. "Hey, I'm up. I'll catch you at the bar later."

"Okay."

He stayed close and watched as Trevor was put into a shot on a hammock with a beautiful dark-skinned model. The model straddled Trevor, who Grant had to admit handled the whole thing professionally. As soon as it was over, Trevor shook the woman's hand and wandered off in the direction of the pool.

"You'll be up next, Grant," the assistant said. "We're pairing you up with Katrina Korsova."

"Sure." He knew who she was. Korsova was a big deal in the modeling world, one of those supermodels whose face and body were all over billboards, in magazines, and on television. She was a beauty and he was lucky to be doing the shoot with her. It would increase his profile, and he was all about exposure.

If he had to be here doing this shoot for the sports magazine, at least he was being paired up with one of the best in the business.

Once they readied the shot on the beach, he was called over and set up on his marks. He stood in the water up to his ankles. They'd already primped his hair, his face, and his skin. It all felt weird to him, but he'd done photo shoots before. They told him it was to combat shine and to make sure his hair would be gelled appropriately enough so it would behave.

Whatever. He was paid to do what he was told, just like in football. So he stood where they told him to stand.

"We're ready for you, Katrina," he heard the assistant say.

The models were clustered in shaded cabanas before the shoot, so he'd only caught glimpses of them.

Katrina stepped out, a gorgeous woman with long hair the color of midnight, wearing a swimsuit bottom that barely clung to her hips. It was more like two tiny pieces of cloth tied together with scraps. There wasn't much to the top, either. Just a couple of triangles that hardly covered her generous breasts.

She was curved in all the right places, and after she bent over so they could spray her hair wet, she straightened, flipped her hair back, and gave him a look.

Wow. Those eyes. They were so deep blue they were almost violet. Maybe they were violet. He had no idea, because he'd been struck dumb as she approached him.

He'd been around plenty of beautiful women before, but Katrina was . . . wow. Photos of her didn't do justice to what a knockout she really was.

"Grant Cassidy, this is Katrina Korsova."

She gave him a quick nod, then turned to the director, obviously all business and not as thunderstruck by him as he had been by her.

He was going to try to not be offended by that. Then again, she likely worked around good-looking male models all the time. He was no big deal, at least not in the modeling world.

"I want your arm around his, Katrina," the director said. "Katrina, your right breast against his chest, with you facing him. Let's see some heat here."

And just like that, she moved into him, her body warm and pliant as she slid her hand into his hair and tilted her head back. Their hips touched, their thighs made contact, and then she looked at him.

He'd never felt that *pow* of instant connection before, but he sure as hell felt it now. It was as if lightning had struck the center of his universe, and every part of him felt it.

Katrina blinked a few times, then frowned.

"Something wrong?"

"The angle. Give me a second," she said. He'd expected some type of Russian accent, but there was none, just the smoky hot darkness of her voice spilling from her lips. It was like drinking whiskey on a cold night. The sound of her voice heated him from the inside out. He'd never been slammed as hard as this before.

Katrina adjusted, her fingers tangling in his hair, giving him just a bit of a tug.

His lips curved. "So, you like that?" he asked.

"Just a job," she responded, then gave him a smoldering look, tilted her head toward him, and jutted her hips out just enough to hit him right in the crotch.

Goddammit. She'd done that on purpose.

He could do it as well. He raised his hand and laid it just above her hip, knowing he couldn't obscure the swimwear. After all, that's what they were advertising. His fingers bit into her skin, just enough that he caught the flash of awareness in her eyes.

"Yes, that's perfect," the director said. "Hold it there."

Grant heard the camera click several times.

"Now move. Get into each other. Lean in, touch. Be mindful of your angles, Katrina. And Grant, follow her lead."

"Yes, Grant," Katrina said, shifting just a touch, then picking up his hand and placing it on her butt. "Follow my lead."

It wasn't like he'd never posed for a photo session before. He wasn't a rookie here. He knew what he was doing, how to move and react to the camera, and when to be still.

Katrina might be the pro here, but he could play the game, too. He cupped her butt, making sure he didn't squeeze—just slid his fingers lightly over her skin, tucking his fingertips just inside the edge of her suit.

He heard every breath she took, saw the smoldering look in her eyes, and his body reacted.

So did hers, as her nipples pebbled, brushing against his chest.

His lips curved.

"Just a job" his ass.

And as he heard every few clicks of the camera, he turned his head, moved his body against hers, making sure their clothes remained the focus while keeping his gaze intently on hers. When he drew a strand of her hair between his fingers, letting his knuckles brush the swell of her breasts, he heard her sharp intake of breath.

"Just a job, right?" he asked, turning her around so her

back was to him, so he could skim his hand down her arm, letting his fingers rest at her hip.

"This is perfect," the director said. "Keep doing what you're doing."

He listened to the sound of Katrina's breaths, got comfortable with her ass nestled into his crotch.

They fit damned perfect together. She was tall—taller than the average woman. He didn't have to crouch down to fit her to him. She had long legs. Really nice legs, too.

"Okay, let's break for a few," the director said. "You both need an outfit change. Then we'll resume."

Before he had a chance to say anything to her, she pushed off and walked away, heading into the cabana. An assistant handed her a bottle of water.

And just like that, she disappeared.

Friendly, wasn't she?

He wandered off at the direction of the staff to change his board shorts and to have his hair and makeup adjusted. When he came back out, Katrina was in a short robe.

He was called out toward a tree facing the sun.

"Ready for you, Katrina," the director said.

She dropped the robe, and Grant blinked. Katrina wore only a thong bottom. She stood while they arranged her hair to partially cover her breasts.

And what fantastic breasts they were, too. He decided to look elsewhere, like out on the water, until she showed up in front of him. In this game they were playing, it was best for him not to show a physical reaction.

"Katrina, you against the tree. Grant, you plant one hand above her head to start, lean into her body."

Some of the assistants positioned them while Grant and Katrina made eye contact.

She met his gaze with a cool one of her own, a challenge to him, as if she'd done this a million times, as if rubbing her breasts against his chest wasn't a big deal. To her, it probably wasn't. She wanted to know if he'd react.

He had a gorgeous, half-naked woman pressed up against him, and his dick was trying very hard to respond to that, while he was trying equally as hard to convince his dick nothing was going to happen out here on the beach with thirty other people watching.

"Ready?" the director asked.

Katrina tilted her head back toward the sun. "Yes."

Grant gave a quick nod, hoping like hell this wouldn't take long, especially since every time Katrina moved, she rubbed her breasts against his chest. And because she was topless, they had to take special care that no nipple was visible, so they took every shot carefully, stopping to rearrange her hair or strategically place his arm or hand.

It was interminable, and seemed to go on for hours. Katrina was patient through every shot, but to Grant, it was like a goddamned eternity.

"Is it always like this?" Grant asked Katrina during one of the many breaks.

Clearly comfortable standing around having her hair and makeup retouched, Katrina cocked her head to the side. "Like what?"

"Hours of this. Click and change positions. Click and redo the hair. Click and clothing changes."

"Oh. Yes. Always like this. Why? Are you bored?"

His lips curved and he glanced downward where her hair barely covered her generous breasts. "Hardly."

She rolled her eyes. "I doubt these are the first set of breasts you've seen. Not from what I've read about you."

"And here I thought you had no idea who I was."

"Oh, I know who you are, Grant. You've dated a few of my friends."

He wondered which ones. None of them were on location with him, and he'd always remained friends with the women he dated, so he doubted any of them had anything bad to say about him. "Is that right. And did you get a full report?"

"Yes."

"So that means you'll have dinner with me tonight."

She laughed, and he liked the sound of it.

"I don't think so."

He wasn't insulted, and he liked her confidence. They

finished the shoot for the day since, according to the director, the light was leaving them. Katrina grabbed her robe and wandered off, and Grant went back to his bungalow to shower off all the makeup and hair gunk. He checked his phone and answered a few emails and text messages.

Trevor texted that he was going to set up a face-to-face call with Haven, so he was staying in his room.

That meant Grant was on his own tonight, which was fine with him. He returned a few calls, one to his agent, Liz Riley. She talked to him about finalizing his contract since the season would be starting soon. He told her he'd come in and see her as soon as he got back to town.

Football season was gearing up, and he was due to the practice facility in St. Louis in two weeks.

He was ready. He'd been in training and was in shape, and was more than ready for the season to start. This was a nice mini vacation prior to getting back to work, though. Soon enough he'd have his head in the game, and it would be all he thought about.

After getting dressed in a pair of shorts and a sleeveless shirt, he made his way to the main bar at the hotel and ordered a beer. He grabbed a seat at one of the tables outside, content to sip his beer and people watch, one of his favorite pastimes.

He saw a few of the models come outside. They sat at a table not too far from where he was, all of them talking and laughing.

They were all beautiful women. Tall and slender, with great hair, pretty smiles, and amazing bodies. But he found himself searching for only one woman.

He had no idea why, when she'd clearly blown him off. She was probably out on a date tonight with some hot male model. He'd seen a few of those guys today as well.

But then he caught sight of Katrina coming through the bar. She was by herself, carrying a tote bag. She stopped to talk to the bartender, who nodded. Then she walked past Grant without saying a word, and pulled up a chair at a table by herself.

Not with the other models, who seemingly ignored her as much as she was ignoring them.

She pulled out a book and a pair of glasses, and one of the waitresses brought her a tall glass of what looked like iced tea with lemon. She opened the book and started to read, oblivious to everything—and everyone—around her.

Huh. Not at all what he'd expected.

He watched her for a while, waiting to see if she was meeting someone. After about thirty minutes, he realized no one was going to show up. He stood, grabbed his beer and went over to her table and pulled out a chair to take a seat.

She lifted her gaze from her book and settled it on him. She didn't offer a smile.

"Did you get lost on your way to some other table?" she asked.

"No. But you were alone."

"Precisely. On purpose."

She waited, as if she expected him to leave. He didn't take a brushoff all that easily. "I thought you might want some company."

"You thought wrong."

"Does that icy cold stare work on all men?"

"Usually."

"Why aren't you with your friends over there?"

She took a quick glance at the other table, then back to him. "Do you think models travel in herds?"

She had a sharp wit. He liked that about her. "What are you drinking?"

"Iced tea."

He signaled for the waitress, then held up two fingers and motioned to their drinks. She nodded and wandered back inside.

"Really, Grant. I'm fine. And I'd like to be alone."

"No one wants to be alone."

"That's bullshit."

"Okay, fine. I don't want to be alone. I figured we'd have dinner together."

With a sigh, she set down her book and took off her glasses. "Just because we worked together today doesn't mean we have anything in common, or that we shared a moment or anything."

"Didn't we?"

She paused for a few seconds, and he held her gaze in his. Damn, there was something about her eyes. He liked women just fine, and always had a good time with them. He'd had a few relationships that had lasted awhile and had ended amicably. But not one woman had ever shocked him with the same spark he'd felt with Katrina today.

He wanted to explore that, see if he could push through her icy exterior.

"I'm reading a book."

"So you said. It's a good one. I've read it before."

She frowned. "You didn't even look at it."

"I saw it when I sat down."

She crossed her arms. "Okay, fine. What's it about?"

"There's this guy, and he works for the CIA. But he's a double agent, working both sides. You don't know throughout the book if he's a good guy or bad guy, or if the partner he hooks up with in South Korea is on his side, or out to kill him. So when they both show up on the train . . ."

She held up her hand. "Stop. I haven't gotten to that part yet. Fine, I get it. You've read it."

"You thought I was bullshitting you."

"You wouldn't be the first."

The waitress brought their drinks. "Thanks," Grant said. "Can we see some menus?"

"I don't want to see a menu," she said to the waitress, who walked away anyway. She turned her attention back on Grant. "I don't want you to sit here with me. Honestly, are you always this rude?"

"Not always. You bring out the best in me."

She rolled her eyes.

"So tell me why that book."

"I like suspense and crime fiction."

"You don't strike me as the type."

Her brows lifted. "Type? Why? Did you expect I'd be thumbing through a fashion magazine? Or even better, that I didn't even know how to read? Do you expect all models to be dumb?"

"That would be stereotyping, and I'd be the last person to do that. And no. You looked like the type to read books on . . . I don't know. Psychology or something."

She laughed. "Why?"

He picked up her dark glasses. "You look so smart wearing these."

"I am smart. With or without the glasses."

He could tell he was digging the hole even deeper with every word he said. "Sorry. I'm not getting this out right. I've dated a few models."

"So I've heard."

He sighed. "A lot of them have different interests. One was a certified scuba diver, so I learned to dive when I was dating her. One was a hiker and a climber. I did some heinous climbs with her."

"You dated Elesia?" she asked.

"Yeah."

She wrinkled her nose. "She's a pit viper."

He laughed. "I'm not even going to comment."

"You have interesting taste in women."

"I like women who intrigue me and challenge me. Not just a pretty face."

"Good to know the modeling world isn't growing old and moldy with no men to date as long as you're around. After all, where would we be without our sports stars to take care of us?"

"Now who's stereotyping? I've also dated a schoolteacher, an accountant, a scientist, and a landscape architect."

She took a sip of her tea. "It's nice you're spreading it around."

He couldn't help but laugh. "So tell me what interests you, Katrina?"

KATRINA DIDN'T WANT to like Grant Cassidy. She didn't want him sitting at her table, yet there he was, drinking his beer and looking absolutely gorgeous.

She'd wanted to be alone, and she'd thought about spending

the evening in her room so she could read. But it was just too beautiful here, and the beach and sea air beckoned, so she'd put on a pair of shorts and a tank top to come sit beachside for dinner.

Obviously a huge mistake, because no matter how hard she tried to insult the man, he simply wouldn't leave.

And no matter how hard she tried to deny the chemistry she felt during their photo shoot today, she couldn't.

She shot with male models all the time. Sometimes fully naked. She'd never felt anything. It was her job. She knew it, and so did the guys. But making eye contact with Grant Cassidy today, there'd been some kind of . . . she didn't even know how to describe it. A zing somewhere in the vicinity of her lower belly. A low warming that had spread when he'd laid his hands on her.

Even now, hours later, she could still feel his touch, the way he'd looked at her. She'd wanted . . . more. And if there was one thing Katrina never wanted from a man, it was more of anything. She was too focused on her career to spend any time at all thinking of men. Work was everything to her, and men were a distraction.

Like now. He sat across the table from her, all big and tan and smiling at her like he had exactly what she wanted.

Only she didn't want it. She wanted no part of anything he might have to offer.

She couldn't want it. Still, she couldn't help herself.

"I'm surprised you read that book," she said.

"Now who's stereotyping? You think I'm a dumb jock, that all I read is sports magazines."

"I didn't say that."

"I actually have a degree in accounting. And yes, I did graduate before I went out for the draft."

She studied him. "Accounting. I don't see it."

"I was going to go for a law degree, but I like numbers better. I minored in finance. I wanted to make sure I could oversee my earnings with knowledge. I've seen too many football players blow it all or not know where their money is going, and a few years after they retire, the money is gone."

He was smart, too. She liked that.

She leaned back and looked at him. "Do you have an investment portfolio?"

"As a matter of fact, I do. With the high income a successful model commands, I imagine you do as well."

"I do. And I know exactly where my money is going."

"See? I knew you were a smart woman, Katrina. Smart and beautiful—a lethal combination."

She couldn't help but appreciate that he mentioned the smart part before the beautiful part. Too many men never paid attention to the fact that she had a brain. All they saw was her face and body and never even wanted to have a conversation with her. Which was why she didn't date. She didn't have time for men who were that superficial.

Grant seemed . . . different. Yeah, there'd been that spark of chemistry at the photo shoot today, but so far all he'd done was talk to her. He didn't sit down to ogle her or hit on her. It was kind of refreshing.

Not that she had any interest in dating him, but when was the last time she'd spent time talking with a man she wasn't connected to in the industry? She wasn't going to bed with him, but she could sit at the table and have a meal with him, right?

"Okay, fine. Let's see what's on the menu for dinner."

From *New York Times* bestselling author
JACI BURTON

STRADDLING
the
LINE

A PLAY-BY-PLAY NOVEL

Trevor Shay has it all—a successful football and baseball career, and any woman he wants. But when he finds out his college mentor's daughter is in trouble, he drops everything to come to her aid.

Haven Briscoe has finally landed a dream job as a sportscaster for a major network. But she can't move past the recent death of her beloved father, and it's affecting her career. A plum assignment following the life of superstar Trevor Shay might be just what she needs…

"One of the strongest sports romance series available."
—*Dear Author*

jaciburton.com
facebook.com/AuthorJaciBurton
facebook.com/LoveAlwaysBooks
penguin.com

Once passion ignites, you can't stop the flames...

From *New York Times* Bestselling Author

JACI BURTON

Hope Flames

Emma Burnett once gave up her dreams for a man who did nothing but hurt her. Now thirty-two and setting up her veterinary practice in the town she once called home, she won't let anything derail her career goals. But when Luke McCormack brings in his injured police dog, Emma can hardly ignore him. Despite her best efforts to keep things strictly professional, Luke's an attractive distraction she doesn't need.

Luke knows the only faithful creature in his life is his dog. After an ugly divorce that left him damn near broke, the last thing he needs is a woman in his life. Fun and games are great and, as a divorced man, the single women in town make sure he never lacks for company. But there's something about Emma that gets to him, and despite his determination to go it alone, he's drawn to her feisty spirit and the vulnerability she tries so hard to hide.

PRAISE FOR JACI BURTON AND HER NOVELS

"Jaci Burton's stories are full of heat and heart."
—Maya Banks, *New York Times* bestselling author

"Passionate, inventive...Burton offers plenty of emotion and conflict."
—*USA Today* Happy Ever After blog

jaciburton.com
facebook.com/AuthorJaciBurton
facebook.com/LoveAlwaysBooks
penguin.com

M1260T0213